To

CW00739317

ROBIN MARR

Finding Jane

Broken Witch i

Best wishes

Robin

Cover Design by Melody Simmons

First edition

This book was professionally typeset on Reedsy.
Find out more at reedsy.com

To that wonderful person who is there for me on every step of my journey, with an ear to hear, eyes to read, and heart to keep me going when it feels the hill is too steep.

Love you.

Contents

Acknowledgement

Quick word of acknowledgement here to my editor, Aaron Sykes, without whom these books would be a lot harder to read.

A Meeting

The crazy old lady was standing at the window again, staring at me.

I'd been at work an hour – the schedule had me on the breakfast shift – and she had already walked past the shop three or four times, her eyes glued to something in her hand. Now she was lurking outside, peering through the window, then glancing down at whatever she was holding. She could be looking at me or the grinder for all I could tell. Creepy old woman.

The bell on the door rang, and my next customer called a cheery "Hi, Jane" as they walked in. I turned on my smile and made small talk as I sold them their morning whizz juice and sugar rush; double–shot flat white and a danish, kick–starting the town of Clifton and America for generations.

Don't bother trying to find Clifton. It's a nowhere town with a few thousand people, two bars, two diners, and four churches. Besides, I've changed the name. And yes, I have a good reason for doing that. But first, coffee.

Rush hour in the morning lasts five minutes, and if I had someone standing behind whoever I was serving, that counted as busy. By 9:05 the shop was empty. At least, until the mommy rush at ten. The place filled up with strollers, chatter, and the screams of a half–dozen children running riot while their moms clucked to each other. I don't like kids. Sue me.

My break started at 9:30. A heavenly fifteen minutes with my own caffeine and sugar rushes, and whatever I'd found to read in the library that week. I didn't have a favorite author, but I had a system. When you return a book, they scan it then put it on that trolley behind the desk, right? I just ask for the last book checked back in. If I like it, I read it, and if I don't, I take it back the next day and get a fresh one. The library was on my way home, and I got to read a lot of cool stuff. A lot of weird stuff too, thinking about it.

But I'd barely sat down, let alone opened my book, when the bell clanged above the door. Betty would deal with the customer, but I still looked up. And flinched. It was the woman from outside, and she was looking at me.

Thing was, she didn't look like some nutsy old bag lady. She was old, yes, but not *old* old, and though her dress sense was – let's be kind and say 'quirky' – she looked cared for.

It was the *eyes* that freaked me. Even across the room they looked too intense, or too bright. She was tall, slim, and had long wavy hair that was mostly gray but still showed hints of golden blonde. And she had one of those faces that never give away how old a person really was.

From the corner of my eye, I saw Betty straighten up, ready to serve. The old woman walked right past the counter and over to the table at the back, where I was. She sat opposite me without asking, dropping her bag on the floor beside her.

"I'm looking for Paulette Tipton," she announced, and looked at me as though it should mean something.

"Sorry. Not a name I've heard."

"Really?"

That annoyed me. I either knew or I didn't. No need for her to make it sound like I was being stupid. "I know it's a small town, lady, but I don't know everybody. Now, if you don't mind, I'm trying to have my break here."

"You look very much like her."

I tapped the badge on the bib of my apron, which announced that I was, in fact, Jane.

Betty had moved along the counter until she was as close as she could get. "Fix you something, lady?"

Betty owned the place and didn't take to freeloaders. If you took up a seat, you'd better have a cup in front of you. The old woman looked confused for a moment, then cranked her head around toward Betty. "Thank you. A medium latte, skimmed."

"To go," I added.

The woman turned back to face me. "Paulette Tipton was a student at my school many years ago, until..." She hesitated, head cocked to one side as she looked at me with uncomfortable intensity. "She left, and under strange circumstances. I need to locate her."

That got me annoyed, and I had an idea what was coming next. It made it worse that she didn't look the type. "Well, good luck with that, but you need to look elsewhere."

"But you look very like her, allowing for the years." She leaned forward and sniffed the air in front of me, like she was checking for body odor. "Are you taking any medication? I can smell Witchbane. Lots of it."

"That's my business. And what the heck is Witchbane? Some herbal or homeo–whatsis remedy? I don't mess around with that junk."

3

"Of course, of course. It's just... Well, if you *are* taking Witchbane, I strongly recommend you stop. These things are not always as simple as they seem to be. For example, Witchbane can suppress..." She mumbled to a stop, but the look she gave me suggested she was assessing me about something. "Let's just say I can't think of a single condition where it could be of benefit to you and many where it could prove most detrimental."

"Like to my memory?"

She looked surprised, like she had never considered the idea. "I suppose it could affect memory, assuming..." Her expression shifted mid word as she changed her mind about what she was going to say. The dreamy expression that seemed so natural on her face disappeared, and her eyes focused hard on mine. "Assuming no neurological or psychological trauma caused the issue."

I popped.

"You people make me sick."

The old woman leaned back in her chair, surprise all over her face. I'd seen the act before, and now she had pushed my button. Hard.

"You find out there's some poor hick out in the middle of nowhere who doesn't have a memory and you think you can roll in and promise me my old life back, or sell me a remember serum, or hypnotize my memories back. Well screw you, lady, and everybody like you. I'm happy the way things are, and I've no money for you to rip off from me."

"Jane!" Betty's voice snapped through my anger and I realized that while I wasn't shouting, I wasn't far off. And the other customers were staring. I waved an apology at her and held my breath for a count of ten.

"You should go. My break is pretty much over; not that I got one, thanks to you."

The woman looked sad and sympathetic, but it didn't matter to me. I'd seen it before.

"I expected this," she said. "And I understand."

"How can you understand?"

"Has anybody else offered to bring you proof? Up front?"

That shut me up for a second. I didn't think so. They all wanted the money first.

"If you will meet me tomorrow, I can bring you enough evidence to convince you that I am genuine, and that I have good reason to speak to you." Her eyes wandered away and a tiny frown wrinkled the bridge of her nose. "I think." Her eyes came back into focus. "Will you meet me?"

Tomorrow I didn't start work until lunch shift, and I had no plans. Normally I would have blown her off, even warned her to stay away from me, but how much harm could an old lady do? I was wise to most of the tricks she might try. And who knew, there might be some truth in it.

"Gino's, tomorrow, at ten thirty. It's a block north on Howard."

The woman nodded once. "Thank you for your indulgence, Paulette."

"Jane," I corrected, and knew I was frowning.

"As you prefer. This will be worth your time, I promise."

She dropped a ten on the table, then picked up her cup and grabbed the strap of her bag before walking out of the shop. Right at the door, she turned her head, looked back at me, and gave me a smile. It was a warm, friendly smile, and I almost bought it before I remembered what she was and what she was trying to do.

5

I lifted my mug and took a swig of my coffee. It was lukewarm and disgusting. While ice – cold coffee – like a frappe – is delicious, a tepid latte is gross. But it was the only drink I would get before my shift finished, so I swallowed the rest of my bear claw and washed it down, trying not to think about the taste.

"My place not good enough for you, then?" said Betty as I came back behind the counter to put my crockery, and anything else that needed it, into the dishwasher.

"I wanted somewhere I could walk out from."

She shook her head. "I don't know why you give those people the time of day. You know she'll try to sell you some snake oil or other."

"They all do, but it can be fun watching them try." I was lying. It was never fun. "Besides, you never know. One of them might have The Answer."

I made light of it for Betty. She was everybody's mom and liked to think she was mine, too. I felt bad that now she would worry. Tomorrow I would find her with badly applied concealer, trying to hide the shadows under her eyes, unable to sleep for fretting about me. I wished she wouldn't. I didn't want to be a burden on anybody. But it was nice someone cared.

Snatching the scissors from the drainer, I split open another bag of beans and poured them into the grinder. They say you stop smelling something if you rub your nose in it often enough. Maybe that's true of some things, but not for coffee. At least for me. Every time the lever on the grinder clicked and a little avalanche of powder tumbled out, I'd breathe in and get that intense aroma rush in my nose. Always wondered if you could absorb caffeine by snorting it like that.

The door clanged open, and the shop filled with the sound

of clucking mothers and babbling toddlers. I sighed and could have done with a minute or two more to settle down. Though I would never admit it, I felt shaky. I always did after these encounters. My life here was great, honest.

But what if she was telling the truth?

For now, I had to let it go. With my best smile glued on, I turned to face The Invasion Of The Moms.

Home Life

"Y ou OK?"

I flinched. "What?"

Bernie was my roommate. Call her Bernadette and she would hurt you. She rolled her eyes at me. "You've been staring out of that window for ten minutes." She came up behind me and looked over my shoulder. "Is something going on out there?"

"No," I said, sidestepping and pulling my half–made sandwich along the breakfast bar to finish building it. The view, if you could call it that, was of the alley between Howard and 3rd, which was where our apartment building was. Nothing but telephone and power poles, dumpsters, and the stripped carcass of a mid–sized Ford.

"So what had you so gripped? Was it a drunk? Or was Scary Mary working a john?"

I finished making my sandwich, cut it in two, and slid the halves onto a plate. We never cooked. Bernie only ever seemed to eat takeout, and I hated her for it. She never put on any weight and had great skin, even though her staple diet was greasy meat pizzas. A shift at the restaurant meant I would get whatever wasn't selling well for free. Otherwise, I lived on fruit, and peanut butter sandwiches.

"Just thinking about something," I said.

"Anything worth sharing?"

Bernie was an OK roommate. She didn't steal from me, she paid the bills on time, and she didn't bring too many of her male harem back to the apartment. And, technically, the place was hers, given she was already here when I arrived. But friends, we were not. I shrugged.

Which was why she knew my secret. Well, it's not really a secret. Lots of people are aware of it, but her more than most. It was only fair. She needed to know what she was going to share her home with. And because she was so clued in, I figured it wouldn't hurt to tell her about the visit.

"I had another visitor today."

"From where?" she asked, still looking out the window. Then she turned back and looked at me. "Oh. One of *them*?"

I nodded. She muttered *fucksake* under her breath – but made sure it was loud enough for me to hear.

"I know," I mumbled, then sighed and waited for the rant. "I know."

"Do you?" Bernie snapped back at me so hard my eyebrows rose.

"Hey, wasn't my idea for her to come."

"But did you tell her to get lost?"

I shook my head, feeling like I was being scolded by teacher, but one with a potty mouth. "I said we could meet tomorrow. She claimed she had proof. If she doesn't, I'll walk."

"Every damned time."

"What do you mean?"

"I mean, every time one of these snakes turn up, you listen to their shit and get all excited. You shouldn't even talk to them."

9

"Betty said the same."

"First sensible thing the old bitch ever said."

"But what if she does have proof?"

"How will you tell if it's real? You don't know what you can't remember, so how can you decide if her so-called evidence isn't just a pack of made-up crap?"

She had a point, but how mad it was making her left me uncomfortable.

"It's not like she's asking for money or anything. Why are you so mad at me?"

"Because she'll come stomping into your world, mess you up, turn out to be yet another fake, and I'll have the joy of watching you mope around the place for a month, pining for your lost life."

That stung. Not that she was wrong, but she didn't have to be so harsh. I had no comeback and was too busy praying that the pricking in my eyes didn't evolve into tears. That would embarrass both of us and make me look weak. Weaker. She already thought I was a wuss.

"What did she look like? All Big City suit and briefcase?"

"Ordinary. Tall, in her sixties, bit of a seventies dresser, long grayish hair. She looked OK."

Bernie frowned at me. "So she'll pull mystic hippy shit on you." She stomped across the room to 'her' chair and grabbed her jacket off the back. "Can't deal with any more of this. Going out."

"Back later?"

"You my mom? Going to play some pool, drink too much beer, and get laid. Later."

The door slammed behind her, leaving me to figure out how I felt on my own.

10

No Show

I got to Gino's around 10:30, hurrying to get out from under an unexpected shower. I chatted with Claire, the barista there, while she whipped me up a flat white. She didn't charge me. It's an *honor among baristas* thing. I thought about a bear claw, or an almond twist, but forced the sugar cravings down. Those I would have to pay for. I get by, just, so long as I don't lose any shifts at the restaurant and the tips are good. That's why I practice my sunny face for the customers. Nobody tips a sourpuss. Doesn't mean I like them, or the work. Like I said, my ends meet.

But I don't have anything to waste. My phone is five years old, and so is my laptop. Bernie pays for the internet, and I buy access a day at a time if I need it. My only luxury is my member's card for the movie theater. The TV and cable are in Bernie's room, and I don't use them. It's no big deal. I can go to the movies every night, if I want, and stay all night. Did that once, about three years ago. Icy harsh winter, and the heating broke down in the apartment building.

People – well, Betty – say I could do better, but I don't understand why they think I need to, or would want to. I've got no qualifications I know of. My resume starts May 11, five years ago, and lists a grand total of two jobs waiting tables.

Besides, like I said, I get by.

Claire is still chatting away about some boyfriend issue. I'm on auto–nod, and grunt when it seems appropriate, but I'm not listening. My eyes are on the door, and on the sidewalk outside the window. I glance at my watch; 10:50.

My stomach twisted. I had a feeling this one might be different, but it looked like I was wrong. Again. Wasn't the first time. In fact, the last two or three had gone this way. I don't know if it was because I didn't seem desperate enough, or if I came over too cynical – which I am – but they all arranged a second meeting and never came back.

It cuts me, inside. I'm resigned to who and what I am. I don't remember any of my life before five years ago. No memory of myself, or any family I might have had, where I grew up, or what happened to me. They found me, sitting on a bench outside the clinic here, with just the clothes on my back. And there's nothing anyone can do for me – at least nothing I could dream of affording. The clinic made sure I was medically sound, the police made sure I wasn't wanted anywhere, and they kicked me loose.

But the scab has pretty much healed over that. The first year was tough, fighting to get a new identity, and work, and the apartment, but now I'm good. Unless people come pick at the scab. And let's be honest; we all want to look underneath and see if it's healed.

And here I was, standing at the side of the counter, listening to Claire's love drama, and realizing that the wound inside was still pretty deep, and still hurt.

She wasn't coming. The bitch had stood me up and I felt like an idiot. My chest burned with anger, so I took a breath, held it for a ten count, then let it slowly out. Getting mad never paid off. Handing the cup back to Claire, I made my excuses, and left. It was time to get away from the chatter and out into the air. I needed to breathe.

Out on the sidewalk, I couldn't help checking for the old woman all the way back to Betty's.

"You're early," she said, catching sight of me in the mirror behind the counter as I walked in. "Your shift doesn't start for another hour." Then she turned toward me, and her face fell. I took another five-breath. I didn't want her pity. Didn't need it.

"She stood you up?"

I nodded. "I just want to work. Take my mind off it."

"Can't pay you the extra, hon."

I nodded again. Janelle, the other barista who worked for Betty, was giving me a look, like she thought I might be trying to steal her shift or something. I jerked my head toward the door. "No point both of us being here. I'll finish your shift. My treat."

Betty seemed to think it over for a while, then nodded. "Fool wants to work free for an hour, you might as well get paid. Hit the road, girl."

Janelle smiled and was out the door while I was still tying the apron strings behind my back. I could feel Betty's eyes boring into my back, so I spoke without turning to face her.

"You holding back on that 'told you so' for later, or just until I turn around?"

"Your business, child."

"But you're still judging me." I turned and gave her a half smile to show I wasn't mad. She shrugged, but I could see in her eyes she was still worrying.

"I don't like to see someone offer candy then snatch it away like that. Maybe it's time you stopped reaching out for it when they come round."

With the cleaning spray in one hand, and a cloth in the other, I set off to wipe down the tables. She wasn't wrong.

Roomie

The door crashed open and Bernie strode in. I don't know if she meant to, but every time she entered a room it was like she was making an entrance. She hadn't come back last night, and this was the first time I had seen her since she had stormed out yesterday. A heady cloud of BO and stale beer followed her around.

"Did you have a good night?"

She grunted and dug a beer out of the fridge. I put my open book face down over the arm of the chair, unfolded my legs from beneath me and turned to look at her. I had a half hour before I had to leave for my shift at the diner, but I sensed my quiet reading time had just come to an end.

"It was OK."

"Who did you end up with? Karl?"

"Dean, as if it's any of your business. Played pool until they kicked us out then went back to his place and...." She chuckled like Beavis or Butthead and I tried not to judge. Tried real hard.

"She didn't show up," I said.

"Who?"

I felt myself frown before I could stop it, and I'd swear she looked away from me for a second, like she couldn't meet my eyes.

"The woman I met yesterday."

Bernie grunted and turned away, disinterested. "Should've guessed."

"Why?"

"You look all pouty and miserable. It's your own fault. Shouldn't give these bloodsuckers air to breathe. You'll just keep getting hurt."

Bernie threw the empty beer bottle into the trash with an expert wrist flick, and I made a note to dig it out in the morning and put it in the recycle box. She went to the fridge and pulled out another beer, twisting savagely at the cap to rip it off.

"Are you OK?" I asked. Two beers so close together was unusual.

Bernie glared at me. "What's it to you?"

I raised my hands peaceably in front of me. Either Dean had given her a hard time about something – or hadn't – or she was just PMSing, and I didn't have time for either. "My bad. Not my business."

She grunted, and the anger faded from the lines around her eyes. The room tension backed down a notch. I closed the book around the bookmark and took it into my room to change for work.

Body

The police came into the diner on Thursday evening. Not sure how, but as soon as I saw them, I knew they were looking for me. Perhaps because they were looking at head height, not down at the diners. I groaned. Thursday was the new Friday, and the place was bustling. And my stomach was rumbling. I had skipped lunch and there had been no shift at the coffee shop that morning. Hungry and serving delicious plates of pasta to other people was a torment unique to serving staff, and why we always deserve generous tips.

One of the cops – his name was Steve – was a coffee shop regular. He would come in most days for two double shot lattes. I kept trying to sell him donuts, but all he ever wanted was giant cookies. I met them halfway across the diner.

"Business or pleasure, officers?"

Steve had a polite smile, but his partner wore a serious expression. I guessed business.

"Hi, Jane," said Steve. "Do you know a Tamsin Whiston?"

I shook my head but got an icy feeling in my gut.

"Mature female, five–nine, long gray hair," pushed the other cop, and I felt sick.

"Oh, her. She came into the coffee shop a few days ago.

17

Seemed like she wanted to sell shares in the Brooklyn Bridge." I tapped my forehead. Like I said, most of the cops had heard of my memory thing. Steve nodded, understanding, but his partner just kept cold eyes on me as though he thought he could make me crack and confess to whatever. Ray, the owner, made a fake but pointed cough from the serving hatch. Cops in the shop weren't good for business.

"What can I help you with, officers?"

"You need to come down to the station, answer some questions." The tough guy reached toward my arm. I took a half–step back to keep out of his reach and kept my focus on Steve.

"Does it have to be now? I'll lose my shift." *And I'll lose it anyway if I don't get you guys out of here pretty much now*, I thought.

"Yes, lady, it has–" started hard cop, all angry business, reaching for me again. Steve casually pushed his partner's arm down before it could grab me.

"Can you make it tomorrow? Morning?"

"About ten?"

Steve smiled, and I wondered if he was hitting on me. "That would be fine, Jane. Ask for Detective Adams. I'll let her know you said you'd drop by."

The hard man turned and marched out, but Steve stopped at the door and turned back. "Sorry for the intrusion, folks. You all enjoy your evening, now."

I appreciated that. It wouldn't hurt my tips, and it would keep Raymundo off my back.

The police station was an unattractive building on the edge of downtown, and far enough away that I needed to use my battered motor scooter to get there – unless I wanted the chore to take the entire morning. It was legal and licensed, but my helmet had a broken strap and a crack through the side. You had to look hard to see it, but I decided to leave it with the scooter while I went in.

The desk officer was brisk but polite. I told him who I was there to see, and he pointed me to a plastic bench bolted to the floor and wall. Clifton didn't have much of a crime problem, mostly weekend drunks. Things could get interesting when a new dealer rolled into town and the crackheads got frisky, but generally it was quiet.

I can't say I've been in many police stations, but I'd visited this one a few times while I straightened out my new identity. The smell never changed: dirty mop water, a hint of old fast food, and testosterone. Or BO.

The door to the side of the waiting space opened, and a woman in plain clothes stepped out. She didn't look much older than me, and somehow that made me feel a little resentful. Five second breath. It wasn't her fault.

"Hi," she said, hand stretched out to shake. She looked at the notepad she was carrying and frowned. "Sorry, but is this name correct?"

I smiled, though I could feel my lips twisted it up some. "Yeah, I get that a lot. It's right. Jane Doe."

And then the penny dropped, and my smile got wider. "You new?"

She didn't like that, though I didn't mean anything by it. I felt the temperature drop as she turned away and nodded to the desk officer to buzz us through the door. I waited to make my apology. We walked through the squad room, where I waved at another of the cops I knew from the coffee shop, and through to a corridor of doors. From the signs, they were interview rooms, and I wasn't comfortable with that. I'd expected to be in an office.

She opened a door for me, and I felt a little better. No table with bolt down chairs or hoops for locking handcuffs to. Just a couple of comfy chairs and a couch, with a table between them.

"Sorry about just now," I said. "I didn't mean anything when I said you must be new. I'm sort of known around here."

She looked up at me, eyebrows raised, and I blushed.

"Not officially," I hurried to say. "I'm the girl with no past, no name. Guess I was just being bitchy when I decided it could stay Jane Doe forever."

She nodded, and a little of the tension went out of her face.

"I see. And yes, I'm new to town."

"Welcome," I said, then worried I was overdoing it.

She gave me a plastic smile and offered me coffee, which I turned down. I had tried the coffee here. Once.

"How can I help you?" I asked.

"What do you know of Tamsin Whiston?"

"If she's an old lady, she might be the one pestering me in the coffee shop a few days ago."

"Pestering?"

"It's the memory thing. Tricksters think they can tumble me to pay them for some miracle cure, or they can find my family if I could just pay them a few thousand in up–front expenses. You know the sort of thing."

The detective nodded absently, looking down at her notes. "And how does it make you feel when somebody approaches you like this?"

I shrugged. "It's annoying."

"We have reports that you were shouting and screaming at

the individual."

Five count breath. "I raised my voice. Some might interpret that as shouting these days. I certainly didn't scream at her. And you can check with my employer on that."

She flashed me a smile that didn't make it as far as her eyes. "We will." Her eyes tracked her pen as she ran it down the page on her pad, then again when she flipped to the next page.

"Did the two of you discuss anything apart from your amnesia?"

I took a moment to run over the conversation in my mind. "Can't think of anything. She said she would meet me tomorrow with evidence to back up her claim. Oh, and she asked me if I was taking something. She called it witchbone – no, Witchbane, maybe."

"And what's that?"

"No idea." I shrugged. "I waited for her at Gino's, where we arranged to meet, but she never showed."

"Gino's? Why not the coffeehouse where you work?"

"I didn't want to bring my trouble into my employer's house," I said. "And I wanted to be able to walk out."

"If you lost your temper again?"

"I didn't lose my temper the first time," I said, keeping my voice even. I was taking a dislike to the eager beaver. She seemed a little too interested in trying to needle me, and not interested enough in listening to what I had to say. And I was getting a bad feeling. "Can I ask what this is about?"

She stared at me for a moment, face still, eyes flat. "We found Tamsin Whiston in a dumpster halfway down the alley at the end of Medford. Blunt force trauma crushed the back of her head, then somebody made a fire out of her belongings. The only thing we found was this, clenched so tight in her right hand the ME had to break her fingers to extract it."

The detective took a photo from the envelope on the table and slid it across to me. "Ever seen anything like this?"

I was barely listening. Why would anybody hurt her? She was just an old lady. Maybe screwy, or crooked, but she was still just an old lady.

"Miss Doe? Do you recognize it? Do you know what it is or why she would think it so important?"

I shook my head and paid attention to the photo. It showed a silver compass. There was more on the dial than bearing marks, and in the middle a silver lid covered a cup of blue crystal. There was something in the bowl, but I couldn't make out what it was.

"No idea," I said, shaking my head. But a crazy thought had come to me. I remembered how she kept looking at her hand, then up to me. What if that was what had led her to me? And what if she had given her life to make sure nobody else got hold of it?

Meds

I checked the mailbox in the lobby on my way back from the coffee shop. Nothing exciting, just a couple of joint bills, Bernie's MasterCard penance for the month, and my meds. I took them all upstairs and threw them on the breakfast bar while I showered and changed. Working in a coffee shop may not sound tough, but I didn't want to stink of coffee grounds and sugar for the rest of the day. It wasn't a hair day, so I wound it up into a bun and pulled on a shower cap. Now that may sound skanky to some, but my hair reaches down to my butt and washing it is an hour-long ritual.

When I opened the package for my meds, I stared at the bottle. I had swallowed a little gray pill while I ran through my morning on autopilot, but right now the plastic tub held my full attention. I popped open the bottle and sniffed. Plastic, hint of antiseptic, but mostly the dusty, slightly sour smell of the pills. Like a pot of dried herbs that had gone way, way past their use by date.

It was two days, or maybe three, since I spent time with the pushy detective, and the old woman's death had left me feeling cranky. Perhaps what she said lingered on my mind and made me pay extra attention to the delivery.

My laptop was still in my room and I rushed through to grab it, hoping Bernie hadn't changed the Wi-Fi password since yesterday. I logged in and grinned; the laptop still had access. There were a couple of downloads I needed to set off while she didn't know I could get in – or she would bill me for the time – then I looked up the name of the pills: Tetranuvenol.

No hits, and no hits on alternative spellings. I tried what looked like a reference number in the corner of the label, but that came up with parts for a pressure washer. Frustrated, and needing to stretch a kink out of my back, I got up and fetched a bottle of water from the fridge. This did not feel good. On the way back I picked up the bubble pouch they had arrived in and checked that over too.

The label held nothing more than my address and the printed postage. It had no logo, and no company name. I'd never noticed before, but I'd never had a reason to. Even the return address was just a street name and a zip code. Then I got another idea. Web maps could do all kinds of useful stuff, and I could use one to see what was there.

I put in the zip code, zoomed in to the address, then switched to a street view. This was no longer funny. It was a bunch of mailboxes, a street maildrop facility.

What the hell was I taking?

More importantly, how could I find out? Damn it, and I was paying for these things.

I grabbed my bag on the way to the door. The mini mall on the next block had a pharmacist, and I wanted some answers.

I found a line at the counter, then I had to wait some more when I asked to see the actual pharmacist, not one of the assistants. When he got to me, he looked as though his day had not been going too well. I took the bottle from my bag and held it out to him.

"Can you tell me what these are?"

He rolled the bottle over in his fingers. "It says right there. Take one a day." He made to hand the bottle back to me, but I didn't take it. I bit back on an 'I can read too' comeback. I needed his help.

"Right. But what *are* they? Can you tell me what they're for?"

I was still getting an 'are you an idiot?' look. "Why don't you ask your doctor?"

"I don't have one."

"Then ask whoever prescribed you the medication."

He was pushing my button, but I clenched my teeth for a moment and smiled again. "It's a long story. Can you just tell me what they are?"

"It should all be in the data sheet in the box, miss."

"They don't come with one. I send a payment out of my bank every month, they turn up in the post, and I take one a day."

His eyebrows went up. "And you don't know what they are? I think I need to see some ID."

"Why?"

"To make sure you didn't just find these on the sidewalk. For all I know, you could be checking to see if they have any street value."

"Do they?"

He shrugged. "No idea. Never seen them before."

Finally, I was getting somewhere. I dug my ID out of my bag and slapped it on the counter. "These turned up when I got discharged from hospital. They said I had dissociative amnesia and I assumed they were part of my treatment. I'd like to make sure of that. Is there some way you can look them up?"

"Well, why didn't you just say that?" he grumbled, then peered at the label again. He tutted and shook his head. "Look at that. Label is so badly printed I can't even make out the dispensing pharmacy. Gimme a minute."

It was more than a minute. It was long enough that I was wishing I hadn't drunk the bottle of water before I came out. I'd reached the point of trying to remember where the mall's restrooms were by the time he came back.

"Nothing."

"At all?" I sounded a little whiny and decided to shut up. I wasn't expecting that. My hands got clammy and my chest tightened.

"Not listed in any of my reference books, not listed in the FDA index, not listed in the homeopathy index, and nothing in the register of dispensaries is a match for what I can guess off the label. If you want my advice, stop taking these. On the positive side, it could just be some scam, and these are nothing more than sugar pills, or vitamin pills and you're being ripped off. Worse case, these could be from some crank and doing you actual harm. Stop taking them and make an appointment to see a doctor to discuss your healthcare needs and monitor any adverse effects."

I muttered "damn" and held out my hand for the bottle. He seemed reluctant to hand it back.

"Do you mind if I take a couple of these? I'd like to send them to the FDA for analysis."

He popped the lid off the bottle when I nodded. "Did you say they arrive by mail?" He shook two into his hand, replaced the lid and handed the bottle back to me.

"It's just a mailbox."

"Still, couldn't hurt to write them."

Suddenly I felt drained and done with the entire thing. And annoyed I hadn't thought of that. I'd worried about hucksters scamming me face to face, when for the last five years the most successful scam of all had been ripping me off a hundred bucks a month for a box of fake pills. I gave the pharmacist the best smile I could. "Perhaps. Thanks. I mean, really. You've given me a lot of your time."

He flashed back a tired grin. "No problem. It was nice to get a little variety into the day."

I waved and walked off to find the restroom.

A Letter

Bernie appeared at my bedroom door, opening it without knocking like she always did, tapping the edge of an envelope against her free hand. "Why do you have a lawyer?"

"I don't."

"Well, you have a letter from one."

"What?"

She gets mail all the time, most of it junk. All I get is my meds, and that's it. I barely exist. My bank communicates by email, and I don't have a credit card or half the other things that make you visible to trash marketing. That's why I didn't see the letter. As usual, I threw everything onto the breakfast bar and left it for Bernie.

She held the letter up so I could read someone had addressed it to me but made no move to pass it over. I'd no intention of playing her version of keep–away. Bet she was a blast in high school. I turned my eyes back to my book. "Either throw it on the bed or let me know what it says when you've read it."

She just stood there for a moment, then I heard a loud sniff and the letter fluttered down between my face and the book – an excellent throw if she meant it. Bernie flounced off, leaving the door open. Again, just to annoy me. She had days like this, where she seemed to need to peck at me. But, like I said, the lease was in her name. My choice to put up or move out.

Once I was sure she left, I put the book down and lifted the letter. Heavy. Very fancy paper, with a logo in the top left corner. The company name, Walcott, Choke & Partners was in *olde worlde* font along the bottom, under the transparent window where my address showed through. Most letters these days seemed content with an off−center stick−on label.

I ripped it open and let the contents slide out: a single sheet of thick paper.

Dear Miss Doe

We would appreciate your calling us to arrange a meeting at our office, at your earliest convenience. The matter is delicate, and may only be discussed in person. We believe it to be to your significant advantage.

Looking forward to speaking to you as a matter of urgency.

Assuring you of our best regards and endeavors

E. F. Walcott

My heart sank. Another con artist trying to sell me legal services to sue the hospital, or some other poor schmuck, for breaking my memory. I tore the letter in four and threw it on the floor, but when I tried to read my book, the words swam through the tears pooling on my eyelids. Why wouldn't they just leave me *alone*?

Two days later a FedEx driver burst into the coffee shop. Ever noticed how they have a certain way of moving? Like they're doing the most important job in the world and everybody else should just step aside. I was just putting my 'can I take your order, sir' smile on when I saw the package in his hand. Business, not pleasure, then.

"Jane Doe?" he called, looking around to see if anybody answered.

I nodded, and he held out a clipboard. Quaint. I dabbed my hands dry on my apron, signed, and he held out the package. It was the size of a sheet from a college notebook, folded in two, and so slim it looked empty. I stared at it, and he gave it a shake.

"You have to take it lady, I can't put it down on a dirty counter."

That earned him a glare. My counter was *never* dirty. Taking the envelope by the corners, I put it on a shelf where it wouldn't get dusty or damp. The FedEx guy turned and whisked away, and I was sure I heard him say 'sheesh'.

Betty glared at me from the door of the storeroom that doubled as her office. I checked around; there were no waiting customers, and I'd wiped down the empty tables five minutes ago. Screw her. She had nothing to gripe at me for. I turned the package over, gripped the little tag, and tore it open. For a moment I thought it really was empty, but then I saw the envelope and my heart gave an odd skip–beat. It was obvious who it would be from, and I was scowling before I pulled it out.

The outer sleeve went in the recycle bin, then I checked again that nobody was waiting and that nothing needed doing. Only then did I tear open the envelope and throw that in the recycle too.

The letter was terse and to the point.

Dear Miss Doe

It would seem either our recent letter did not reach you, or you have not yet acted upon it.

I urge you most strongly to call me on the number above, asking for me by name, to discuss a serious matter that will be to your advantage.

I look forward to hearing from you soon.

Your servant,

E.F. Walcott

The bell clanged over the door. I crammed the letter into the back pocket of my jeans and forgot about it as I focused on serving a posse of moms that surged in. Only when my shift finished did I feel the letter crinkle in my pocket. I pulled it out and read it again, then went into the storeroom. Betty was sitting at the desk she had crammed into the corner, doing paperwork, and it was a few seconds before she looked up. She frowned.

"Don't bring your personal life to work, Jane. It doesn't look good in front of the customers."

I wasn't taking that. "There weren't any customers. You saw me make sure of that. And this wasn't my idea, and I never gave them the address here. Let me use the phone and I'll do my best not to have it happen again."

I don't usually bite back at Betty. She doesn't moan at me that much, and when she does, I often deserve it. But this was unfair, and I wasn't going to let her get away with it.

She looked up at me, eyebrows raised. Remember I said she thought of herself as everybody's mom? Well, like most moms, she didn't like back talk. I hurried into an explanation I didn't know I was going to offer.

"I know it's long distance. My cell phone company will charge me a fortune and my roomie will pry about it. You want them to stop bugging me at work? Let me call them here and shut them down." When I finished, I winced at how lame I sounded.

Betty glared at me. "If it's over five minutes, it will come from your pay. And I have work to do, so if it's private I suggest you go elsewhere."

"Thank you. I'll deal with it, I promise."

The line purred once after I dialed the number on the letterhead. A prim-voiced receptionist, who managed to turn being polite into an insult, told me Mr. Walcott wasn't available. She made me feel so stupid I snapped at her.

"Well tell Walcott if he wants to see me so bad, he can damn well come down here himself. And he can stop pestering me with letters and FedEx—"

"FedEx?" The receptionist's voice sharpened, and she paid a lot more attention. "May I ask who is calling?"

"Jane Doe." I was waiting for the 'I'm afraid I need your proper name', but that wasn't what I got.

"Sorry to have kept you waiting, Miss Doe. Mr. Walcott will be with you immediately. Please hold."

The line clicked and I braced myself for the on—hold music. I was betting on something boringly classical, but not a note played before the line clicked again.

"Miss Doe?"

He sounded mature, but not old. He came over as crisp, no nonsense, but not short. I curled my lips and tried to wipe the impression away. That's what cons want you to do, build up an image of them they can build on.

"Yes. Now would you please stop—"

"Might I enquire when you can take the time to come and see us."

We sort of spoke at the same time. It was easier to let him finish rather than talk over him.

"I've no intention of coming to see you."

"Indeed? May I ask why?"

"Can't we deal with this over the phone?"

"I am afraid not. The matter is confidential, and we can only discuss it here."

"So what are you trying to sell me?"

"Nothing, I assure you." I was sure I heard a soft chuckle. "Might I ask again why you chose not to come?"

I took a breath. "Because I can't afford to lose a day's wages to come to whatever time–share or realty investment opportunity you're trying to sell me. Hell, I'm not even sure my scooter will go that far."

"I see." He went quiet, but I could still hear background noise at his end, so I knew they hadn't hung up. "We will send a car for you and arrange one to take you home. We will reimburse you for any lost income, and we will pay any reasonable expenses incurred on the journey, for refreshments and so forth. Would the day after tomorrow suit?"

I knew I should say no, but he caught me off guard. Being stuck in an Uber for three hours didn't fill me with joy, but I'd get a free lunch out of it, even if I walked out of his office as soon as I got there. And I was curious why they were so crazy eager to see me.

"I guess."

"Wonderful. Give me your cellphone number. I will have the driver text you when he arrives at your address."

I gave him the number of my cell, said my goodbyes, and

hung up.

Betty was looking at me. Not glaring, just looking, and with a certain amount of sympathy.

"When are you going to learn, child? One day you'll have to accept there ain't no answers out there for you."

I shrugged and gave her a half–smile.

"One more favor?" I begged.

Lawyers

My phone pinged. The car was outside. I had planned to be all rebellious and wear my angriest t−shirt and ripped jeans, but I changed my mind at the last minute and rushed into something smart, or as smart as I could. It didn't make me feel great that most of it was from my work uniforms.

I was glad I did. He hadn't sent an Uber. He sent a limo. Not a big one, but it was still most definitely a limo, and I stood on the sidewalk and gawped at it. The driver got out and opened the door for me, like I was going to prom or something. No, not something I remembered, something I saw in a movie.

I got in, sliding my backside across the soft leather seat, and settled back, trying not to stare at the gadgets, the smoked windows, and the partition between me and the driver. The driver got in but didn't pull away. After a moment his voice sounded through an intercom.

"Seatbelt, miss. I can't leave until you're wearing it."

Face burning, I pulled the strap across and clicked it into place. The car pulled off so quietly it could have been electric. I turned my head and stared out the windows, looking for anybody who saw me get in. Part of me wanted there to be someone, but part of me hoped nobody had been there to report back to Bernie. I didn't want to come home to an interrogation about what I'd been doing.

Once we got onto the freeway, the driver came back on the intercom.

"Please help yourself to any of the facilities. There are cold drinks in the mini fridge, and to your right is the coffee machine. For your safety, please don't take the lid off the cup once it's removed from the machine. In the center armrest are the controls for the entertainment system. We have Netflix and Spotify, or you can pair your phone with Bluetooth."

I wished. My phone had heard of Bluetooth but wanted nothing to do with such new–fangled technology.

"On the door is a button to raise a privacy screen between us. I'll shut up now and leave you in peace. If you need me, press the button that looks like a Lego man and that will open the intercom."

"Thank you," I called, then wondered if he heard me. He smiled at me in his mirror, so I guessed he did.

I had three hours in a comfy chair, with decent coffee and I even found chocolate in the mini fridge. Mellow music and my book. What more could I want? I even took a nap.

The sights didn't interest me that much once we reached Lancaster. I recognized City Hall when we passed it, and the gates to Memorial Park. That was where on–the–spot reporters always seemed to set up their cameras. Other than that, the place just looked like the downtown district of any other major city. Like Clifton, you'll never find this Lancaster on a map either. And yes, I have a reason for that, too.

The limo drove through to the business district, and swung into a smaller, quieter street, before it turned down a ramp into an underground garage. The driver pulled up level with a line of elevators, and a concierge appeared out of nowhere to open the door for me. Swanky. I got out and turned to thank the driver, but the door was already closed, and the car was whispering away. I felt bad I hadn't said something sooner.

"This way, miss." The uniformed concierge gestured toward the elevator doors, getting there ahead of me to press the call button. A door opened right away.

"Mr. Walcott?"

"Fifteen, miss." The concierge touched the brim of his hat and faded away to wherever he had been hiding when I got there. I poked the appropriate button, and the elevator whirred into motion.

The lobby was trying to be modern and edgy, yet reassuringly traditional. I didn't like it. The receptionist sat behind a wood-paneled counter, all bee-hive hairdo and cat's-eye glasses.

"Miss Doe?"

I nodded, and she gestured at the register with an elegant hand. "Mr. Walcott will be here before you finish signing in."

I thought it was a bold promise, but she was right. Walcott was at least ten years older than he sounded, but his eyes were sharp, and his body trim. His suit had to be worth four thousand dollars. And I still didn't trust him.

"Miss Doe." He closed on me with an outstretched hand. "So good of you to find the time to visit us. Please, come through to my office." He led the way, somehow getting in front of me to open each door we came to.

His office was nothing like the lobby. As you walked through the door it felt like you had stepped back a hundred years. Ancient wood panels covered the walls and portraits of a dozen stern—faced men glowered down at me. The desk was enormous and looked like it cost more than the apartment I lived in. I started toward it, but he edged me toward the comfy leather chairs huddling around a low table.

"Please, make yourself comfortable. Would you like coffee? Water?"

I shook my head. "Can we get to the bottom of this? I have to get back in time for my shift tomorrow."

Walcott pursed his lips and didn't say anything. He had a problem with that, but I didn't care. Taking a file from his desk, Walcott settled into one of the other chairs. He opened the envelope and sorted through it until he found what he wanted.

"I will be frank with you, Miss Doe, this is the culmination of one of the strangest sequences of events in my career." He looked up from the paperwork and smiled. "And I have seen some very strange things indeed."

I could see him shift mental gears as he finally got to the point.

"I understand that you made the acquaintance of a Miss Tamsin Whiston a week go, or thereabouts?"

And the crazy old lady was back in my life, messing me up again. I nodded.

"Good." He paused again, looking at the sheet of paper in his hand, and I swear I saw his head shake. "We received instructions from Miss Whiston to amend her will. Barring a few conditions, she has bequeathed her entire estate to you."

"Shut. Up."

"I am most serious."

My brain switched on again. "I get it. All I need to do is provide you with a few thousand dollars in advance fees so you can start the process off, right?"

Walcott did a magnificent job of looking offended. "Young lady, this is not some cheap scam. The majority of the estate comprises a single property in this city, and a small financial settlement in the form of an annuity. The bequest is unencumbered by taxes or fees."

"You said there were conditions?"

"You must stay in the property for twenty–four hours, directly from here once we have concluded our business for the day. Unless you do so, or should you leave the property for any reason before the twenty–four hours have elapsed, we must revoke the bequest and reinstate her previous will.

"Once you have stayed in the property for the required period, it is yours. You may dispose of it as you wish, but with the proviso that the disposition does not disadvantage the existing tenants. If you sell the property, the annuity lapses and the balance is settled elsewhere."

"That's crazy. Is the place haunted or something? Axe murderers ready to jump out the doors?" My head was reeling, and I knew I was being stupid. But seriously, what the f–?

Walcott chuckled. "Miss Whiston was something of an eccentric, but I doubt the building is possessed. Except by you." He laughed at his own joke, but it faded away when I didn't join in. He coughed and ran his finger around the front of his collar. "Do you agree to abide by the requirements?"

Betty would go nuts when I told her I wouldn't be working tomorrow either, but I nodded.

House

Another car was waiting when I stepped out of the elevator and whisked me back up to the street. Only an Uber this time, which was disappointing. Being chauffeured around in a limo was something I could get used to. I expected a long drive out to a leafy suburb, or to some gated community where little old ladies lived. What I got was a three–story condo less than fifteen minutes away.

The street was nice enough. I couldn't tell if developers had gentrified it, or if it had always been as nice, but I wouldn't want to walk down some of the streets we drove along to get there. Thinking about it, I wasn't sure I'd want to ride my scooter along them either.

The car dropped me off. I checked the address on the note Walcott gave me when he handed me the keys. Right place. The buildings were all the same, set in a small plot of land, just enough space on either side for a set of stairs at one side, and an alley for trash cans on the other. Looked like they were all built as three apartments, with the stairs giving access to the upper units. What did that make them? Stacked triplexes? A memory from a book I'd read suggested I use 'third floor walk-up', but I decided to stick with my original choice of 'condo'.

Narrow windows at ground level suggested a basement. Walcott said the old woman had lived on the ground floor, and I guessed the front door served that. I walked up the steps and put the key into the fire–engine red door. Goosebumps ran up my arm as I pushed the door open. Weird. The longer I stood there, the more it felt like static electricity was crawling over my arms. As I stepped inside, the prickling ran across my whole body.

My jaw swayed in the breeze as I wandered around. I don't think I'd had time to form much of an expectation, but I didn't come close. The living room was almost austere. The original floorboards had been sanded, and polished to a pale finish. The seating was all white leather, with low chrome frames. A huge flat–screen sat next to a sound system – with a turntable of all things.

One door led off to a guest room, another to what was obviously her room, and a third to the bathroom. An arch led back to the kitchen. White units, with matching dark floor tiles and work tops. Breakfast bar. A six–seat dining table in black and chrome.

And on the table, propped up against a mug, an envelope bore the name the woman had called me by – Paulette Tipton.

I came close to walking out of the house. It had already creeped me out by making me tingle when I got here. And no, I didn't accept that was just the excitement of the situation. Now I found she'd planned to get me here all along. Who the hell did she think she was? That wasn't my name, even if it once had been. *My* name was Jane Doe. It worked just fine for me, and I didn't need a new one, or an old one. The front door handle was an inch from my hand before my natural greed struggled back into control.

Storming out wasn't an option. Even if I didn't want the place, what I could get for it would set me up for life. Maybe I would buy a place back home, get out from sharing. It was too good to give up. I let my hand drop, turned away from the door and sulked back into the kitchen.

The letter I left where it was, still wanting nothing to do with it. I wanted beer, and something to eat, but all I found was wine and ice cream. On the breakfast bar, a pepper pot in the shape of a porcelain toadstool held down a couple of twenties and menus for local pizza and Chinese restaurants that delivered. Sorted. The TV had cable and movie channels, so I slouched on the couch, getting a taste for red wine and stuffing myself with pizza until I fell asleep.

My head throbbed, and I felt sick if I tried to move. I knew it was morning, because I remembered it getting dark and now it was light again, but that was about as much thinking as I could do. I found coffee pods, filled the machine with water, and kept running pods through until I had a full mug. That cut through the hangover enough for me to toast some bread.

Balancing plates was second nature to me now, and I took everything to the table and set it all safely down. Then I cursed. The breakfast bar would have been better. That damn letter was staring at me, taunting me. Biting into a slice of toast, I glared right back at the envelope.

I knew I was being stupid. The old woman wasn't taunting me, or trying to offend me. Unless this was still all some crazy, over–engineered scam she was trying to pull off. Or *had* been trying. Somehow, I kept forgetting she was dead.

Pushing the toast to the side, I picked up the envelope. I had another six hours to wait in the house; that was time enough to find out what she had to say. I ripped open the flap, pulled out the single sheet, then dropped it onto the table. It bore just one word, handwritten, maybe with a fountain pen.

Breathe.

My fists clenched, and my heart pounded in my ears. Stupid old bitch *was* trying to mess with my head. Was this a test? Wind up the amnesia girl, dangle a carrot in front of her and see if you can piss her off enough to make her throw away the prize? Well, I would be damned if I would let her win. I drew in a ten–count breath and let it out so hard it made the paper flutter.

The word faded away, leaving the page blank. I stared, then felt my eyes open wide as more words appeared on the page, floating up and bobbing around on the surface of the paper sea before settling into place.

I stood up, knocking over my chair, and nearly tripping over it as I took a step back. What the hell was going on here? From where I stood, I could read the first few lines.

Dear Paulette.

I am deeply sorry for the hoops and tricks, but I must be sure it is you. If you are reading this, something has gone wrong, and I must assume I have been killed. A pity. I would like to get to know you, and to help you through what is to come.

I stepped back to the table. The letter didn't look like it was going to explode, or suck out my soul, but what the hell did she mean, *what is to come*? Ominous, much? I kept reading.

If I am dead, then I have no use for the things that made up my life. I have no children to leave them to, so I shall leave them to you, even though I've yet to meet you. Or is that to meet you again?

There are forces in play, now and when you were much younger, that you cannot know, and I will understand if you do not wish to pursue them. I was hoping to tell you this in person, to soften the blow somehow, but this you must know. Your situation is not a result of some neurological or psychological condition. Someone did this to you, deliberately.

I dropped the letter on the table and turned away. A belt had pulled tight around my chest and my eyes stung. Bitch. How could someone play on me like this? It went beyond cruel. I would sell this pile of crap for a penny, or throw the tenants out and have the place pounded to dust. I'd put a sign up as a memorial to show other rat–bastard scammers what would come of their schemes.

The water from the faucet was ice cold and I let it pour over my wrists before I splashed my face. Wow. Talk about touching a nerve. I picked up the letter and nearly dropped it again. The message had disappeared, and the only word on the paper was Breathe. Creepy. I huffed at it and the writing came back. I felt one side of my mouth hitch up in a grin at the same time my eyes opened so wide they nearly fell out on the table. Creepy it might be, but it was also incredibly cool. I scanned down the page to find where I had left off and the grin upgraded to a chuckle. The next line read *This may make you angry or upset.* Dead center, lady.

This may make you angry or upset. You have every right to be, and it will upset you again as you find out more. I don't want to put you through any more of that than you want. If this is already too much for you, the house is still yours.

If you want to know more, not just about what they did to you, but about the magnificent world around us and the wonderful thing that they stole from you, go down the basement stairs, and stand with your back to the door at the bottom. Place your hand on the wall in front of you, then breath on it, just as you have with this letter.

One word of caution. Once you leave this house, neither the letter nor the portal will work for you again, and if you attempt to break the portal down, the space beyond will destroy itself. I don't mean to sound melodramatic, but there are certain things within that must either be protected or destroyed.

Well, she failed on that. Couldn't have got more melodramatic if she had been trying for it, but it did the job. If what she was aiming for was to make me curious, she just put a box with a hole in front of a cat.

I put the letter down, gently this time, and picked up my mug. It was cold, so I killed time and avoided having to think about anything until I made another. I didn't want to spend another eternity stuffing pods into a machine, so I hunted around until I found some ground and made it in the filter machine. Turned out it took about the same length of time, but it gave me some separation, some space to think. I felt like she wanted me to react, that she – or something – wanted me to be rash. Or could I be blaming her for my own curiosity? I still felt like I was being manipulated, even if I was doing it to myself.

I sat at the breakfast bar and sipped my coffee. It was good. It hadn't been ground that long ago, and it was strong without being bitter. Tamsin Whiston had excellent taste, and

I wondered if I would be able to get more. Which brought me up short. I hadn't made any decisions. Why was I worrying if I could find her coffee supplier?

Or had I decided? Was I at least edging toward a decision? Who wouldn't want to live here? I even liked the furniture and the decor. And then fear slapped me again. Fear of leaving the cozy safety blanket of Clifton. Fear of starting all over again, of retelling my story another thousand times. Fear that something lurking down in the basement would send all this to shit.

At least I could do something about one of them. I set my mug on the counter and strode to the basement door.

Workshop of the Weird

The stairs down to the basement were wide, and the door at the bottom was strong like an outside door. Made sense. It was a shared space, and anybody could have forgotten to lock the outside door. The top half was glass, but frosted. I twisted the catch and opened the door. If living here was becoming an option, I should have a good poke around.

I found nothing out of the ordinary. Industrial grade washers and dryers, shelves with soaps and conditioners, and a couple of chest freezers. One was big enough to freeze whole bodies. I closed the door, locked it again, and turned my back to it, like the instructions said.

The letter said I had to put my hand on the wall, and I needed to take a half–step forward to do that. I raised my hand but taking the step didn't happen. Was I scared? Or was I afraid that it was still a hoax, or that whatever was beyond would be... disappointing? I made myself take a deep lungful of air and shuffled my feet forward, then I touched my fingers to the wall and breathed out.

A tracery of black rippled out from my fingers, looking like lace or a raggedy cobweb. They crawled over the surface of the wall, then collected in lines about the size and shape of a door. The outline got thicker, until I felt the wall move under my hand, like it had settled inwards. As I pressed harder a panel set back into the wall, then slid sideways. In front of me was a curtain of rich red velvet. I leaned forward and put my hand to that too, and when it parted down the middle, I took a deep breath and walked through.

I gasped. The room was already lit, maybe by me opening the door, or maybe by some movement detector I couldn't see, and it looked like a set from a fairy tale. I took a couple of cautious steps inside. A soft scraping made me turn around in time to see the door slide back into place, but I saw a handle catch the curtain. If I had a way to get out, I had no reason to panic, right?

Half the floor was clear of furniture and had a crazy circle and star design laid right into the concrete. The same design as half the stuff in the hippy shop on the next block over from Betty's. The metal inlay shone like it had just been polished, but the color was richer than chrome or steel – silver, maybe? The other half of the room was dominated by a table, and I edged closer. It looked like the kitchen table from an old farmhouse, but breakfast bar high. She kept the top scrubbed clean, but there were burns, gouges and pits all over. A real workbench.

The only thing on the table was a manilla office envelope, covered in little boxes with names crossed out in them. Something else I'd seen in the movies, for sending memos around offices in the days before electricity. On top of that sat another of those damned envelopes, again addressed to her, not me.

I ignored the letter, at least for now. Wandering around the rest of the room was too interesting, and I didn't want to burst the bubble. The old girl was either a total nut–job, or serious about what she did. All the walls around the table—end of the room were full of shelves. Some were stacked with books older than anything I'd seen in a museum, and even some honest to goodness *scrolls*. Most of the titles I couldn't even read, but I made out one that said *Greater and Lesser Demons of the Lower Hells* by some guy called Geoffry of Whitby, and another I could just make out said something about *Ye Undying and Their Habyts*.

Another set of shelves held boxes full of candles, all shapes, sizes and colors, even with stuff crusted into them or words written around them. I wandered from shelf to shelf. Some of the old girl's trinkets and knick-knacks made me grin, others were gross, like a jar that said it contained pickled frog's hearts. I swept by countless bottles of herbs, some tied in bunches. She even had a space for blank notepads and a box of pencils, and the plastic sharpener screwed to the shelf looked utterly out of place.

But I stopped in my tracks when I saw a label that said *Witchbane*.

I took it off the shelf and closer to the light that hung over the table. It didn't look like much. If anything, it reminded me of dried oregano, though maybe yellower, like it had gone stale.

She said I smelled of this, that day when we met in the coffee shop. I pulled the stopper out the top of the jar and sniffed. Carefully. I didn't get much of anything, so I tried again, harder. It smelled familiar, but I couldn't place it. Once I'd replaced the stopper I stared at the label. It had nothing else to tell me, so I put the jar back on the shelf.

There was more. Cool knives, and wands, and a staff with stuff carved along the edge. I even found a crystal ball. The place smelled of time and ancient books, and I loved it. But I was running out of things to explore, and I knew I was looking for excuses to keep me from reading the letter and looking into that envelope.

A pair of stools had been tucked under the table. I slid one out and perched on it, then reached for the envelope. My finger brushed against something, and I noticed a ring, sitting next to envelope. It made no sense I hadn't seen it before. Perhaps I wasn't paying attention. God knows, there was enough in the room to distract me. I left the ring where it was. For now, at least. I wanted to get the letter out of the way. It got right to the point.

I have made copies of some items from this envelope and shall bring them to show you when we meet. I cannot shake the feeling that the trip will not go well for me. That's why I'm making sure the originals stay here for you to see.

Your name is Paulette Tipton. I have never been a major part of your life, though I was one of your teachers for a time.

This is so very difficult to explain, and I am sure I would do a much better job in person, but perhaps that is not to be.

Many years ago, I felt something in your aura – and I expect you are rolling your eyes right about now. (She was right, I was.) *I do not expect you to believe me. Not yet. But please don't give up on me. Let me say I got a powerful hunch, and my hunches are usually right. I never connected it with you until many years later, and for that I apologize. If I had seen you had any abilities sooner, I might have been able to avoid so much. But I'm chasing the wind again.*

(Abilities. What the hell did she mean by 'abilities'?)

A terrible tragedy happened to your family, and you disappeared.

Again, perhaps I could have done more, but by the time I understood, it was too late.

And to tell another painful truth, I would not have come looking for you had I not felt that same strange event, that hunch, happen again.

But this time I knew more of what it might be, and the implications. I believe they have found another child with whatever ability the fates saw fit to grant you, and that the same things they did to you are being done to another. In looking to find out more about her, I rediscovered you, and when I realized what they had done to you, I had to find you.

And when I set out to find something, or someone, there is very little in this world, or any other, that can stop me from doing it.

They have stolen a wonderful legacy from you. I so regret that I cannot be there to help you rediscover it.

On top of the envelope is a ring. Please wear it. It will help you.

Inside the envelope is all I could uncover about your first life. I think you should read it. You must be in possession of all the facts before you make any more decisions.

Regards your legacy, inside the envelope there are contact details for a very dear friend of mine. Speak to him. He will help you, I am sure.

NOW THIS IS VERY IMPORTANT!

This house is protected, and so is this room. The house has made allowances for you this once, but it will not do so again. I know you may think this absurd, and will feel rather silly doing it, but you must go kneel in the middle of the silver circle, place both your hands in contact with the star, and say these words:

In Tamsin's name, I am now mistress of this domain
Then breathe upon the metal.

Find your peace, become who I know you can be, and carry my

love with you.
   Tamsin

My eyes were stinging, and I blinked the tears away. Crazy old lady had a way with words. And she was right. Just thinking about all the nonsense with the circle made my lip curl. But then I pulled out the letter from upstairs, breathed on it again, and re–read the bit about nothing working again once I left the house.

I rolled my eyes. This place was contagious. It was making me as crazy as her. And yet... I looked around the room, at all the books and the wonderful trinkets.

And yet...

What if it was true? What if I didn't do it and I got locked out of here? I don't know what the protections were against, but what if I needed them? Yes, it was ridiculous, but would it hurt to do it? Just in case?

I walked over to the circle, the letter still in my hand. I kneeled in the middle, and put the letter in front of me, where I could read it. Then I sat back on my heels and paused, looking around. The strange thing was not what I was doing, but that somehow it didn't feel weird. It felt almost familiar.

I shook my head, leaned forward until I could rest my hands on the silvered surface of the star, then read the words.

"In Tamsin's name, I am now mistress of this domain."

Then I leaned forward until my lips brushed the silver and breathed.

Something happened. Don't ask me what. I've no idea, but it felt like a wind blew out from the center of the circle. The paper wafted away a foot, and the curtains moved. I got up and went back to the table, rubbing the gooseflesh on my arms.

I picked up the ring. It was pretty enough, and looked like a mesh of different colored metals, with a black stone set in a simple mount. A bit emo, but that suited what passed for my 'look'. I tried it on, but it was too loose or too tight for every finger, even my thumbs. I put it down next to the letter and moved on to the envelope.

I couldn't undo it. It wasn't a physical thing, just that the part of my brain that did things wasn't ready. This was not the place, or the time.

I looked around the room again, not rising from the stool. Somebody who took this stuff seriously built this. If they were crazy, fine. If they weren't, and there *was* anything to this BS? I got a shiver down my back that someone screwing around in here could cause all kinds of mayhem. The place made me edgy, and it wasn't where I wanted to find out about my other life – if I wanted to at all.

I picked up the envelope but left the letter and the ring. There were still a few hours to wait until my day was up, but the minute it was I was heading back to Clifton. I needed to get back to what I knew before I started shaking my world again. When I got upstairs, I left the envelope on the breakfast bar while I set about tidying the place – something I'd never intended to do.

A little less than twenty–three hours had passed, by my reckoning, and I was wondering how the lawyer would know what time I left when someone tapped on the door. Walcott was standing outside.

"Good afternoon, Miss Doe. May I come in?"

I stood aside to let him pass, and he hiked off toward the kitchen like he knew the place. I closed the door and followed him. By the time I caught up, he had taken a seat at the table and was taking papers out of his case and arranging them in front of an empty chair. Just to be ornery, I sat somewhere else.

"I thought I had an hour to go?"

"In the strictest sense of the instructions, yes, but I'm sure that the spirit of Miss Whiston's instruction is satisfied, if not the letter. Should you be considering returning to Clifton for any reason, leaving matters to the last hour would cause you to be late for your evening duties, should you wish to perform them."

I had to give the guy points for thinking on his feet. I hadn't thought about that, and missing the shift without warning would get me into trouble with Ray.

"First question, Miss Doe. Do you accept the bequest as specified in the last will and testament of Tamsin Whiston? You have fulfilled the primary requirement. Provided you accept a responsibility to behave with consideration toward the existing tenants, there are no other restrictions."

I spoke deliberately, thinking as I went. "If I accept, I don't have to decide what I'm going to do with the place right away, do I?"

"Not at all."

I couldn't see a downside. Didn't mean there wasn't one, but for now it was live with whatever catch was waiting around the corner, or in the basement, or let the deal slip through my hands. Changing chairs, I sat where Walcott had laid out the papers.

"Where do I sign?"

Papers Past

My purse was nothing like big enough for all the paperwork, so I needed to find a bag. There was nothing in the living room, so I crept into Tamsin's bedroom, feeling like an intruder. A satchel hung from the back of the closet door, empty. I snatched it and left the room one gear down from a run. As I closed the bedroom door, I wondered how long it would take me to start thinking of the place, and the stuff in it, as *mine*.

Walcott had two cars waiting outside; an Uber to take him back to his office, and the limo to take me home.

I tossed the bag on the seat next to me. All the way home I tried to ignore it, but I could feel what was inside watching me, daring me to read it. I guess I could have, but I wanted some privacy. I didn't want some emotional Pandora situation freaking me out in front of the driver – or should I have said behind? So I sat and I ignored and I wondered what the old woman had found that she thought could make me believe her.

I could smell it before I opened the apartment door. Bernie was playing contortionist on the couch while she painted her toenails. The place reeked of varnish remover and cheap nail gel. I opened some windows before I did anything else.

"Where did you go? Find a guy for the night?" The grin she flashed me was sleazy and made me feel dirty. She poked at me all the time about not having a boyfriend – or more to the point, not whoring myself around like she did, for laughs and free drinks. I didn't rise to it.

"I had some business."

"Ooh, very mysterious."

I picked up my bags and took them with me into my room, then I changed into sweats. As I came back into the living space, I took the key from the inside and locked the door from the outside.

"And what do you think you're doing?"

Bernie was glaring at me, cold–eyed, body tense.

"Just want to see if it worked."

"Why? Got something in there you think I'm gonna steal?"

Wow, she was getting crazy about this. "Like that stupid lock would keep you out if you wanted in," I said. "It's just copies of stuff that crazy old woman was bringing to show me. The one that got killed."

"I remember," Bernie snapped. "Old bag got what she deserved.

I let that go. She got crazy moods from time to time, but this was worse than any I'd seen, and I didn't want to push her into anything we might both regret.

"Cops can't say why someone murdered her. I figure it makes sense to keep it locked away. It's the last copy."

"Should burn it," Bernie muttered as she turned her attention back to her toenails. "Nothing but trouble. You got a good life here, dontcha? Why mess with it?"

I didn't answer. It felt like a trigger and I had no intention of pulling it. "If it worries you, I'll unlock it."

And now it was her turn to fall silent. I stood there until the silence got awkward, then a grabbed a bottle of water from the fridge and went back into my room, closing the door behind me. Let her burn.

I did some more staring at the envelope. It was almost an hour before my shift at Ray's, but I knew when I got home, I would be too tired to concentrate. The envelope wasn't that thick, so there couldn't be that much in it. I had time, if I got up the nerve to open it now.

A length of string, wound around two paper buttons, held the flap shut and it took me a moment to figure it out. I expected an avalanche of newspaper cuttings and scraps of notes, but it looked more like photocopied pages from a scrap book. Tamsin was very methodical and organized; each sheet had a number and a title, and there were extra notes wherever she thought things needed clarifying.

The name she called me by was on the first page, top and center, and I took a minute to think about that. Paulette Tipton wasn't an unpleasant name, but it still didn't feel like *mine*. Then, in short order, I found out my birthday was wrong, and I was a year older than I thought I was.

That set me back. In the hospital, I had no identity. I suppose I should be grateful that they helped me arrange one before they kicked me onto the street. When I filled out the forms, I'd taken that day's date as my birthday, and my age had been an average of the best guesses of the specialists who had looked after me. But this still felt as though I lost something, that somehow I was a year closer to dying than I thought I was. It made no sense, but I had to brush away a tear that tickled down my cheek, and it was a moment before I could look at the next page.

I turned the sheet over and saw photos, of me or so I supposed. They looked like copies of copies, not scan and print, and were all posed. Maybe they were school photos. I guessed they looked like me, but not enough to convince me. I moved on. There were copies of a school record, too. I had a father, David, and a mom called Elanor, but the names meant nothing, and my only thought was where they might be now. That was as far as I'd let those ideas go. I knew I should be angry at my parents, hate them for leaving me alone, but that part of me was cold, dead. They weren't people to me.

By middle school, I couldn't deny the photos were of me. The hair was longer, the face happier, but it was me. And then something happened when I was about fourteen. In the space of a year my grades dropped from a fairly impressive A– to a much more believable C. Whatever happened, it had been traumatic, and my grades stayed that low until I was about to enter high school.

The next to last sheet was a letter to the school, badly photocopied so that the top of it was missing – no letterhead, no senders address. Just a reference number that meant nothing.

Further to your objection regards the transfer of Tipton, Paulette to the Gifted Students Program, I can assure you that the relevant federal and state departments for education are fully aware and have granted approval under the relevant special education protocol, which can be obtained in full by calling the number at the top of this letter and asking for the administration team. A fee will apply, as will postage.

The letter went on, but it was just legalese and bureaubabble. I skipped to the bottom, but nobody had typed a name and it was signed with an indecipherable scrawl.

There were two more photos of me, posed like a school picture or for a yearbook. I didn't look good. My skin was terrible, as was my hair. It was like I had stopped taking care of myself. And I looked miserable. Not just unhappy, but like I was being beaten up on, or bullied. The pictures made me feel cold inside.

I reached into the envelope for the last sheet, but I dropped it onto the bed as I slid it out. It was a newspaper cutting, front page, or so it looked. A family portrait, and above it a bold headline.

"Family Slain in Tragic House Inferno."

I put the sheet back in the envelope, unread, and I placed the others over it in the right order. At least I knew what they looked like now. And I knew I had a little sister.

And I knew why they never came to look for me.

Need to Think

Milk foamed over the lip of the jug and ran all over the machine, the counter, and the floor. Betty snapped my name at me like an angry kindergarten teacher, and I bit my lip to keep the curse words inside. Two snooty moms waited at the counter, and there would be hell to pay if I swore in front of their kids. I grabbed the other jug, splashed more milk into it, and frothed it one-handed while tearing off paper towels from the dispenser and dropping them on the floor to foot—wipe what I could before I slipped in it.

I was not having an outstanding day, and this was the second time I had danced to this tune. After dispensing the drinks and sugar fix without further mishap, I set to cleaning up while I tried to stay on top of the mom rush.

It was all because of that envelope. Not that I had read any more of it. I told myself I hadn't had time, but I think I was scared of it. Or scared of me. I couldn't shift that picture from the paper out of my mind. Those four people smiling out of the page, next to the picture of the ruins of their home. My family. Further down the article there were two more pictures, one of the fire raging, and the other of the burned—out ruin.

That was all I had been able to look at before I put the sheet away.

But I didn't *feel* a thing.

In my head I felt sorry for them, but no more than I would for anybody else I didn't know. They were strangers to me. Nothing bound them to me—no memories, no emotions—but I couldn't get them out of my head. Was I a bad person to be so empty? It wasn't the pictures that troubled me, it was the way I didn't feel.

The mom rush faded. I took a bus tray and the cleaning spray to wipe down the empty tables, getting ready for lunch time and being extra careful I didn't drop or miss anything.

The thoughts still circled around in my mind. If I was so empty inside, was there any point in chasing this nonsense? I was fine where I was. I liked my jobs and I had what I needed. My bubble wrapped itself around me and I was warm and safe. And I could stay comfortably cocooned inside it for the rest of my life if I sold off the house. It had to be worth a fortune.

"Jane."

I looked behind over my shoulder. "Yes, Betty?"

"You've sat rubbernecking through that window for five minutes. I believe you already took your break."

When had I sat down?

"Sorry."

The bus tray almost ended up on the floor as I jumped to my feet and hurried back to the cleaning station. Was I even safe to be out today? Was I going to walk in front of a car as I walked to the library? I made sure Betty wasn't looking, then splashed lukewarm water from the sink onto my face.

I dried myself with some paper towels, but as I took them away from my face, everything looked different. It was like

I was watching my world on some high−def TV, with super sharp focus in the center, and soft−shot around the sides. At the same time hyper−real, and yet unreal, there but not there.

My eyes wandered around the coffee shop, knowing everything I would see before I saw it, but seeing it all with a new clarity. Was this *all* I wanted? Can you know something so well it's no longer a comfort? The vision seemed to expand, to stretch outside the shop, touching memories of the apartment, the restaurant, the library and the cinema.

My entire life.

Was that really all I wanted?

"*Jane!*"

I jumped like Betty had poked me with a fork. I made another apology, but she was still frowning when I turned to serve the customer I'd been ignoring, apologized to him too. Concentrating hard, forcing down the nagging thoughts, I got through the rest of the shift without any more mishaps.

"That wasn't your A−game today, Jane."

I had gone out back to pick up my bag and my coat. Betty wasn't wrong. I drew a breath to apologize. "Yeah, I need a break. I'd like a week off."

Judging by her face, that came out as much of a surprise to Betty as it did to me, but it felt right. My head was all over the place. I needed time to pull it straight. If I didn't, I'd get tangled up in it for months, or forever.

"When?"

"Right now."

"You can't." Betty's penciled−on eyebrows climbed up toward her hairline. "You have to give me notice, so I can arrange cover. And this won't be paid vacation."

"You really want me to bumble around in there like I did today for another month? I have things to sort out, personal things. Stuff is messing with my head."

"What can *you* have to sort out?"

You know when you say something, then are utterly shocked that you would ever have said anything so thoughtless? That was Betty's face right then. She started babbling apologies, but I knew what had gone through her mind. Jane doesn't have a life. Jane doesn't even have a memory of a life. She's a nothing.

She gave me the vacation time.

Though I walked out of the shop like nothing had happened, I wanted to kick chairs and smash cups, and sweep my arm along the counter and throw all the cakes and cookies to the floor.

I also wanted to sit on the sidewalk and cry like a baby.

Instead, I walked down the block to the library and checked my book in. Didn't want to come home to a late fee. That's my rock–and–roll life. I also stopped at the ATM. I needed fuel for the scooter. And it was only then I realized I meant to take the timeout in Tamsin's house – my house – not the apartment. That was a surprise, too.

I had enough for fuel, and twenty for just–in–case. I took out the cash and hurried back to the apartment.

The door to my room was open.

I knew I had locked it. The key was in my pocket. I had to unlock the outside door when I came in, and I could see from where I stood that none of the windows were open, so there hadn't been a beak in.

Bernie was such a bitch.

I kicked her door open and stormed into her room, but she wasn't there. Probably out at some all–day bar getting drunk and trying to figure out how she was going to talk her way out of this one. And probably pissed at me that the envelope hadn't been in my room.

I stood in the middle of the living room and grabbed my hair with both hands, like I was going to pull it out. Today's weirdness started the moment I woke up and seemed to get worse with every minute that passed.

That morning, I went into the bathroom to do what you do, brushed my teeth, and picked up my bottle of meds. I popped the cap as usual, tipped one out into my hand, and raised it to my lips. But as I went to toss it into my mouth, I got a hit of the smell. Same old smell, but somehow different. I closed my mouth and took in a breath through my nose, holding the pill close, then did it again. It took a second for the penny to drop. On top was a general smell of anonymous dust, but below that I could make out the tang of the Witchbane I had found in Tamsin's underground lair.

What was I supposed to do? Someone wanted me to take the pills, and two other people had told me I shouldn't. I think that was when my head started spinning. I put the pill back in the bottle, but dropped the bottle in my bag.

That was when I came up with the crazy idea that I wanted to look inside the envelope on my break. It didn't happen. It was insane that I would spread all these papers over a tiny table in the coffee shop for a whole fifteen minutes. But I hadn't been thinking that far ahead. Last night, before I went to sleep, I bent the envelope in two and stuffed it in my work bag. I had left it there and taken it to the coffee shop.

Seems a good thing I did.

I wanted to stay furious with Bernie. I wanted to find her and tear her a new one for messing with my stuff. But I needed to get out of the apartment more. And I would be damned if I would leave a note.

I grabbed a duffel bag and filled it with clothes to last a week, which was close to all I had. I didn't bother with toiletries and stuff. The bathroom in Tamsin's house — *my* house — was full of stuff, and it was all better than anything I had here. I just threw in a lipstick and an eyeliner. Then I put Tamsin's smaller bag and the envelope on top.

That, plus my work bag, got strapped to the scooter with bungee hooks. I crammed the crash helmet on my head, suddenly wishing the strap worked, and hit the road.

Voice from the Grave

I t was terrifying. Don't ever ride a small bike on the freeway. The regulations say it's ok, but it's not. I almost turned back. But a combination of pigheadedness—plus some determination that I wasn't going to let the bullies in their 18–wheelers intimidate me—mixed together with a need to see the house again and pushed me through four hours of hell.

I got there. Pretty much collapsed on the couch when I did, too.

The first day I did nothing. I took a long hot bath, which was new, and to which I might have become addicted. The apartment in Clifton only had a shower, so I had no idea what I'd been missing out on. I explored the house more, too, and found a small garden out back, with a square of concrete big enough for a mid-size car. A gate led out to an alley. It would be great for the scooter, which was parked in the front yard and looked untidy.

But I couldn't go into *her* room. I went to the door more than once, even as far as turning the handle and opening the door an inch. Then I closed it and stood there for five minutes, staring at the grain in the wood.

It was too soon.

It felt I was a guest, like I didn't belong, and nosing around in my host's room was not an option, yet. Clearing the room out would have to wait until I felt I had the right.

The second day, I rode around on the scooter to get a feel for the area. It seemed nice enough, but a place of people, not families. Some parks and green spaces filled a couple of blocks to the west, but all the local streets were small apartment complexes, or condos like mine. Professional people. Couples without kids. That sort of demographic.

Things took a dive to the east and I got out of there quick. In that sort of area, it seems they can smell when you shouldn't be there, and I didn't want to attract attention. Half a dozen blocks north, I was on the outskirts of downtown. I buzzed around there for a half hour, then rode back to the condo.

The envelope accused me of neglecting it, staring at me from the dining table. I walked past it, refusing to look at it, but unable to move it. It needed to be there to bully me into opening it again, but I wasn't ready yet.

The next day I read through the mail that had collected since Tamsin had left the house. I even found one for me, from the lawyers. They wanted my bank details to send me money. I had nothing better to do, so I took the bus downtown and found the office.

Walcott himself came out to see me and ushered me into his den.

"Are you in town long?"

I was concentrating on filling in a form with my bank details and didn't answer for a moment.

"Don't know." I finished the form and slid it back over the table toward him. "I came up for a week."

"Do you know what you intend to do yet?" He was chatting, not pushing for decisions or information. It was nice he was taking an interest, though I would bet he was still hoping to get business out of it. I shook my head.

"Still trying to fit my head around it, or squeeze it all into my brain."

"I know what you mean." His voice was light, but his eyes seemed to droop at the edges.

"Did you know her?" I knew I was way inside his personal space, but the question seemed to fit the moment. He nodded, which both did and didn't surprise me.

"Tamsin Whiston has been a client for many years. She was preparing for this eventuality for several months."

"Months?"

"I knew she had been looking for someone. She had been struggling with it for more than a year. There were certain inquiries she asked us to make on her behalf. Your particular situation raised some interesting challenges, and there will be more to come, I am sure. It worried me when she called and told me to put all our preparations into place post haste. I was sure she knew she was in danger, and I was most upset when she refused to follow my advice to call the police, and even more so when she did not call back the next day to tell me all was well."

"She knew? Why didn't she get out, run for it?"

He spread his hands. "One can only assume finding and convincing you of what she had found was that important to her."

Well, that got me. Obvious, in a sense, but to hear it from somebody else gave it sharper focus.

Walcott gave a fake cough and looked at his watch, but I

thought he was more embarrassed about letting his guard down then hustling me out for his next appointment.

"Please, get in touch when you have thought things through. We are always here to help, and it might be better to start in on the identity issue sooner rather than later."

"Identity issue?"

He looked surprised. "You haven't read the file yet?"

"Once."

He hesitated, thoughtful for a moment. "I may be speaking out of turn, but I believe Miss Whiston assumed you would, on finding your true name, takes steps to claim it. But it is not urgent and can wait."

I nodded, though I wasn't sure which bit I was agreeing with.

I took the envelope back down to the workshop the next morning, right after breakfast. Not sure why, but it felt right to bring it back where I had first found it. It would have been easier upstairs; the light from the ceiling lamp in the – what was it? A den? A workshop? I settled on that. Whatever, the overhead was very yellow, and I wondered if I should light some candles, or a lantern. Instead, I found a brass lamp. Same green shade as a Banker's Lamp, but with a tall, adjustable neck. It had an LED bulb and a USB charging point in the base. Grandma Tamsin was hip to the tech gods.

I opened the file and read everything again, slowly, and only when I took the time to go over the last article in detail did I realize more was printed on the other side. Two additional photos of the ruin of my family's home. These were better quality, like someone had copied them with a camera or a phone. Most of them were destruction and heartache, but the last one caught my eye.

It showed an undamaged area. Not excessively big, from the picture, but to my eye it stood out. A chunk had fallen intact from the second story. Clearly the edge of a room; a slice of floor with a corner of two walls, all untouched up to a very defined edge. Tamsin had left a comment.

"Spherical? Protection? Herself or artefact?"

I looked at the picture again and saw that the shape of the charring did look like a bubble had held back the fire. But that was ridiculous, wasn't it? At the bottom, in red pen, she wrote 'All declared dead'.

Beneath that, also in red and underlined, 'But she survived?!'

Now I understood Walcott's comment a little better. If I was dead, or thought to be, how could I prove I was who she said I was. Endless messing around in courts and offices trying to get my identity back – no, my *old* identity back, stretched into my future and I shuddered. Would I be fighting to become somebody who wasn't me anymore?

The last line was faint, in blue ballpoint that didn't show up too well. It looked like it was scrawled in a hurry.

'Grant Peterson – speed dial 03'

I didn't have her cell phone. A landline? I went upstairs and looked around the kitchen, then realized I was looking for some house brick sized thing hanging on the wall, complete with rotary dial. I tried again.

It was in the living room, near the window and tucked away on a low table like it was embarrassed to be there. A handset standing in a base station that had controls for an answering machine. Maybe Tamsin wasn't as hip to the tech as I had given her credit for. I reached out for the handset, and paused. The message counter read 01, so I pushed the play button instead.

"Hi Paulette, or Jane. I don't know how you think of yourself.

So sorry about our meeting today. I had so much to tell you, and it's all gone so wrong. Coming to see you at work was a terrible idea.

"But if you are listening to this, something even worse has happened. Somebody is following me. I'm safe in my motel, I think, but I need to explain things to you. This is too important.

"I was hoping they hadn't stolen your memories, but it would make sense they have. I wish I knew who *they* were. There is an envelope in my workshop. All my research is in there. And don't forget the ring."

She sounded scared, which explained why she was muddling things up. I would never have found the voicemail if I hadn't already found the envelope.

"But this is the most important thing. We live in a world bigger and more wonderful than you could imagine. Don't overthink it. Accept it and go with me, at least for the next five minutes. I think you were once a part of it, or learning to be. Years ago, I sensed something I should have paid attention to but didn't. And I didn't pay attention to you either. I should have sensed your powers were waking. I might even have been able to help. It hurts me I failed you."

Powers? My guts twisted and I couldn't be sure if the thought scared or excited me.

"Finding you was an accident, in a way. You see, the same event that should have woken me to what was going on in your life has happened again, and by everything I can discover, that should be impossible. But beyond that, I think it means that whatever they did to you is being done to somebody else.

"It was only when I was going through some boxes, to remind me of the first time... Anyway, I had one of your schoolbooks. I think I may have kept it after the fire. I found one of your hairs inside, and out of curiosity I cast a finding on it. It astonished me when it said you were alive.

"I'm rambling, repeating things I already said in a letter you will read soon. I think I'm just putting off the inevitable. Hopefully, I get to see you tomorrow. But if I don't, take my gift with all my blessings and love. I was hoping to work with you, to help whoever they might force to follow in your footsteps, but I won't lay that on you. Ring Grant Peterson. He will guide you."

I heard her sigh. "I've been foolish. There are things I should have written down, and more I should have left in the envelope. But I didn't want anybody else to find it. You must listen, and be careful. What I felt, both times, was the awakening of a power that shouldn't be. A power so—"

I heard a crash of splintering wood, a shriek, and the line went dead.

My legs weren't there anymore, and my vision faded into a gray tunnel. I stumbled back until I fell onto the couch. Maybe I hadn't actually heard her die, but that had to be her murderer breaking into the room. Guess I didn't have to worry I couldn't feel things anymore. I felt that; tears ran down my face and I wanted to puke.

I made it into the kitchen for a glass of cool water and sat for a while, looking out the window. Was this all my fault? If I had listened to her in the coffee shop, would this have played out differently? Of course it would. But *was* it my fault? Could anyone blame me for being suspicious of her?

And how could I accept these gifts from her?

Back in the living room I picked up the handset and scrolled through the contacts until I found Grant Peterson. My fingered hovered over the button for a moment, wondering if it was too soon, then tapped to connect the call.

"Tam? I was worrying about you."

"Sorry. This isn't her."

"Who the blazes is this?"

"My name is Jane Doe."

I waited for a gag through the predictable pause, but all I got was "You don't say. And what might you be doing calling me from this number?"

"I was told to. By Tamsin Whiston."

"And why ain't she speaking to me herself?" The voice got deeper, almost snarling.

"She can't. I... She's dead."

The line went quiet for a long time, but I waited it out. Eventually he gave a lengthy sigh. "I thought I felt her leave." The words were almost a whisper, so that the next sounded like a bellow. "So what're you pestering me for?"

"She left a message I should call you. She thinks I should ask you for help."

"About what. Wait. Are you the girl in this crazy bloodfire hunt she's been nagging me about?"

"I don't know about that. All I know is she believes someone has stolen my memory from me, and that I might have some talent or ability I don't know about."

Who was I, and why was I being so polite to this miserable old bastard? Maybe because Tamsin told me to call him? Maybe it was the shock of hearing her message. The last words she spoke . . . Either way, Grant Peterson was staring to push the limits of my civility.

"I don't know what I should do, Mr. Peterson. Tamsin said something about smelling Witchbane on me, and I can smell it in my medication."

"Who in all the gods gave you that to take?"

"I don't know."

"Pretty damn stupid taking medication you don't understand, missy."

"So should I stop?"

"Of course. Wait, maybe not. Maybe better you keep taking it, crawl back under whatever rock she lifted to find you. Maybe best you forget this ever happened. Now stop bugging me."

He hung up. I put the handset carefully down in the charger, did a ten–count breath, then snatched a cushion from the couch and kicked it across the room.

Bad Bar Boogie

I stormed out of the house. It was either that or break things, and I'm not a smasher or a thrower by nature. But that miserable old fart had pushed me over the edge. I had enough of my own shit to deal with right now, and I didn't need him to add to it with his attitude. Why was he pissed at me? I wasn't the one that killed his friend.

I pushed that thought and everything else to do with Tamsin Whiston right to the back of my mind. From my cruise around the area I remembered a bar about a block and a half away. Right now, I wanted a beer, or something stronger, some seriously unhealthy food, and maybe a little music.

The place was clean enough. The bartender gave me a weird look as I walked in, but she seemed happy enough when I ordered food and a beer, and even exchanged a few words with me while I waited for the burger.

I took my food to a table, sat down, and stuffed my face. Only when I looked up, wiping the grease off my chin with a paper napkin, did I realize what a lonely place an empty bar was. I bought another beer, changed a few dollars for coins, and set myself up on the pool table.

I was hopeless, and had been for the last five years, but I

couldn't face going back to the house. Not yet. The first year I lived in Clifton, I went drinking with Bernie a few times. I had scored, and been scored, but I wasn't the slut she was. Then, one night, while she was making all kinds of promises to some guy in exchange for beer, she told him she only brought me along so everybody could laugh at the freak with no memory. I'd not gone out with her since.

I racked them up again, throwing the balls into the triangle in any order except the right one, and smacked the cue ball into them as hard as I could. It bounced off the top of the head ball, leaped over the set barely disturbing them, and rolled down the length of the bar.

Face burning, I set off in pursuit, and found it trapped under the toe of a fancy red cowboy boot. Thankfully, the rest of the boot hid its glory under the guy's jeans. I followed the leg up to the face that owned it. He was slim, not particularly pretty, but he had a smile that went up to his eyes and a full row of teeth.

"I admire your enthusiasm, but I think your technique needs work. Want me to show you a thing or two?"

I said yes. He bought beers and more change for the table. We played, he did indeed give me pointers, although I was still hopeless, and we didn't object when someone who knew what they were doing kicked us off the table.

We moved to a booth. The place was picking up with workers on the way home, stopping off for a quick one to wash the dust out of their throats. He bought us more beer, and fries and wings and rings, and we talked. He told me about his life, and I told him a story that had nothing to do with mine. Time passed. Customers dwindled over an hour or so, then the evening rush kicked off in earnest. I don't know when I decided to take him to bed, but right then was when I decided to do something about it.

"Getting loud in here," I complained. "Wanna go somewhere quieter."

"Where might that be?" His grin was leery and lopsided.

I giggled. Yes, I actually giggled. "Somewhere private."

"Well, that sounds just fine to me."

We slid out of the booth, weaved through the crowd in the bar, and pushed our way out to the street. He took my hand. After a moment to figure out which way we had to go, I led him back toward the house.

After half a block, in a place where the shops were closed and the foot traffic was light, he jerked me sideways into a doorway, pushed my chin up with his finger, and kissed me. Nothing chaste, no romance. Full-on high school making out. And I went with it. I enjoyed it. I was a little on the wrong side of a mellow buzz and I just wanted to cut loose.

Eventually I pulled away, dragged him back onto the sidewalk, and we staggered closer to the house.

"Nice place," he said as we came up to the gate. I pushed it open, grabbed his hand, and pulled him through, dragging him toward the door. But he only took two steps through the gate before he stopped, his hand slipping from mine. I turned back, caught his arm again and pulled him forward. Except he didn't move, and he wasn't looking at me, he was looking at the house.

"Come *on*," I whined, but he was the immovable object, and I was a very resistible force. He slipped from my hand again and I staggered a little closer to the house. "Wassa matter? Doncha wanna have fuuuun?" I did a cutesy little tushy–wiggle, but the fun, and the buzz, was fading from his face.

"Sure I do, babe, but let's do it somewhere else, huh?"

"Why?" I whined. "It's nice here."

He held to his hand. "Come on, baby. We can find some fun somewhere else."

"I like it here."

His weight shifted forward, and he took a short step toward me. Then his face transformed into something angry and frustrated. "Get the fuck back here, bitch." He pointed to the ground in front of him. "Get your ass over here."

I took another step back, terrified. He looked around him like a trapped animal and glared at the house. "You bitches are all the same. Whores. All of you. Whores."

He turned and ran.

I stumbled to the door. Somehow I got the key into the lock and turned it. I fell into the house, ran to the guest room, and threw myself on the bed, sobbing.

No News is Better

Orange juice and black coffee were all I could face the next morning. I slumped on the couch wearing sweats, the drinks beside me on the table. The shower I'd forced myself to take was a necessity. The stench of the bar was so strong I doubted I'd ever get it out, but the feeling of inner soiling wouldn't scrub away, and I wasn't sure why. My hair stunk of it, and I'd washed it twice.

I grabbed the TV remote, fumbled at the buttons and finally switched it on. Its default station was the local news channel, and I figured that was good enough to be a background to my pain while the coffee and Advil tried to reboot my aching brain.

'Cowboy boots' filtered through my consciousness and I grabbed the remote, winding the TiVo back to the start of the article. The picture behind the anchor was the terribly bruised face of a woman.

"Police are warning women to be alert following another assault in the Four Meadows district late last night. Tonya Sullivan was found by a jogger this morning, savagely beaten and sexually abused, apparently left for dead by her assailant. Police say they are making inquiries in the area, and want to speak to anybody who owns, or knows anybody who owns, a pair of distinctive red cowboy boots..."

I didn't hear the rest. My ears were ringing, and my body trembled so hard I spilled OJ down my sweatshirt. I got the glass to the table without dropping it, then my knees drew up to my chest and my arms squeezed tight around them.

"...with violent rape in the city this year, and police, initially reluctant to confirm a serial rapist was at large, today admitted this was the case."

The picture cut to a grizzled police officer surround by people stuffing mics and cameras into his face. He looked angry, and a little ashamed, but I wasn't listening.

Did she get raped because of me? Was I supposed to be the one? He picked me first. If I had gone with him, given him what he wanted, would he have hurt me as much? Would he still have gone out and hurt her?

I took a ten-breath and forced my arms to relax. My hands itched where he had touched me. The skin on my arms cringed where he had tried to line up pool shots with me. I wanted to vomit at the thought of his lips on mine, his tongue in my mouth.

But her pain was not my fault. My heart ached for her, but it was him, not me, that hurt her.

I picked up the phone. The old cop on the news had ended his statement with a plea for anybody with information to call the nearest police station. I was halfway through dialing the number when I paused.

Would it help? Could I tell them anything more than they had already? I had showered. Forensics would get none of his DNA from me, though they might get some from my clothes. The police must have a description. They knew about the boots. And if I did call in, some bastard would be sure to leak it to the media. The name alone would get them hovering around the house, especially when they found out I had inherited the place from a murdered woman I had only met once.

I let out a frustrated sigh and dropped the phone onto the couch. If I thought anything I had to say might make an actual difference, I would have tried to find a way, but I couldn't see that it would. Not enough to destroy my life over, to make me a victim twice.

I picked up my OJ and took a sip, then almost dropped it again.

"Now over to our on–the–spot reporter for live updates on the terrible house fire in the heart of the Barrows."

I tingled all over.

"You join us just as the fire department has reported the inferno is under control," said a short–haired brunette, all action–figure and fake horror on her face. "There are reports of four fatalities, two of which are young children. A fire department spokesperson says they have no information on what started the inferno at the moment, but they have ruled out neither arson nor domestic terrorism. All we know is that name of the registered occupants: parent's Jake and Mary Pennell, and daughters Katherine and Vonnie, who was only nine years old."

I pushed the power button on the remote. The TV switched off and I stood up to walk away. Instead, I stared at the empty screen, a black mirror reflecting my image back to me from the neck down and I knew.

I knew what happened to me had just happened to Katherine Pennell.

Visiting an Echo

I left the scooter half a block away and carried my helmet. Not sure which was worth more, but I could lock a chain through the scooter.

Emergency vehicles filled the street right from where I parked. TV news vans cluttered up what space was left, and the crews got in everybody's way. One reporter was poking her camera in through doors at shocked, angry neighbors.

I wove my way through it all, giving way to anybody who bore down on me, trying to be invisible but expecting shouts of *Hey, you!* or *Move back please, miss.* I managed to get right up to the police tape. Not directly in front of the house. Those who got there early snagged the best views, and the newshounds were still trying to shove people out of the way to get better sightlines. I stood a little farther along, where I could still see the house, or what the fire left of it.

And that was close enough, anyway. Most of the fire crews were packing down now, rolling up hoses and pulling ladders down. A single engine was still pumping, one team fanning a wide, drenching spray back and forth like they were watering a flower bed. Another team shot narrow, targeted blasts at stubborn hotspots like they were playing an arcade game.

Every breath I took reeked of damp, smoldering wood, with an overtone of chemicals, all being carried about by unenthusiastic smoke and water vapor from the hoses. My nose told me it could smell barbecue, too, but I ignored it. I was probably imagining it. I hoped.

But I didn't *feel* a thing. This should have been like a trigger. Any normal person who had been through Tamsin's notes would be on their knees sobbing or screaming. I felt nothing. A cop, scanning the crowd for trouble, gave me a look and moved on, but I still felt guilty.

I didn't even pity them. The news report had said two adults, two children. The same as my family. Why didn't I feel for them? Should I? Or should I be more worried about myself? Was Tamsin wrong and the amnesia due to some brain damage after all, or an illness the quacks hadn't found yet?

The pins and needles that had run along my arms and legs when I saw this on TV had stopped too, and I wasn't sure when. Did I imagine that too, or was it just some lingering shock from the bastard that had nearly raped me?

The cop looked at me again, and a tiny frown dug into his forehead. He was short, wide, and had a hard face. Not someone I would want to meet, professionally or down a dark alley. Though I wasn't doing anything wrong, even I knew that when a cop keeps looking at you, it's time to consider being somewhere else. I edged away, getting myself behind the rest of the crowd and out of his line of sight. Still, his eyes seemed to follow me along the back of the crowd until the first of the news trucks hid me.

I made my way back to the scooter the same way I had arrived, keeping out of everybody's way, being invisible. I didn't want to touch their feelings, and I was afraid of someone questioning mine. When I got to the scooter, I squatted down to undo the chain.

As I rose, a hand fell on my shoulder.

Tasha

My arm came up as I turned, ready to push the intrusive hand away, but it had already gone. Angry words jammed up behind my teeth, but the only one that got out was a grumpy "Hey!"

She was taller than me, slim build, dark hair, and oversize wraparound shades. The wide brim hat was a bold fashion statement too, but the rest of her outfit was smart without being dressy.

"I wanted to make sure you were OK."

So much for blending into the crowd. "I'm fine." I turned away to pick up my helmet, but she didn't take the hint.

"That's good. It's just, well, I'm a bit of a people watcher."

"And?"

"Most of the people here are excited, enjoying the spectacle of the fire. It upset a few, some sad faces. But you didn't show a thing. Not a single emotion crossed your face from the moment I saw you."

"And?" I repeated, with extra snarkiness.

"Well, I wouldn't play poker with you, for one." She chuckled at her own joke, but it died away when she saw I wasn't joining in. "It's unusual, and I wondered why you made the effort to visit if you were so uninterested, and why you spent so much time here?"

"Doesn't that come under 'none of your damned business'?" I flicked the straps out of the helmet, ready to put it on. She pulled off a glove I hadn't noticed she was wearing and shoved her hand out toward me, all long delicate fingers and burgundy polish on short nails. She introduced herself.

"Tasha Campbell. I should probably tell you up front that I'm a private investigator."

That should have made me snatch my hand away, jam my helmet on my head and ride off without another word, but I took the hand and shook it. I could see why she wore gloves. Her hand was freezing.

"Jane Doe."

I saw muscles twitch on her forehead, but the shades were so big I couldn't see her eyebrows move.

"By choice?"

"Long story."

"Best ones always are."

I took my hand out of hers and she put the glove back on.

"Is this going anywhere?" I asked.

"I think you have an interest in this fire and I would like to talk more about it with you. Right now, I am out of time and need to be somewhere else. Can we get together this evening, or tomorrow?"

"I'm really busy..."

"With what?"

Normally, if anybody asked me that, they would see the back of my head as I walked away, and it cut almost as deep as Betty had when she used almost the same words When Betty said it, I heard contempt, disbelief that anyone as stupid, as limited, as me would have a life. But from this woman I got her quirky

86

smile, and nothing more than curiosity in her words.

"I moved up a few days ago, from Clifton. I left some things behind and I have to hire a car to go back to fetch them. Too big to carry on the scooter, and I don't like the idea of playing death race with the rigs again."

"You rode up the interstate on *that*?"

I didn't know whether to feel she had offended my scooter or pleased by the implied heroism of my death-defying ride. Though I couldn't see her eyes, I felt she was studying me, and I don't know why I didn't move.

"I'm free tomorrow. Why don't I drive you down?"

That was unexpected. "Lady, it's three hours each way."

"Two, the way I drive." And she gave me that quirky smile again.

I didn't understand why I wasn't walking away. Or riding, more to the point. I had somehow just avoided being raped twelve hours before, and now I was seriously considering taking a ride from a woman I didn't know. But it would be so much easier than arranging a hire car.

The woman held out a card. "Text me your address. I'll pick you up at two?"

I took the card. She gave me one more of those odd little smiles, then turned and sashayed back toward the crowd. And I do mean sashayed.

I rode back to the house, parked the bike in back, and let myself in. My head was thumping and my mouth was dry, so I went into the bathroom for more Advil. When I ran water to wash the pills down, I caught a glimpse of my meds staring back at me from the mirror shelf, right next to the toothbrush I hadn't used yet.

This was the new, full bottle. I shook one out into my palm, but I didn't toss it into my mouth. I looked at it and raised it to my nose to sniff at it, again getting that strong tang I had smelled in the Witchbane jar.

What was it that miserable old bastard had said to me? First, he said not to take them, then he said I should and forget all this happened. Interesting choice of words. Did he know about me, or was I reading too much into it? He *couldn't* have known anything about me; Tamsin didn't have time to speak to him after we met. So was he just talking about the pills?

The more I found out about them, the less I liked them. I put the pill back in the bottle and closed the lid, then put it back on the shelf and picked up my toothbrush. What must that investigator woman think of me? My breath must smell awful. But while I was scrubbing for a sparkling smile, I had a thought. I spat, rinsed, and went down to the workshop.

There had to be a book in there that would tell me more. Unless what I wanted to know was primer level stuff too stupid for Tamsin to need a reference on. It took a while, but eventually I found *The Occult Applications of Herbs and Other Fauna*, by some guy called Simonus. It was almost as heavy as I could lift, but I hauled it over to the table, then almost dropped it on the ring she left me. I brushed the ring aside far enough not to flatten it, or dig it into the cover, then let the book down with a thud.

I picked up the ring, thinking to put it somewhere safe, and turned it over in my fingers. It was so much prettier than I remembered. Not in an expensive, gold and diamonds kind of way, but it had a grungy, folk–art vibe that spoke to me. I started trying it on fingers again with a similar lack of success – until I tried it on my left thumb. It slid on like the maker sized it to go right there.

I held my hand out and admired it. I had always liked the idea of a thumb ring, but I had also liked the idea of various piercings and getting a tattoo. Didn't mean they were a sensible idea or that I would get one. The ring looked magnificent there, but I was sure it would keep catching on pockets and snagging clothes. But I could leave it there for now and feel cool, couldn't I?

The book on herbs was older than anything I had ever touched, and I was extra careful with it. It was difficult to read, too, until I figured out a few things – like 'f' with no bar is actually an 's', and substituted 'y' for 'i' and 'u' for 'v'. I decided Wych looked cooler than Witch and plowed on.

The entry was about halfway through the book – don't ask, I didn't understand the order either – and I had to read it twice before I was sure I had all the weird spellings ironed out.

Wychbane: A tall shrub of dark green leaves and yellow blossom, with a distinctive scent like that of the Rose commingled with the mash of the brewer. In use, dried and ground to a fine powder, it can be mixed with a host of other substances to modify its effect or mask its presence. This said, in stem form at a threshold it can proscribe a lesser Wych from passing. Ingested, it prolongs the efficacy of magicks inflicted upon a person, or if that person be a Wych, or some other practitioner of the arts, it can circumscribe, or even destroy, whatsoever ability they once had.

What the hell had they done to me?

Road Trip

Another pounding headache announced the start of the day, but I knew this one wasn't a hangover. I'd drunk no more than a half bottle of wine the night before. The other half was still down in the workshop. I had gone through the envelope again. Dinner had been a glamorous peanut butter sandwich accompanied by an oversize bag of chips. There might be greasy fingermarks on some of the papers.

But I still knew nothing more than the first time I read through the papers Tamsin left for me. No sudden insights, no missed pages or skipped notes that would enlighten me or give me some idea of what I should do next.

I did text the woman who offered me a ride. I'd given it more thought and hell, if she wanted to put herself out for me, I'd be a fool not to use her. But if the car looked like a rental, I wouldn't even step outside the house.

So there I was, thick headed and sulking, with four hours to kill and nothing to do. I didn't even have enough laundry to make it worthwhile going down to the basement, and there was enough food in the kitchen that I didn't need to go shopping – not that I knew where the good stores were anyway. And somehow just going out for a walk had lost its glitter. I had always felt safe in Clifton. There were places I knew never to go through on foot, but I never felt in any danger.

Here, the thought of going outside scared me. Not totally, but enough that every time I thought about it, I managed to find a reason not to. Wasn't sure I wanted to live like that. And yet, here I was driving down to collect the rest of my life from Bernie's apartment and move it here. I spent the morning trawling through the cable channels and box sets for something to watch. I had found nothing.

My phone rang, and a number I thought I recognized came up on the display.

"Are you ready? I'm outside."

It was her, and she was early. I got angry wondering where she had hacked my number from. Then I remembered I had sent her a text and felt dumb.

"Two minutes."

I grabbed the few things I needed, made sure I locked the door, then hurried down the steps and out to the street. But I didn't go straight to the car. I walked around back, checking for rental decals in the rear window, and opened a new text. I typed in her license plate, then got into the car. She was pulling away before I had the belt done up.

"What was all that about?"

My bag went through the gap between us and into the rear seat, then I finished the text and sent it to Walcott; a note saying "please be aware I am traveling in this car with someone I don't know that well. Clifton and back. 911 if no message in three hours."

"Insurance."

Her chuckle was low and bubbly. "Excellent idea. Want to

send a photo, too? That's not my good side."

I pulled a face. "This thing can just about manage texts, and I'm on a crappy contract. If I asked it to send a photo, I'd owe the phone company most of Nebraska by the time it exploded."

"So where are we going?"

I started to tell her, but she just tapped the center of the dash. "Put it straight in there; zip code first, then building number."

Hey, I don't have a car. I don't hang out with anybody who has a car less than ten years old. Don't mock me for not being up on the tech. I put the address in, and a pleasant androgynous voice told us we had two hours and forty minutes to run. That was a long time to be in a car with a stranger. I decided to roll the first dice.

"What's it like being a private investigator?"

"The pay sucks and so do the hours, but it's better than working for a living."

If the pay sucked so bad how come she was wearing leather pants, a silk blouse that would have cost me a month's wages – from both jobs – and driving a BMW less than three years old? But I let it pass.

"It's a mix," she went on. "Some stuff is really interesting, much of it is pay–the–bills grind; missing dogs, following husbands, unfaithful either of the above."

I let her run on. While she was talking, I didn't have to, and it was interesting. Some of it was funny, too. It sounded like a cool job to me, and the longer she told me about herself, the longer it would be before she started asking about me. The privacy lasted until we were halfway to Clifton, and losing it was my fault.

"So what were you doing at the fire yesterday?" I asked, and as soon as the words left my lips, I realized I had slipped up.

The question was too close to my own life.

"A case," she admitted. "I can't tell you too much about it because its active and open, so there are a few rules about confidentiality. Let's leave it that a client of mine had an interest in somebody connected to the address."

"One of the family?"

She took a hand from the wheel and wagged a finger at me. I saw she wasn't wearing gloves today, then realized she was also missing the hat and the shades. Nice eyes, but the wings were a bit heavy for me. "Naughty," she said. "No digging. Penalty switch. Now you have to talk."

"About what?" But I already knew she would grill me. I'd been waiting for this, dreading it, and I'd realized I would win no points being coy. She had my cell, both my addresses, my scooter's license plate, and my name. She could figure out most of my life from that, if she was any good. I was just saving her time.

"Start with the name. Who chooses to be Jane Doe? And why?"

I went with it. Told her the memory thing and the living in Clifton thing, dragging it out with as much unimportant detail as I could to either make her bored or just pass time. I ran out of words way too soon.

"So how come you moved up to the city?"

I was going to lie, a half–formed idea of a long–lost relative leaving me the house. But I realized it couldn't work. If I claimed an estranged relative, I'd have the backstory I'd been claiming I didn't. Why were lies so complicated?

"Some weird woman I didn't know from Eve wandered into my work saying she knew who I was. She got killed overnight, and then I found she'd left everything to me?"

Another mistake, and just as bad. She turned her head to look at me so long I was drawing breath to scream 'eyes on the road', but she never veered out of the lane for a second. I was staring forward. I didn't want to look into her eyes, to see the incendiary curiosity that I would fight off for the next hour and all the way home.

"Bull. Shit. Why would anybody do that?"

"I'm still waiting to find out."

She paused, slightly awkward, slightly too long.

"Sorry, I was prying. I do that. But if I push too hard, just say so."

Another pause, longer. It was obvious she was waiting for me to say more, but I had nothing more I wanted to share. She was a clever host; she only let the gap go so long, then stepped in to fill it.

"Did I say I was a cop before I was a PI?"

And she was off again. The cop stories were almost as good as the Private Investigator ones and lasted us until the off ramp for Clifton. She shut up then. Might have been because I was staring out of the side window as my life rolled past. Maybe she sensed I needed some time inside my head.

I was thankful for that. As we turned onto the familiar roads, my home streets, I got cold feet. Was I doing the right thing? Here, the world didn't bug me. Everything was how I liked it. True, Bernie could be a bitch, but maybe I could buy her out now, or find somewhere else in town. Then I realized I had other business I needed to attend to.

"Are you OK?" Tasha asked.

I nodded. "Big day. Lived here all my life, or all of it I remember. Can we make a side trip? Two, actually?"

She gave me a sideways look. "Sure. We aren't in any hurry,

are we?"

"Take the next left."

She turned, and the GPS immediately started bitching about 'route recalculations' until I found the button to switch the voice off. We pulled up outside the restaurant. I jumped out, dashed inside, and was out again inside three minutes. But that was the easy one.

"Where next?"

I gave her directions to the coffee shop.

Tasha waited in the car again. I stood on the sidewalk and looked at the place. Was I doing the right thing? Might it be easier on all of us if I just got back in the car and drove off. I could quit in a text.

But I wasn't just quitting, was I. The bell made its familiar, tuneless clang as I walked through the door. Janelle did a double-take, then glared at me, her hands planted on her hips.

"Well, it's about time. Do you know how many double shifts I've had to work while you've been off doing whatever you were doing?"

"Hi, Janelle. Is she in back?"

"Don't expect her to be pleased to see you. She's had to work extra shifts too. I told her, hire a new girl. You can't just walk out and expect someone to hold your job."

She was making it a whole lot easier, but it wasn't her I needed to see. I knocked on the back room door as a courtesy but went in without waiting. Betty was sitting at her desk, and I got another double-take off her.

"Well, look what just got dragged in. If you think you can just walk in here and expect your old shifts—"

"I'm not."

"We can probably organize something for you next week…
" Betty had seen something in my face, and her mouth was drooping.

"I'm not coming back, Betty."

"You're quitting?"

"I'm leaving. Leaving Clifton."

"Oh, child. Are you sure? That's such a big decision to make in a hurry." She got up from her desk and took my hands.

"Don't I know it." I grimaced. "But it's the right thing for me to do. I have somewhere to live. Unbelievably nice, and it's mine. And maybe I can go back to school. Being a barista has been fun, but…"

She smiled, understanding. "But you think you can do better?" She gave my hands a squeeze. "I think you can, too. You're like a butterfly, crawling out of its chrysalis. I can feel the change in you, the strength growing inside you. You can be whatever you want to be."

Damn, but she almost had me in tears right there. "Thank you. For everything. You know I don't remember my mom, but you've always been the next best thing."

She let go of my hands and wrapped her arms around me, and I hugged her right back. When the ref called break, we both had tears down our faces, but we were smiling. She kissed me on the cheek. "Go. Explore your wonderful new life. And when you've made a success of it, come tell me all about it one day."

We held hands a moment longer; I kissed her back, and I walked out of the one place that had been more of a home to me than my old apartment.

Tasha didn't say anything when I got back into the car, but she reached into the glove box and pulled out a pack of tissues. In the same motion, she switched the GPS back on, and pulled away from the curb. She didn't speak until we pulled up opposite my apartment building.

"Are you alright?"

I sniffed and nodded. "Harder than I thought."

"I understand." She peered through the windshield and up at the cornflower blue sky. "Can you bring your stuff down on your own? I'd rather not leave the car."

"Sure, I can manage." It would have been rich to expect her to help me drag my crap down to the car as well as giving me the ride. I unbelted and got out the car. As I passed through the lobby, I checked the mailbox. Nothing for me, but it reminded me I'd need to get it redirected for a while. Collecting the junk mail for Bernie, I started up the stairs.

Separation Issues

"Where ya been?"

I hadn't expected Bernie to be home. This would be awkward.

"I need to get some stuff."

"Why? And you still haven't told me where you've been. You can't just disappear."

I had planned to go to my room and get on with packing, but I stopped and stared at her.

"And exactly when did you get made queen of the world? I go where I like when I like, and I don't owe anybody, least of all you, an explanation."

"Ray's been talking smack about you. Telling everybody you lit out on nothing but a text and that he fired you."

"He can tell me that to my face."

"Are you going into work tonight?"

"What's with all the damned questions? Get off my back." I stormed past her and into my room. The more I spoke to her, the less I realized I needed to take and the quicker I wanted out. She could keep the bedding – it was old, anyway. Hell, I was one step away from walking out on my clothes too. Most of what I left was uniform skirts and blouses, and I had already taken my laptop to the house.

The only thing I really wanted was my poster.

I heard her creeping across the floor behind me, but I didn't expect her to grab me. She took my shoulders, spun me to face her, then pushed me back on the bed.

"This is my house, and you show me some damn respect. You don't talk to me like that."

Was she for real? *Did* she think she was my mom? Her voice was full of anger, but what I saw on her face was fear.

"I talk to you how I want," I snapped, rolling off the bed and rising to my feet. "And you're welcome to your house. It's been a tiny version of hell living here, and I'm out. I'm leaving. Now."

"The hell you are." She planted herself in the doorway and made it plain that was where she planned to stay. "You can't."

"Stop me."

"You owe rent. And you owe for damages."

"Send my lawyers the bill. I'll leave you his card."

"You ain't got no lawyer."

This was getting stupid. I took a five-breath and tried to calm the situation down.

"Look, I know this may be a shock, but I'm going. I have a ride waiting for me downstairs. Just let me get my stuff and we can sort the rest of it out later."

"You have to give me six months' notice."

I turned my back on her, found my other duffle bag, and started emptying drawers, tossing what I didn't want onto the bed. She could give the clothes to the thrift shop or wear them herself if she could cram her fat backside into any of it.

"You can't leave. You have to stay here, where I can watch you."

I screamed. I mean proper battle–cry scream. Then I scrambled over the bed to the other side, put my head down, and ran at her.

I must have caught her by surprise. She weighted a good twenty or thirty pounds heavier than me, and four inches taller. But I hit her low, in a good tackle, shoulder in her gut and my arms wrapped around her waist. We stumbled back into the living space and collapsed onto the coffee table. And that was the last thing that went right for me.

The coffee table splintered under us. I tried to roll away and put some space between us, but I trapped my hand under her. By the time I could pull it free, she had her fist bunched in my t–shirt and was on the way to her own feet.

She picked me up like a doll. I mean heels off the ground picked me up, like in the movies. Then she threw me across the room. I don't know if she meant for me to have a soft landing, but I hit the chair like I was sitting in it and it tipped over backwards.

"You can't leave. You *mustn't* leave."

I scrambled away from the chair, grabbing the heavy glass ashtray that had fallen from the coffee table. I rose to my knees and threw it as hard as I could. Bernie swayed to the side like a ninja and it flew past her, smashing its way through a window.

I pushed the chair upright and tried to hide behind it, but Bernie grabbed it by the arms and tossed it aside like it was a lawn chair. Dodging around her didn't work either; she moved lightning fast and gripped my upper arms in a vice grip. Pinning them to my body, she lifted me from the ground again.

"You will stay in your room." She shook me. "Stay in your room." Something weird was happening to her; the angrier she got, the more stupid she sounded, and I don't know if it was a trick of the light, but her forehead seemed to jut forward like a neanderthal.

She didn't seem to notice I was kicking her, so I smashed my forehead onto the bridge of her nose. She screamed, and the next thing I knew I was flying through the air again.

I twisted in the air, but crashed into the doorframe of my room, arm first. Something cracked. I thought the pain from the headbutt was the worst I had ever felt until I bounced through the door and landed on the arm I had just broken. We both screamed then.

Cradling my broken arm with the good one, I scooted backwards on my butt, trying to keep away from her, while I looked for anything I could use to keep her off me. I had nothing to hit her with, nothing to stab her with. She put one hand on the shoulder of my broken arm, forcing another scream out of me until she cut it off with a hand around my throat.

No matter how hard I squirmed, it was like trying to push a mountain off me. The bitch was going to kill me, which left me terrified but furious. How *dare* she take all this away from me, just when life was starting to look something other than bland and meaningless? I wriggled harder and managed another gasp of air, but she settled her weight and squeezed tighter around my throat.

My vision stared to fade. My heart was thundering in my ears, its rhythm faltering, and I was losing the feeling in the hand I was using to rake nails across Bernie's wrist. There was a flicker of motion, then an angel stood behind Bernie. There was no more point struggling. I was dead, and the angel had come to take me to heaven.

Then the angel got a furious face and punched Bernie in the back of the neck, which was great, but not what I'd expected from a member of the Heavenly Host.

Bernie's hand came off my throat and the stale air in my lungs whistled out before they dragged the cool, sweet oxygen rich replacement back inside. The angel threw a headlock around Bernie, but my roomie struggled to her feet. The angel, whose face was rapidly turning into Tasha, looked surprised before they both staggered backwards out of my room.

By the time I crawled to the doorway, the room was a wreck. Bernie and Tasha tossed each other from one wall to the other, throwing kicks and punches so fast I could barely see them.

Then Bernie took a clumsy fall, smashing her head against one of the cast iron radiators that failed to heat the place during winter. It should have killed her, and caved in the back of her head, but her eyes blinked owlishly for a moment, then she tried to get up. Tasha took two fast steps, grabbing one of the metal stools we used at the breakfast bar. She spun on the ball of her foot and smashed the stool into the side of Bernie's head.

Bernie groaned and slumped to the floor. Tasha stood over her, stool raised high, until she was sure Bernie was staying down, then she dropped the stool and hurried over to me, a wide grin across her face.

"Well, that was fun." She brushed down her trousers, then held out a hand to help me up.

I stared up at her, and I know my face was as blank as the inside of my head.

"Did you know you had such an interesting roommate?" she added, like polite conversation.

"Interesting?" Deep down I knew I wasn't being helpful.

"Did you kill her?"

Tasha frowned at me. "Of course not."

"But you smashed her over the head so hard..."

"She's a pledge. By the way she moved, she's juiced up, or not entirely human. She can handle it." She looked around the apartment. "We should get out of here. Do you have what you need?"

I shook my head. I was fairly sure that what Tasha meant by pledge had nothing to do with sororities and college, but I guessed now may not be the time to ask.

"Then grab it and let's go."

I turned in the doorway and looked into the wreckage of what had been my room, then back to Tasha. I needed her help, but she was taking a photo of the tattoo on the back of Bernie's neck. That done, she dug Bernie's purse out of her bag and started going through it. For a moment I thought she was taking stuff, to make it look like a robbery, but all she did was take pictures of what looked like two different driver's licenses and IDs.

I tiptoed through the wreck of my room. Packing with one arm, wasn't an option but I wasn't going without my poster. I don't recall whether it was here when I moved in, or if I brought it with me, but every time I looked at it, I felt things were a little less bad, or I was a little more in control. It was a picture of an old British motorbike, like a fake blueprint, made by somebody called Norton. It was a little ragged on the corners and had a sharp crease where I must have folded it, but it was mine. The only thing holding it to the wall was sticky putty. I managed to get it down one handed but rolling it up was impossible. Tasha came into the bedroom and saw what I was trying to do.

"Is that it? We came all this way for a *poster*?"

I tried to think of words to use for an answer, but settled on, "Help?" I think that was the first time she noticed my broken arm. She took the poster from me, rolled it into a tube, and found a hair band to keep it in place.

"This is it?"

I looked around the room again. It would take me too long to sort through it, and I was certain I'd find nothing I valued. "Seems that way. Sorry."

"Then let's get out of here before someone calls the police," she said, which sounded like a smart idea.

Drive Home

I managed to hold it together until we were back on the interstate, but that was when I started to cry.

"Is it that bad?"

"Of *course* it's that bad. My roomie just tried to kill me and smashed up our apartment, I have nothing I came to get, and she broke my arm. How bad do you think it should be?"

But it was more than that. My head was pounding again, and I was getting flickers of light at the edges of my vision. Was that something Bernie had done to me? Had she truly been trying to kill me? And why? I'd done nothing to her. If anything, I'd been a little afraid of her since I met her and had been walking on eggshells ever since. It wasn't something I noticed before, but now it seemed so obvious.

I expected Tasha to snark back at me, but she just nodded. "Did anybody see you go into the building?"

"I don't know?"

"Think." Her voice was like a whip cracking. I tried to play the scene back in my head. "No. I don't think so."

"I didn't see anybody on the street, and I don't think anybody saw you get into the car outside your home."

"So?"

"Plausible deniability. Unlikely your roomie would try to say you wrecked the place. Any cop would take one look at you and laugh at her. Could be awkward if they try to tie me in."

I hadn't thought of that. "Shit. Sorry. If anybody asks, you weren't there."

"Thank you, hon, but more to the point if anybody asks, *you* weren't there. She was running fake IDs, and she had a pledge tattoo on her neck. I have some friends in low places who can have a word with her. Or maybe with her sponsor."

The car hit a pothole, and I cried out from the pain. "Can we go to an emergency room?"

Tasha thought for a minute, then shook her head. "No."

"You're kidding. Broken arm here."

"It's your call, but if you go into an ER with a broken arm and those bruises around your neck, they'll want to run a rape kit on you, take– What did I say?"

For a moment I didn't understand, then I realized I had hunched against the door, pushing as far away from her as I could get. I forced myself to relax and sit straight in the seat. "Sorry. Nothing."

She took her eyes off the road too long again, staring at me, then turned her eyes front again. "They will have cops all over you. And that's wherever you go. Can you hold out until we get back? I know someone who can check it out under the radar, fix it up if it doesn't need too much surgery."

"I don't know. I have some painkillers in my bag."

Tasha angled her mirror down until she could see into the seat. "Can't reach it." She stared at the road for a while, frowning, biting her bottom lip under her top teeth. "Can I trust you?"

"Isn't that supposed to be the other way around?"

"Not joking. Can you keep it together if I do something, well, weird? Quickly."

I was going to ask, *How weird?*, but the car jolted again, and fire shot along my arm as the ends of my broken bone grated together. If it would stop the pain, I would do about anything. I nodded.

The car slewed sideways as she took the off ramp we had almost passed. She switched the lights off, even though the sun had set. It was the wrong end of twilight, and I couldn't see where we were going. I didn't say anything because I was too scared of distracting her. Three turns and a half a mile later we were rolling up a dirt track. She pulled off the road and killed the engine.

"Are you going to kill me?" I wasn't sure why I said it. The pain was making me woozy, and I think I was in shock. My voice sounded like a little girl's. I heard her low chuckle, but at that moment it sounded sinister, not friendly.

"If I wanted you dead, I'd have killed you at the apartment," she said. "So I'll let that slur on my professionalism and ability pass as delirium. Now, I want you to listen, and to do what I say. I am not going to hurt you."

"OK." But I'm not sure she had convinced me. "I can reach the Advil now."

"They're won't be enough to help. My way is better. Scootch around in your seat, so you face me."

I took off my belt and turned as far as I could. In the dim light, I could just make out Tasha doing the same in the driver's seat.

"Now, I'm going to touch your face, and the sides of your head. Don't flinch, and don't pull away."

The tips of her fingers touched my skin, cool and soft. No, not cool. Cold. My skin twitched, but I didn't move.

107

"Think about the pain. Focus on it. Make it the center of your thoughts."

It wasn't difficult. The gnawing ache from my arm was a constant nag in my thoughts, as was the dull throbbing of the headache that had plagued me all day. I shifted my weight to keep my head still and got a sharp spike of agony for my trouble, and I was sure I heard Tasha gasp, soft and low. But once I had started thinking about it, a well of pain bubbled up from deep within me: Bernie's betrayal, Tamsin Whiston's death, the fear of change.

And as each came to mind, they seemed to fade away, or become less important. The grinding in my arm faded to a minor ache, and everything seemed more bearable, more manageable. I felt languid, relaxed, like I had a soft beer buzz, and I felt the tension ease from my muscles.

Tasha took her hands away and settled back in her seat with a groan.

"Are you all right?" I asked.

"I'm... going to need a minute." Her voice was thick, like she was on the wrong end of a row of shot glasses. I sat back in my seat, still feeling warm and fuzzy myself. After a few moments, Tasha started the car and, lights still out, drove back toward civilization.

By the time we got back to the freeway, my head started to clear. "What the hell did you do?"

She didn't answer me for a few breaths. "I'll tell you, if you tell me why you are wearing that ring. And no lies, no matter how much you think the truth is unbelievable."

I don't know if it was the warm and fuzzy I was still floating on, but I didn't stop to think before I answered. "Everything I told you is true, except the old woman who found me is freaky witch. She thinks – thought – I had powers, and that someone was trying to use me. Then she told me she reckoned they tore all my memories out and dumped me in Clifton. And she said someone was dosing me with Witchbane."

"*That's* what I can smell." Tasha thumped the steering wheel. "It's been nagging at me since yesterday. Anything else? Do you believe her?"

"I think I might be starting to. Some of it, at least. Oh, and there's this cool witch's lair under the house." I thought for a few seconds. "That's it. I think. How did you know I –?"

"Lied to me?"

"Kept some things back."

"The Ring of Magni. Don't see them often, and not everybody can wear one. They're picky about who they work with."

"You know magic?"

"I know *of* magic, but I can't do it."

"So what did you do back there?"

She didn't answer straight away, and I saw her head twitch toward me, like she wanted to look at me before she answered. But she kept her eyes on the road. "I'm an emophage."

"Is it catching?" Which I thought was hilarious, but apparently Tasha didn't. I stopped laughing. "What a – what's one of those?"

"I'm a vampire, sweetie. But I feed on emotion, on feelings, not on blood."

That sobered me up some, but not as much as it should have. "Are you going to eat me?"

"Already did. But I'm not going to kill you. I don't do that."

"I thought that's what vampires did?"

"Some do. Most, even. The taste of death is the sweetest meat of all. My Dam – the one who made me a vampire –

warned me not to even think about it. Once you taste death, you lose your soul, become an unhuman animal. If you can fight the craving, you get all the benefits but stay you."

"And the crosses and garlic and stuff?"

"Once you lose your soul, crosses and holy places are abhorrent. Wooden stake to the heart works on anybody, not just vampires. But I love Italian food. I'm stronger, quicker, heal faster, and I'm almost impossible to kill. I just have to be careful I don't get too much sunlight."

"But you drove us here."

She tapped the windscreen. "UV filters in the glass. The car is one of the safest places I can be."

My eyes were drooping. "Did you make me trust you? When you shook my hand?"

She let out that low, sexy chuckle. "No, Jane, you decided that all for yourself."

"Yay me," I muttered as I drifted into sleep.

Witch Doctor

I woke when Tasha switched off the engine. "Are we home?"

She shook her head. "Side trip. Might as well get this done now."

I looked at the clock on the dash. It was a quarter after midnight. "This late?"

"All the best people are night people," she said, and winked at me. A sleepy conversation came back to me and I gulped.

Tasha came around to my side of the car and helped me out.

"Where are we going?" We were on a street full of shops, closed except for the all−night liquor store at the corner. Lights shone in the windows over some of the shuttered shopfronts. "And where is this place?"

"28th and Happy Valley. Most of the lights are whorehouses, but we want this door."

We stood between a hardware store and a vape shop. The door intercom had four buzzers. Tasha pressed the bottom one.

"Get lost."

"Bite me, Louis."

The lock clicked, and she pushed the door open. It led

straight to a steep flight of stairs, and I was aching by the time we got to the top. I think the day was catching up on me and that Tasha's magic, or whatever she called it, was wearing off. At least we only had to climb one flight. On the landing, Tasha hesitated, then turned right. She put her hand on the door, then paused again. "Always have to think twice when I come here. Get the wrong door and you're in a fetish parlor." She looked across the landing at the other door. "And I'm not in the mood tonight." She gave me a big wink, a grin that said *You're not sure, are you*, then pushed the door open.

It was a waiting room with five plastic chairs along the hall. A middle-aged woman sat at a desk at the end.

"Waddaya need?" she called before the door had closed behind us.

"Broken arm, we think. Simple, no exit wound."

"You're lucky. Quiet night. Ten minutes." She held out a clipboard with a pen. "Fill this out. You got insurance?" She was looking at me, and I shook my head. Her face started to freeze up.

"Put it on my account," said Tasha. "The old quack still owes me."

The receptionist's face unfroze a little, but now she was glaring at Tasha. I don't think she liked the 'quack'. Actually, I don't think she liked Tasha either. "He'll have to OK it. Fill out the form."

It looked ordinary at first, but then some of the questions got weird. Like under 'sex' was male, female, and four or five other words I didn't understand, then a box for 'species', and another to enter your 'rage index'. I was doing the best I could, but it was my right arm Bernie had broken, and I was getting bogged down on some of the questions. Tasha grabbed the clipboard off my lap and tugged the pen out of my fingers.

"Gimme, or we'll be here all night."

I wasn't sure if she was getting impatient, or if she found the situation funny, but I felt useless either way. Then I saw the torn knuckles on the back of her right hand, and when I looked at her face, I noticed a cut on her cheek, and a bloody scrape on her forehead. The sniffles evaporated and got replaced with guilt. I couldn't even remember if I had thanked her yet.

A man walked up to the receptionist from a side corridor. She looked around him and pointed to us. "You can go in now. Leave the form on the desk."

Tasha dropped the clipboard as we passed, then led me down the hall and through another door. She obviously knew the place, and I wondered how often she took injuries that didn't need to appear in the public system.

The room was a cross between a consulting room and an OR. A desk sat against one wall, complete with a computer, a blood pressure cuff and a stethoscope. Next to it was a shelf of books that wouldn't have looked out of place in Tamsin's collection – or should I call that mine, now? A dentist's chair and an adjustable table took up the rest of the room, with a station in between them that held a light and trays for instruments. All spotless, very professional, and not what I expected.

Who was I kidding? I had no idea what I expected.

"Hey, Doc."

"Tasha? What brings you here?"

"Friend with a broken wing."

"Really?" The doctor looked excited.

"Arm, Doc, arm."

"Ah." Disappointment filled his face for a moment, then got washed away by irritation. "Do please say what you mean."

"My apologies. It's my friend here."

"The pale skin and cradled arm gave it away. Over here, young lady. Sit on the chair." He turned his head back toward Tasha. "Can you help with the analgesia?"

"Sorry. Already helped. This happened three, four hours ago."

"If I use conventional medication, someone will need to be with her."

"It's covered."

He pushed a stool on wheels to my good side then pottered around the room gathering stuff into a stainless-steel tray. I'm not good with needles, but the syringe came out of a sterile packet and I watched him break the seal on the ampoule of milky fluid he drew into it.

"This will ease the pain, but it will leave you feeling a little odd for the next few hours. Somebody should stay with you until morning."

I drew breath to say that I had nobody living with me, but Tasha beat me to it.

"Like I said, I'll be with her."

I looked away as he pulled the tourniquet around my arm. The pinprick was very sharp, very short, and seconds later a vast softness wrapped around me. It wasn't as warm as Tasha's touch, but it made me comfortably numb. So much so that when the doctor pulled on my wrist to align the bones in my arm, the best I could come up with was an unconvincing "Ouch."

Things got a little less comfortable after that. The doc put his hands around my arm, right where the break was, and squeezed. That was sore enough, but the flesh between his hands warmed up, then got hot. Feeling heat *inside* my skin was very odd, and when he took his hands away, I felt like he had wrapped an ice pack there instead.

And then he was looping a sling around my shoulder, and it was all over.

"How much?" I asked, though I was in no state to deal with money.

"Trade you for that pretty ring," he replied.

I tucked my thumb into my fist and held my hand against my chest. "Noooo. Mine."

"Leave her alone, you old crook. I thought you promised to stop abusing patients under sedation at your last court date."

"Hilarious."

"Put it on my account." Tasha put out a hand to shake.

The doctor, who had just taken off his gloves, looked at it for a moment, then smiled and patted her on the shoulder. "Always a pleasure doing business with you."

She held out the same hand to help me up from the chair. The floor was a trampoline, and I felt like I would bounce up to the ceiling with each step. Only her hand held me to the earth, and I clung to it for fear of floating away. The stairs were terrifying. I freaked out under the empty night sky, but Tasha got me back into the car.

It seemed I had no more than blinked and we were pulling up outside the house. I managed to stay upright by holding on to the car, but as soon as I tried to walk, my knees turned to jello and Tasha just caught me before I fell in the gutter. She scooped me up like a child and carried me toward the house, only to come to a stop a pace or two beyond the gate, right where redboots had decided I wasn't worth his time.

"Your house ward doesn't trust me," she said.

"My what doesn't what?"

She sighed and shook her head. "What did he shoot you up with? Just invite me in, by name."

"You have to say knock knock first." I giggled.

"I can drop you right here," she growled. "Literally." I think she was trying to sound mean, but her voice just sounded sexy.

"Come in, Tasha," I said in a voice I meant to sound like Nosferatu.

She propped me against the wall while she rifled through my bag for the keys, then she carried me into the house. "Where's your room?"

I waved a hand toward the guest room. She managed the door without putting me down and dropped me carefully onto the bed. The last thing I remember is feeling my boots being tugged off and wondering what would be next.

Show and Tell

Tasha was asleep on the couch when I got up. I had no memory of ever seeing anybody asleep. In the movies, yes, but not for real. She was on her right side, facing me, her head resting on a cushion, and her left hand tucked under her cheek. Something they don't get right in the movies is how sleep softens a face. Maybe it's down to the makeup, or the fact the actor isn't really sleeping, but Tasha looked years younger, like a teen. She wiggled her nose like a rabbit, and a faint frown wrinkled her forehead. Cute. I almost laughed. And then I realized standing in front of her and watching her breathe was creepy.

I got as far as taking a drape in each hand to pull them apart and let in the morning sun before yesterday's revelations began to resurface in my mind. Letting go of the drapes I turned to look at Tasha, then pressed pause on everything my mind was screaming at me. I walked out to the kitchen and put coffee on.

Back into the living room, protected by my caffeine armor, I sat on the chair opposite the couch and stared at this being who had exploded into my life. It took half the mug just to go over what had happened, to test my memories and see if I had maybe had a knock to the head and hallucinated it all. But it all seemed authentic, if difficult to believe. Even the guy who fixed my broken arm. The sling was still hanging sound my neck, and I belatedly hooked my arm through it even though I felt no more than a dull ache where he had clamped his hands.

What the hell was I supposed to believe about yesterday? That vampires were real? That someone could heal a broken bone with the touch of a hand? Difficult to ignore when the evidence was right before my eyes. Maybe Tasha had hypnotized me to take my pain away, but that didn't account for her and my roomie smashing each other around my old apartment like Batman versus Buffy. But then I remembered the cut on her cheek, and the graze. Now, her face was flawless again.

What made me trust her? I had told her so much, more than I shared with anyone else in my life. She said I made that decision myself, but if she mind—mojo'd me into trusting her, she would say that.

Trust wasn't something that came easily to me, with anybody, so what made her different? Because even as I struggled with it, a voice inside my head told me she was genuine, an OK person.

"Do I get one of those or are you just going to sit there looking at me."

She hadn't moved, but her eyes were open.

"I have a broken arm. Get your own." But I rose from the chair and padded out to the kitchen. "How?"

"Everything."

By the time I brought it back into the living room she was sitting up and had turned on the table light.

"I thought private dicks drank their coffee black and bitter."

118

I put it down on the table next to her.

"Thank god I don't have one of those then." She picked up the mug, sipped, and purred. "I hate that term. Too many jackasses think it's funny."

I said nothing but made a note she was not a morning person.

"Thank you for yesterday."

She swept a dismissive hand in front of her. "No worries. I enjoyed it."

"Well, I'm glad *you* did."

Her eyes came up to my face, but her lips broke into that twisted grin when she saw I wasn't being bitchy.

"Do you want to stay here today? While the sun is up."

"I can take it for a while. I'm still a baby. The older a vampire gets, the more sensitive to ultra-violet they become. Besides, it affects blood-suckers more than those like me."

"Oh." I didn't want her to go.

"I do have a request, though, and I'll trade you breakfast for it."

"Cereal I can pour for myself."

"Funny. May I look in your basement, at the previous owner's workshop?"

"Why?" It was reflex, an automated response, and I was sorry as soon as I opened my mouth. Tasha looked hurt, and I wanted to kick myself. "Sorry. So used to answering questions that way. Can I try again?"

The faint traces of hurt disappeared in the light of that grin.

"Of course. Breakfast first?"

Ham, sausage, mushrooms and scrambled eggs later, I led her down the steps. The eggs were heavenly, lightly herbed, and spiced with finely chopped chorizo. I stopped at the bottom, while she waited two steps above me.

"Will you turn away. I feel like I'm showing you my PIN."

She turned her back, and I quickly placed my hand on the door and breathed at it. The door clicked open, and I told her she could turn back. Tasha stopped outside the door.

"You can come inside," I said.

"I would, but your wards have other ideas."

She said something about wards last night.

"My what?"

"Protection. Wards stop undesirables from entering your house. Souped-up version of threshold magic."

"Of what?"

"Stops a lot of unpleasant people, especially night-dwellers, from entering personal spaces... You really don't know a lot about this, do you?"

But I was thinking back two nights ago, when I tied one on and brought that disgusting animal back to the house with me. Was that what had scared him off? Some magical barrier that Tamsin had put in place who knows how long ago. Did I owe her my life for that too?

Tasha called my name. I took a breath and refocused. "Sorry. What"

"Try inviting me in."

"Come in please, Tasha."

She raised a hand and shook her head. "This one is more stubborn."

"I really want her to come inside with me." I said the words out loud, feeling foolish. Putting my arm back through the doorway, I grabbed her by the hand, then pulled her into the room. It wasn't as easy as it should have been, like I was pulling her through something.

"Wow." It was long, low, and very heartfelt, and I felt

tremendous pride that the place was mine. She took the same tour as I had done when I first saw the room, but I noticed she was very careful to stay away from the big silver circle set into the floor. She ran her finger along the spines of some books, and almost touched a few of the objects, but it was that finger–graze you do when you like something, but you can't afford it. "This place is amazing."

"I know, right?"

She came back to the table and pointed to the envelope that was still resting on it. "Are those the notes she left you? May I look?"

I hesitated, and Tasha froze with her butt halfway down to the chair. "Sorry. I'm pushing, aren't I."

"No," I said before she could get up. "It might help to have another pair of eyes on it. Some of it still hasn't sunk in, and some I don't understand."

She opened the envelope and glanced at each page as she took it out and laid it on the table. At least I thought she was glancing, until I noticed her eyes vibrating as she looked at each page. She was reading it. All of it. She covered in seconds what had taken me half an hour, and when she got to the picture of the fire, the incineration of my family and my home, she pounded her fist softly onto the tabletop.

"I knew it."

"What?"

"I knew I remembered this story from somewhere, but I needed the details to bring it out again."

"What do you mean?"

"This investigation, about the fire. It was my last case before I got kicked out of the police."

I had never believed in fate, but I equally didn't trust coincidence, so right now I was sitting on an uncomfortably high, narrow fence. Tasha read the back of the last sheet, then put everything neatly back in the envelope, while I tried to decide if I wanted to ask any of the questions bubbling up inside me. When she finished, she looked around the room again before finally turning to me.

"Do you understand any of this magic stuff?"

I shook my head.

"I think you ought to learn some. Quick."

Advice from a Grumpy Old Man

The place felt empty without another body in it. Maybe that was why I sometimes felt edgy in the condo; I wasn't used to being by myself. And Tasha had left in a hurry, saying there were things she wanted to check out. I couldn't shake the feeling that something in the file had made her run. So I sulked in front of the TV for most of the day, popping painkillers like M&Ms to keep the nagging and probably imaginary pains in my head and arm at bay.

The next morning I felt much the same. I gave myself a mental kick in the ass and tried to figure out what I could do to feel better. It was too early for wine and I had no chocolate left in the condo. I had even checked in Tamsin's room, cringing every minute I was in there. Those were temporary fixes anyway. And I was already maxed out on Advil.

With a bottle of water from the fridge, my cell, and the phone from the kitchen, I went down to the workshop thinking that might make me feel better—though I didn't have any idea how. I stared at the books for half an hour before I even picked one off the shelf. It would have been helpful to find 'Witchcraft for Dummies' (which I later found out actually existed) or '100

Days to Magical Stamina'. I figured there might be something more on Witchbane, or a potion for headaches, but I couldn't see anything that might help.

Still, I took down two that didn't look too intimidating, and leafed through them on the table. The first one could have been written in Greek for all I understood, and I think the second one was. I closed both and put them back.

This was getting get me nowhere, but what else could I do? Tasha said I needed to learn magic, and Tamsin obviously thought I had something about me. And here I was, giving up after glancing inside just two books.

My jaw firmed up, and I stood straight. Maybe I didn't know enough, but I could do what Tamsin told me to do. Taking the phone out of my back pocket, I pressed the speed dial for Grant Peterson.

"I thought I told you not to bother me."

Deep breath, don't snap back. "Sorry, Mr. Peterson, but Tamsin isn't here to help me, and I think she meant for you to. There's nobody else I can turn to."

"Don't you dare tell me what you think she might have thought, and never try use her name to guilt me into anything again." His voice got quiet, and I felt like a big old family dog had just snarled at me. He also made me mad.

"I'm sorry you think I'm doing that, but I'm not. These are things she wrote to me, or told me in her last voicemail. Why else would she give me your number and tell me to ring you?"

The line stayed open, but he didn't speak for an uncomfortable time.

"Not on this line. Never know who is listening. Are you in her chamber?"

I looked around, realizing for the first time that the room fit the description of 'chamber' perfectly. "Yes." My eyes roamed around the space, seeing details I had missed before as if the name had been a trigger.

"Well, at least you managed that. Look around. Can you see a crystal ball? About four inches across, on a black iron stand?"

I already knew where it was. It seemed to pull my eyes into it the first time I saw it. "I have it."

"Hang up and put it in the middle of the table."

He cut the line before I could say anything. I put the phone to one side, slid the books back into the right spaces on the shelf, then lifted the glass ball and its stand. As soon as I dropped them on the workbench, the crystal began to glow. A fan of light shone out from the side away from me, and Peterson appeared, in full 3–D, on the other side of the table. I could see through him, but I was still obliged to let out an awed, "Wow."

"Grow up," he grumbled. "Sit down and stop fidgeting about."

I sat opposite him and put my hands on the table. He stared into my eyes, then down at my hand.

"When did the Magni accept you?"

I looked at my hand, then realized he meant the ring. "I got it on the second time I tried it. Two days ago, I think."

"So you stopped taking that disgusting Witchbane?"

"Yes. Was that the right thing to do?"

He grunted. "Depends."

"On what?"

"I told you. On what you want to do."

"Well, someone just told me I needed to learn some magic, and to do it quickly. I was going to experiment with some of these books–"

His eyes opened wide, and even in the weird light the crystal cast, I saw his skin pale.

"Gods and fishes, girl, don't do that. If you're what she thinks you are, you could accidentally cut a hole through the planet."

It annoys me when people overreact to make a point. "Then what *should* I do?" I was a little more forceful, a little less respectful. I was giving him another chance because Tamsin seemed to respect him. So far, I couldn't understand why.

"Are you serious about this?"

"I think so?"

"You *think* so?" he thundered, and pushed me over the edge.

"Stop shouting at me. How can I know if I'm serious when I don't have the first clue what I'm talking about? I *want* to, but I don't know if I *ought* to, or if I even can." That last thought caught me off guard by how deep it cut. I brushed it aside, for the moment. "Now either help me or switch this thing off."

He glared at me for a moment, then his face softened. "Well, you have some fire in you. And you'll need it." He sighed. "If you really want to know more, don't dabble. Get your memories back."

"Why?"

"Because learning this all from scratch will take you three years before anyone can trust you not to blow yourself up, and another three before I can trust you not to blow the world up. And I hear you saying you don't have that sort of time. Assuming, of course, the memories are still in there."

"Pardon?"

"They can make memories inaccessible by hiding them, or by destroying them. If someone destroyed them, there's no bringing them back. Now, be careful who you ask for help, and do not trust anybody who says they are from the Concilium Nexus. They look like priests with black collars."

"Then what should I do. Can't you help me get my memories back?"

He shook his head. "I'm good with combat magic, and I'm an average to good thaumaturge, but messing around in people's heads is beyond me. You need a healer, and a specialist at that. Got a pencil?"

I fetched one, and a notepad, from the space on the shelf where I found them what seemed like so long ago, and brought them back to the table.

"Find Justin Sands. He moves around a lot, so you may have to hunt for him. Do you have any contacts you can trust?"

"Yes."

"Then use them, but cautiously. Justin can be hard to find when he wants to be. And tell him I sent you. Probably just make the old crook charge more, but it might get him to see you. Now get off the line and stop bothering me. I've already said too much. If Justin says he can't recover those memories, destroy that chamber. Forget you ever heard about magic, sell the house, and move out of the country. Somebody went to a lot of effort to shut you up and hide you away. They won't be pleased you've started poking about where they didn't want you to."

Bernie Who?

The doorbell made me jump. *Any* sharp noise was making me jump today. The pounding in my head was non-stop, no matter how many painkillers I took. As if that wasn't enough, the flickering in the edge of my vision was back, and I kept thinking I could hear someone talking in the next room, or outside the apartment door. It was so real; I even jerked the door open to shout at whatever kid was playing this whispering variation of knock and run.

But this time it was a wide hat, oversize shades, and a pair of gloves. It was exciting to see her, to see anybody, but I did my best to play it cool. She threw her hat onto the couch as we walked through to the kitchen, where her gloves and shades ended up on the breakfast bar.

"I have news."

"Not a social call then. Do I get billed for this?"

"I'll trade you for coffee," she offered.

"Cook lunch and I'll upgrade you to wine."

We made small talk while Tasha threw lunch together. I suppose I was taking advantage, but she didn't seem to mind, and it put another voice in the condo for an extra hour. Besides, I couldn't cook worth a damn unless it involved the microwave.

When she served lunch, I reminded her why she came.

"Oh yes. I spoke to a friend who spoke to a friend. Neither of the driving licenses carried her actual name, but one was a known alias. She's wanted for assault in three states, robberies in another two. A friend dropped a dime on Clifton PD for me and passed on some of the details. They won't be looking for anybody local over the state of the apartment, and they'll start liking her for the murder of your friend, too."

I stopped with a fork full of food halfway to my mouth and let it drop back to my plate. "She killed Tamsin?"

She wagged a finger. "It fits her style, but that proves nothing." Something in Tasha's expression suggested she only said that to cover her ass and to stop me doing anything rash. "It will give the local boys in blue something to think about. Not that they'll catch her. Either someone will have extracted her, or she'll be starting new Bigfoot rumors in the nearest forest. I heard a whisper she was working for someone or something going by the name of Crodax, or some such. That was all I got. I also had word sent back to her sponsor that she'd been drawing attention to herself. They don't normally like that, so she could end up with a price on her head too."

The ravioli sat heavy in my gut, and I wished I'd not eaten it. Such words of violence, so casually spoken. A killer, who might have murdered me if I had gone back to the apartment without Tasha. That was twice in one week someone had tried to hurt me, and I'd done nothing wrong. At least, that I knew of.

I changed the subject before my heartbeat got so loud Tasha would hear it.

"Sponsor? The person who set them on me?"

"Possible, but unlikely. But her sponsor may have done a

deal with someone who wanted you watched. Can't imagine why a pledge would stay so far away from her sponsor for so long." She looked into the distance. "Unless someone negotiated local biting rights." She stabbed another ravioli parcel and popped it into her mouth, whole, then must have seen the abject confusion on my face.

"A pledge is a human, or a near-human, who enslaves themselves to a vampire master or mistress, usually to feed on. Most of them hope if they are loyal enough, they'll get turned. To people like your old roommate, being a bloodsucker is glamorous, desirable." She shook her head. "And it's almost impossible to convince them otherwise. If the sponsor trusts them enough, or needs them to have an edge for some job, they may let the pledge feed from them. It can make a human stronger and quicker."

My head was still spinning. So many new, outrageous ideas. The pasta sauce was delicious, but I pushed the plate away. "There are vampires after me?"

"Not necessarily. They may just be supplying the muscle."

"But Bernie could still come after me?"

Tasha's eyebrows rose. "Hadn't thought of that. Anything's possible, but it would depend on how important you were to whoever had her watching you. Or if she carries a grudge. Operating without her sponsor's blessing would be tantamount to a divorce, though. And bloodsuckers don't take well to being divorced by mere humans."

I felt small and helpless. "And what do I do if she finds me?"

"Do you have a Taser?"

"Of course not. Why would I?"

She pulled a face, scrunching her lips together and rocking her head from side to side. "Because you never had a demon chasing after you. I'll get you one. If she comes up to you, shock her to her knees and run like hell. Or get yourself a crash course in some kick–ass combat or defensive magic."

"Demon?" My voice came out as a squeak, and I cleared my throat to cover it.

Tasha rolled her eyes. "Not literally."

Well, how was I supposed to know?

"Mind you, she was either juiced up on something, or not pure–blood."

So very, very much I didn't know. The conversation with Peterson came into my head, and I almost asked Tasha to help me find this Justin I had been told to look for. But I was already asking so much of this woman – or whatever she called herself. Adding to the list seemed ungrateful. She was wiping the last chunk of a bread roll around her bowl, picking up the last of the sauce.

"By the way, I'm busy for the next few days. Do me a favor – don't try to call me."

A chill ran through me. Had I done something wrong? Was this a brush off, a shedding of the demanding, clingy thing she had taken under her wing and now wanted rid of?

"I'll give you a call when I'm back in circulation."

Small and helpless came back in spades.

Fire

I ran out of clothes. More to the point, I ran out of clean panties. My size or not, no way I was raiding Tamsin's room for those. It was time to brave the other door in the basement. The ice box in the kitchen was looking empty too. I gathered my laundry into a bundle and shuffled down the stairs to the basement – where I had to drop it all on the floor to open the door.

Inside, of course, were the laundry baskets. One washer was already running, so I dumped everything into the other machine, 'borrowed' soap from the fullest container, and trusted to luck.

Someone had numbered the chest freezers one through three, and I figured it was safe to assume that the numbers referred to the condos. I opened '1' and started rooting around inside.

"Well, hi."

I'd made it near to the bottom and almost fell inside. When I pulled myself out, a perky blonde about my age was looking at me with a confident smile so fake it made her look like a victim on legs.

"Hi." My originality and wit stunned me.

"Have we met?"

Passive–aggressive much? I shook my head and held out my hand. "Jane."

"Amanda." Her handshake was limp, like she expected some suave dude to turn her hand over and kiss it. I was struggling not to invent a bad first impression for her, but she wasn't helping. "And you are visiting...?"

"I own the house," I said. I realized I was standing with my arms folded tight over my chest and my weight on one leg. Now who was being passive-aggressive? I stood straight and tucked my fingers into the back pockets of my jeans. This conversation already wasn't going well.

"Oh. I thought you'd be... Never mind. Was Miss Whiston a relative? We were both so sad to hear of her passing."

Crap. Another busybody. Did I give off some pheromone that attracted them, or was the rest of society bent on sticking their noses into my business? "Yeah, terrible shock." The silence got awkward, and I struggled for something to lighten the mood.

"Hey, I really don't know the area. Is there a good grocery store around here? One that delivers, maybe?"

"GreenMart is good. Little expensive, maybe, but they have an online delivery service. A couple of miles north up Armstrong. Difficult to miss – it has a giant inflatable broccoli on the roof."

I had to raise eyebrows at that, and I felt my lips ghost into a grin. "Subtle."

"We got the letters," Amanda said, changing track so hard the conversation almost fell over. "From the lawyers."

"What letters?"

"Telling us of the change of ownership. We were sort of

expecting you would come meet us, or something. Have you made any decision yet?"

"Sorry, I've been busy," I replied on autopilot, then something she said waved a flag at me. "Wait. Decision about what?"

"About serving notice on us?"

"Did they tell you that?" If they did, Walcott was in for a conversation with unkind words.

Amanda shook her head. "Not exactly, but it's the way it usually goes. Buyout, new landlord can't hike prices because of rent protection, tenants evicted because of 'renovation'–" she made air quotes with her fingers "– then new tenants brought in at higher rents. Oh. Maybe I shouldn't have told you that?" Her hand covered her mouth and her cheeks burned bright red.

And I laughed. Not nasty, not at her. "Thanks for the evil plan. It's much better than the one I had."

She gave me a look that said she wasn't sure if I was for real, then laughed too.

"Sorry," I said again. "I have a tremendous amount on my plate right now, and I assumed the lawyers would explain it all. Tamsin – Miss Whiston – took care of you. You're both safe right where you are. I have no intention of selling, at least not for now. Can you tell–" it was my turn to go pink when I realized I didn't know the name of the other tenant.

"I'll tell Nathan," said Amanda. "Then maybe we can have dinner and get to know each other."

I raised my hands. "Perhaps we should start with coffee. I'm not good with crowds."

"Three's not a crowd."

I put on a smile to take any sting from my words. "It is to m–"

Amanda raised a hand, sharp and imperative, and cut me off in mid word. She cocked her head like a dog, listening.

"Did you hear something? Glass breaking."

I listened. Instead of a sound, I felt fear – but it wasn't mine. It was outside of me, around me. A moment later something tickled my nose, then a smoke alarm started to shrill upstairs. I shoved Amanda toward the outside door.

"Out. Call 911."

She grabbed my arm as I turned away. "You, too."

"Go," I shouted, and pulled my arm free. I had only just got this house, and no damned fire would take it away from me. There was an extinguisher in the kitchen.

I burst through the door at the top of the stairs. Smoke clung to the ceiling, so I kept my head low as I scuttled around the breakfast bar. Only when I tore the extinguisher from the wall did I realized how ineffective it would be. It was tiny and meant for pan fires. But it was all I had. Still keeping low, I scurried into the living room.

The drapes were alight on one side of one window, and that was making the smoke, but a pool of fire was creeping over the floor like a stain, heading for my beautiful couch on one side, and the TV on the other. The thought of losing either made me feel sick. Popping the safety off the extinguisher, I let the fire have it full blast.

I might as well have blown it a kiss.

This was not happening. Life couldn't do this to me. It wasn't fair. But as I stood watching the fire creep across the floor, the sickening realization sunk into my skull that I was helpless, and that I had to watch my new dream destroyed right in front of me.

Pain stabbed into the back of my eyes, the same as the

headache I had been getting, only a thousand times worse. If that wasn't enough, my heart felt caught in the fire, burning in my chest as crackles of light danced around the edge of my vision.

I knew I should run. I could still get past the fire and out the main door, but that part of me didn't seem to connect. In fact, it felt like I was wearing a Jane–suit, and it didn't quite fit.

My arms spread open, hands wide, and I faced the fire. Sparks danced between my fingers, though I felt nothing, and the fire backed away from me. The flames swayed back as they rose, as if they were afraid of me.

Stepping closer, I herded it back across the floor to the drapes. My hands made a scooping gesture and the fire gathered in on itself. It became a ball, hanging in the air in front of me and getting hotter as it got smaller. Bright light burned my eyes. My hands didn't touch it, yet they pressed down on it, pushing harder as it condensed to a beach ball, then a basketball, a baseball.

It fit in my hands now, and felt as hot as the sun. I kept pressing, squeezing, rolling it between my palms as it got smaller and smaller. Then it disappeared, leaving a smear of heat across my palms.

The pain in my head faded, and I seemed to fit inside my skin again. I looked down at my hands. White blisters were erupting across angry, red flesh. "That's gonna hurt," I muttered, and it immediately did.

The fire department would break the door down if it wasn't open, so I ran over and unlocked it before I hurried into the kitchen in search of cold water. I was standing at the sink when the sirens wailed up the street, and I was still there when I heard a "Hello?" from the door.

"Back here," I called.

A burly firefighter, all craggy faced and action man, poked his head into the kitchen.

"Where's the fire lady?"

"It was out there, by the window. I got it."

"You hurt?"

I thought about being brave, but my hands were telling me that was stupid. "Little bit," I admitted, and held out my palms.

He twisted the radio on his jacket round and pushed the button. "Stand down. Safety inspection, hand units only. Medic to the kitchen." He looked back at me. "We'll just check it out, make sure it's safe."

The smoke detector was still screaming, and he casually reached up and reset it as he passed. I would have needed a stool.

Another firefighter appeared a few minutes later, wearing less protective gear but still looking almost as hot as the fire I put out. That bounced around inside my head for a moment and made me want to freak; the fire *I* put out.

What was it about firemen? Cops did nothing for me, nor paramedics, but something about firefighters made me come over all flirty. He put his med pack on the table and started unzipping pockets.

"That was brave," he said. "Also stupid. Looked too big to take on with just an extinguisher." He took my hands out from under the running water and looked at them for a moment, then pushed them back underneath. "How long you had those there?"

I looked at the clock. "Coming up on ten minutes."

"Keep them there a while longer. The more heat we can take

out, the better." He started laying supplies on the table. "I'm surprised such a small extinguisher could take on anything that size. Did you have another one?"

Another one full of questions, but I could let him off. It was his job. And if I said yes, they would look for the other fire extinguisher, and I couldn't just tell him that the fire extinguisher was me. He'd have me locked up as crazy. Hell, I still wasn't sure if I wasn't nuts.

"I only had that one," I said, nodding toward the empty red cannister just visible on the living room floor. "I was going to run out the door if it didn't work, but the fire seemed to die right under it."

He took my hands from under the faucet and touched them all over like he was brushing them with an angel feather. "Feel that? And there? And there?"

I nodded, my lips passed together. My hands we so sensitive this was like foreplay, and I would die of shame if I let out a moan. Then the happy fantasy shattered as the cooling of the water wore off and the pain came back.

"That's good," he said

"What?"

"Pain."

"Maybe for you."

He grinned. "If it hurts, it's still alive, and the burn is only on the surface of the skin. If you can't feel anything, the heat got deeper, did more damage. This looks okay, though."

"Do I need to go to the emergency room?"

He looked up from my hands. "Normally, for burns this severe. Don't you want to?"

"Not if I don't have to." I made a sour face. "No insurance."

He nodded, then took my hands in his to examine them again.

Then he turned them over, and he froze for a moment. He was staring at my ring, and I was staring too. The gemstone wasn't black anymore – it was a swirling orange-white. He looked back at my face.

"Yup, sometimes those little extinguishers can work like magic."

I was sure I heard an extra weight in the last word. I struggled to keep a straight face, but he wouldn't take his eyes from mine.

"But I'd be really careful if you felt like trying that trick again. Dealing with a fire can get out of hand real fast."

He held my eyes a moment longer then turned his attention back to my hands, spraying them with something then wrapping them in plastic film. He knew. My heart was hammering and I couldn't breathe. I didn't know how he could, but he knew. Was I supposed to have kept this stuff secret? Would he report me, and black hats in unmarked SUVs were going to raid the condo and spirit me away?

"They'll hurt like hell for a couple of days. Try to keep them covered. Contact with air makes it worse. No soap or creams, but you can use food wrap to renew this. Any signs of infection, or numb areas, you get yourself to the emergency room. Understood?"

I nodded. He gave me a smile that made everything feel better, and the fear of men in black suits and sunglasses faded away. He turned his attention to packing his kit and I felt abandoned. I sighed inwardly, watching him until he finished, then matched his parting smile with one of my own.

The older man came into the kitchen. "It's safe. Weird little fire. Looks like an accelerant was involved, but we're damned if we can see any trace of it. Did you spill anything there?"

I shook my head. "But I only moved in a couple of weeks ago.

Could it be something the previous tenant spilled?"

"Who knows? Nothing to see there now." He looked at my hands. "You take care of those. Get help if you feel anything unexpected. And next time, call us and get out. What you did was brave, but stupid."

His voice was stern, but his eyes were caring. I saluted.

"Yah, already got my hand slapped for that. Figuratively."

He smiled, waved, and left. Amanda poked her head around the door. I kept my face calm. I was still enjoying the buzz of the hot firefighters and didn't really want to confront reality just yet.

"Are you ok? The medic said you hurt your hands."

I ambled over to the door and held my hands out for inspection. Also, I wanted to discourage her from coming in. It was nice she was showing an interest, but I didn't want visitors right then. She peered past me and into the room.

"Did it do much damage?"

I kept my body in her way, and she got the message. "A little. Damaged the drapes, part of the floor. None of the furniture, and nothing structural. Have to clean it up before I can get a clear look."

"Can I help? You might find it..." Her voice faded away, but she had a point. I gave her one of my friendly smiles.

"That's kind of you. I have to get it checked out first, for the insurance, but as soon as that's done, I'll let you know. A day or two?"

"OK. Nathan's out. I'll write a message for him and slip it under his door."

"Thanks, that would be a help." Maybe I had her wrong. I do that sometimes. "I need to go. Hands really hurt, and I just want to process things for a while."

Amanda put her hand on my arm. "Call me if you need me. I expect I'm still in Tamsin's phone list." She gave my arm a gentle rub and ambled up the stairs to her level. Definitely may have got her wrong. And I noticed the subtle shift from 'Miss Whiston' to 'Tamsin'. Maybe I was being invited into the little circle they had before I crashed into their lives.

I closed the door and turned back to face the living room.

The damage didn't cover much space. The drapes, smoke damage above it and on the wall, then the burned patch in the floor that was about ten feet by six. As a percentage of the room, it didn't add up to much – but it felt like a scar across my face. I hated it.

And now the flames and the smoke were out of the way, I could see a hole in the window, just wide enough to put my hand through. Shards of glass littered the sill and the floor, so whatever made the hole had been coming in, not leaving.

An icy knot grew in my gut. This wasn't a question of *what* had caused the fire, it was a question of *who*.

Suspect

Someone hammered on the door, imperative and impatient. I peered through the spy hole and saw two bodies, one in uniform. As I struggled with the latch, I heard more pounding and yelling.

"Open up. Police."

I got the door open. "What the hell is your problem? I'm burned."

"Watch the language, lady. That's enough for 'disorderly conduct'." snarled the uniform. He grabbed my arm and twisted it behind me. While I screamed, plainclothes grabbed my other arm and snapped a cuff onto it. Uniform held my other arm steady while plain clothes put the cuff around that too. I don't know which of them did it, or if it was deliberate, but somebody scraped the skin on my hand and I screamed again.

"Mind the damned burns, jackass."

Uniform tugged on the chain between the cuffs, and the hurt started all over again. Then he let go and walked around in front of me.

"Any more attitude, we'll add resisting."

"What the hell are you doing? Do you have a warrant?" I didn't watch a lot of TV, but I was sure they couldn't just burst in like this.

"Probable cause, lady. We got a solid tip that someone at this address is connected with the arson attacks." The uniform tugged at the cuffs again. That he could cause me so much pain so easily threw my mind off balance.

"To what?" I wailed.

"Arson, attempted arson, reckless endangerment, insurance fraud, attempted murder." The detective paused and looked up at the ceiling. "That's all I can think of for now." He stood in the middle of the room and turned one full circle.

"I've seen enough. Let's get her down to the station. Forensics can tear this place apart while we go over it with her."

The uniform chuckled. "Tear apart is right. Those guys are on a mission."

"Hey, tear what? Why are you doing this?"

"Shaddup." The uniform snapped, then took out his notebook. "Name?"

"Jane Doe."

He slapped me. The son of a bitch actually slapped me. "Watch that smart mouth, kitten. You're in enough trouble already."

"Check it, moron. My bag, on the couch."

He upended the contents onto the couch and rooted through everything until he found my ID and my driver's license. He waved it under my nose.

"This is out of state."

"I moved here a couple of weeks ago. From Clifton."

"Enough of this. Get her in the car."

"Hey. At least get my keys and my purse. How will I get home?"

Uniform pushed me so hard I bounced off the door frame on

my way through. I heard a nasty chuckle. He growled in my ear, quiet enough that nobody could overhear him.

"What makes you think you're coming back here, bitch? Place is too good for trailer trash like you anyway."

Up to then I'd just been mad, but now my gut clenched around a sharp fist of fear. This was for real. They thought I had something to do with the fire, that I had set it. Walcott would be able to sort it all out, or I hoped he would, but the damage these creeps would do would be a hundred times worse than the fire. Beyond that, I was helpless. They had already made their mind up, and even I knew arguing with a cop was a quick way to get beaten up. Or shot. Especially with nobody else around.

The uniform hustled me outside, chanting the Miranda mantra into my ear as we went. When we got to the car, I realized this was my last opportunity to change anything. "Please, get my purse and my bag. And my phone."

"I ain't your baggage service. Get in the car."

"You want me to sit on my burned hands."

"Oh, boo hoo. My heart is breaking for you. Get in."

Plain clothes was coming out of the house. He didn't even close the door, never mind lock it. If Amanda didn't notice, the place would be looted overnight, and I'd be left with nothing but squatters the law wouldn't help me get out and bills. Tears started rolling down my face.

"Last chance, bitch. Get. In. The. Car."

His hand dropped to his gun and a finger flick off the strap.

"Oh, please do it. Do it for me."

I was so relieved I almost pee'd myself.

Tasha was standing, somewhere behind me.

"Lady, put that fucking phone away or I will arrest you for

assaulting a police office, causing a disturbance, and aiding and abetting." The uniform sounded a little less sure of himself.

"While you pull your weapon on a handcuffed woman with burned hands offering no resistance. And you just said it." Tasha's voice was bright and cheerful. She was enjoying herself. That made me feel even better

He turned and took a step toward her, gun elbow crooked. "Gimme that damned phone."

"Ah ahhh." Tasha refused in a singsong voice. "Direct feed to the cloud, sweetie. You can smash the phone into a thousand pieces and your charming face will still be stored up there. And if I don't stop it in the next 30 minutes, the system will mail the video to my lawyer, her lawyer, and every news desk in the state."

His face was bright red now. As he took another step toward Tasha, his gun slid out of its holster.

"What the hell are you doing?" Plainclothes' voice cracked across the sidewalk like a whip. "Take your hand off that weapon or I'll shoot you myself."

Uniform, gun still drawn, turned his head. "One day, pretty boy. One day we'll see how that would have gone."

"And I have that on record too," said Tasha.

"Tasha, put the phone down."

What? Plainclothes knew Tasha?

"Nah–ah. Not until you tell me why you're cramming an injured woman into the back of your car, cuffed, after somebody tried to burn her house down."

Plainclothes looked at Tasha, the uniform, me, then back to Tasha. "Take the unit and go" he said to the uniform. "I'll bring her in my car."

"The hell you will. Come on, man. She fits. She an outie. It's always an outie. Remember what the Commissioner said? He wants this arson thing closed, and he wants her for it"

"Go."

"Pussy whipped," the uniform snorted. "Bitch had your balls when she was your partner, and she still has them now."

He turned away and walked toward a black and white a little up the street. Tasha called out to him.

"Hey, O'Malley."

He looked over his shoulder and she waggled the phone at him. "Don't you want to say goodbye on my leverage tape? Want me to send it to your captain now or later?"

He turned away, kept walking, and flipped her off over his shoulder.

"Do you know this woman?" Plainclothes demanded of Tasha, but his voice was different, less edgy.

"Eddie, what the hell do you think you're doing? What are you rousting her for?"

"What's it to you? Client?"

"Friend, asshole. You should try making some. Or keeping some."

"The mayor is on the commissioner's case, he's riding my captain, and my captain is giving me a hard time. With the house last week and this, people are getting angry about a serial arsonist as well as the rapist. Captain said the Commissioner has hard evidence that involves her."

"In what? A genius serial arsonist, who hasn't left the slightest crumb of evidence for you to go on, drops a match and sets her own house on fire? A house fire so serious that the fire department didn't even get wet?" She lowered her phone and switched off the video. "You're slipping, Eddie. Didn't believe you'd turn into one of *them*."

"When you walk away from it, you don't get to judge any more. Department's changing." He looked away. "You can only swim against the current for so long."

This seemed as good a time as any for me to butt in. "I saw glass. Inside my window, like someone had thrown something through."

"Did you tell him this?" Tasha asked.

"I tried." I glared at the cop. "Nobody was listening."

She glared at Eddie the Cop. "Check it out." He took my arm to lead me away, and I shrieked. Tasha thumped his other arm. "She has burns, you dickhead. Lose the cuffs." Something caught her eye elsewhere. "You go on ahead. I need to speak to somebody."

Eddie didn't say a word as he took the cuffs from my wrists and followed me back into the apartment. I walked over to the window, then pointed to the hole and the shards. When I turned back, Eddie was bright red.

"Would have helped if you'd mentioned this at the time."

"Did you give me a chance?" I walked away from him, careful not to give the impression I was leaving the room, but I couldn't stand to be near him. Every sound echoed around the living room until Tasha strode in. She walked straight to the hole, pointedly staring at the obvious burn ring centered around the hole, then gave Eddie such a withering look that he scuffed one of his feet like a boy being lectured by the principle. Or his mom.

"I spoke to the fire department." She still looked at Eddie. "Something you might have wanted to do before you came storming in here looking to frame someone. You'll want to drop this."

"Why? Commissioner won't be happy."

"Let's say it's one of those he doesn't want to admit happens."

I saw Eddie's eyes roll, and he threw his arms up in despair. "Oh, come on."

"No accelerant detected, burn pattern doesn't match any standards. No ignition source or point. Official FD report will read unexplained. Push it and yours will end up the same. Blame it on an ornament catching the light in the window. That's what they usually sign this off as."

"Well, if she didn't do it, someone did." He still looked like a sulky little boy, but Tasha was offering no sympathy.

"Get out there and square it with the watch commander before he drives off."

"What about O'Malley?"

Tasha looked like she wanted to slap him, for real. "Want me to hold it and shake it after you piss, Eddie? He's a thug. Stand up to him." She waved the phone. "And if I hear a word from him, or of anybody from the station harassing my friend, this goes to the Mayor and the press. And you can tell your precious captain that."

"Hey, I'm on that too."

"Then make sure I don't have to use it." She was as cold as ice now. "And you might want to mention to them that she has Walcott for a lawyer."

Eddie winced, then gave her a long look and shook his head. "You were always a pain in my ass."

"And I always will be." She took two long steps until she was in front of him, then kissed him on the cheek. "Now get out of here before one of us says something the other can't forgive."

Eddie touched her arm, made a grab for the phone that didn't come close, and strolled out as if nothing had happened.

Tasha closed the door behind him, turned the latch, then came back to the middle of the living room. I was still there, motionless. She pointed to my hands.

"Do you want me too...?"

It took me a moment to understand, and a moment to decide. It would be so easy to say yes, but I shook my head. "I need to feel them, in case they get worse. And to remind me not to do things with them. Besides, the medic was hot." As humor went it was weak, but I was trying.

"Darius?" She grinned back. "He's OK, for a fire demon."

"A what?"

"Nearly every station has one, though they won't admit it. They can feel things about a fire, like what started it, where the hotspot is. It was him I spoke to."

She put her hands on my arms, just below my shoulders. I could feel her coolness through my top. "Are you OK?"

I tried. I really tried. But the tears started rolling down my cheeks faster and faster. I sniffed. "No."

She took me in her arms and held me, standing in the middle of my wounded home, until the sobs stopped.

Evidence

Tasha stayed all evening and only left once I had settled down for the night. Drinking red wine through a straw was different, but got me no more drunk than swigging it the usual way. Being fed was possibly the most personal thing I had ever experienced. At one level, utterly demeaning. At another, a curiously deep connection between you and the person feeding you.

By the time she got back in the morning I had managed to bathe, pee, and dress myself, but my hands made me pay. Without the wrap they were so painful, but I couldn't cover them on my own.

She breezed through the door, all bubbly and bright, takeout coffees in one hand and a bag from the grand temple of fast food in the other. "Sausage, bacon or egg, you get first choice."

"You bought *three*?"

"I thought we deserved a treat. By the way, do you have any honey?"

"I have no idea. Why?"

"You're going to have a guest later. And I arranged for a glazier."

"Who wants honey, the guest or the glazier?"

She glared at me under lowered eyebrows for a moment, then tapped the side of her nose. "Breakfast first."

I took the sausage muffin – and half the egg – and managed to feed myself. Though I have to admit my mind did wander back to the meal last night. So intimate, each morsel offered to me on the end of a fork, my lips plucking it off. I nearly dropped my muffin and shook my head to clear it.

Tasha stabbed the lid of my coffee with a straw. "Be careful, it might still be hot."

I nibbled and slurped. "When are these people coming?"

"The glazier should be here around ten," she looked at her wrist. "In about an hour. If they managed to find him, and if he's stopped running, Maximus should be here around noon."

I tried to prod for more information, but Tasha was enjoying keeping her surprise, and I let her keep it. For now.

The glazier came, measured, put a board over the hole where he took the broken pane out, and promised he would be back by the weekend with the replacement. Then we had nothing to do but wait for this mystery visitor.

Fifteen minutes before noon, Tasha sent me off on the hunt for a sheet of good, white paper and a mechanical pencil. By the time I got back, she was sitting at the kitchen table. The window was open and an egg cup sat on the table, half full of honey.

"Put the paper in the middle of the table, then come sit next to me. Don't act surprised and don't make any loud or sudden noises."

An iridescent purple dragonfly hovered outside the kitchen window and tapped against the glass. It was huge. And it looked even bigger when it buzzed in through the open window. I drew a breath and shot Tasha a worried look, but she put her

151

hand on my knee and I let it ride.

The odd thing was that the closer the dragonfly got, the bigger it got. Yes, I know things do that, but it got bigger than it should have, if that makes any sense.

And then something stood on my kitchen table. A seven inch up–scale model of a male Tinkerbell, dressed in a purple tunic and green leggings, and complete with pointy boots and a cap with a purple feather. He offered us both an extravagant bow, and I copied Tasha when she gave him a slow, grave, nod.

"If I might make the introductions," said Tasha. "Maximus, meet Jane. Jane is my friend, and Maximus is one of my most trusted Information Privateers."

"Privateers?" I muttered.

"He disapproves of pirate," Tasha whispered back. "Or informant, or snitch. Immensely proud."

Maximus made a loud cough and looked as though he didn't approve of the side conversation. "Apologies," said Tasha. "Just bringing Jane up to speed with a few points that would bore you, my friend."

Maximus accepted the apology with a regal nod. "Shall we begin?"

His voice was loud, given his size, but pitched like a child's.

"Could you tell us what you saw?"

"A man. With a bow. He blended himself with the back of a parked van, then shot two arrows at your house. The arrows carried bottles. As soon as he fired the second arrow, he got back in the van and drove off. He was a competent archer; the second arrow passed exactly through the hole made by the first."

"Was his face hidden?"

"Not to me." Maximus said, smug.

"What happened after that?"

"A hundred heartbeats later I saw fire through the window. I watched until the noises came. They annoyed me, so I left."

"Can you show the archer to us?"

I wondered how a seven-inch critter would use a five-inch pencil to draw, but reality chose to be weirder than I could imagine. Again. He picked up the pencil like it weighed nothing, clicked out an inch of lead, then put it back down. Then, from inside his jacket, he took a silver spoon with a long handle. He put the bowl of the spoon to the pencil lead, and the lead melted into the bowl and vanished, like solder touched by an iron.

While I was still trying to process that, he kneeled down on the paper and began drawing so fast I couldn't see his arm move. Tasha leaned closer to me, cupped her hand to my ear, and whispered. Her breath tickled and sent a tingle down my spine.

"Max is a fairy. I asked him to hang out in the tree across from your house and watch. Nothing creepy, just had a feeling something like this might happen after Clifton. Fairies don't like noise, so Max ran away when the fire trucks turned up, but he sent word as soon as he saw the arsonist. That's how I got here so quick. Don't thank him, though. It's considered insulting to offer thanks for carrying out an arranged task."

I nodded, a hundred questions battering at my lips, but no way to whisper in Tasha's ear with my hands shrouded in plastic film. Maximus stood up, brushed off his knees, then shook a tiny pile of black dust out of his spoon and onto my table.

"It is done."

The sketch was exquisite and highly detailed, but it was from the back, behind the shooter. It didn't help us at all. My heart sank to my boots.

"Is the work not sufficient? Does it in some way displease?" Maximus had his hands on his hips and was glaring at me. From the corner of my eye I saw Tasha glance at me, then she nudged me with her elbow. I forced a smile.

"Forgive my friend. She is new to our ways. The work is as exemplary as always. Might I mention one minor detail?"

"Oh?"

I marveled, I really did, at just how much attitude it was possible to fit into such a small body.

"We were rather hoping to identify the miscreant," Tasha finished.

"Oh. You want to see his *face*?"

It was a 'well why didn't you say' moment, obviously our fault, and he turned back to the paper. I waited for him to start drawing again, but he put his hands on one side of the image and slid them across it.

The image rotated. Turned all the way around until we are staring at the guy from my side of the street.

"And if you could bring the face closer, please. To fill the picture?" Tasha was apologetic, but Maximus put his hands together on the middle of the tiny face, then swept them apart. Twice. The sketch zoomed in until the archer's face was pin–sharp and visible.

My contribution to the conversation was a heartfelt *wow*. Tasha grinned at me and whispered. "Where do you think they got the idea for smartphones? Nobody could have thought up something so crazy on their own." She turned her attention back to Maximus. "Perfect and complete. You have truly earned your fee."

She ceremoniously offered the egg cup of honey to a beaming Maximus. His spoon reappeared from his jacket and he dipped it into the honey, then brought it dripping to his mouth.

"Not unpleasant. I prefer a more natural nectar, but this is acceptable for payment."

He dipped his spoon and sampled it again, and I wondered how long it would take him to eat the entire eggcup full. The cup held almost as much of it as there was of him. But he had an answer. The spoon went back into the egg cup and he started to stir. The level went down, and the more he stirred, the faster the honey disappeared. No more than a minute passed before he was running his hand around the sides to catch the last drops of the fluid.

"Do you wish to continue surveillance?" he asked Tasha. She nodded, and he bowed to us both again. "Then I shall return to my task. Farewell. And a pleasure to meet you."

This last was news to me, so I gave him one of the odd head–bows. "Likewise, sir." I almost said thank you, but remembered not to at the last instant.

Maximus took to the air, getting too small too quickly. The dragonfly shot out of my kitchen window and away into my garden. I stared out the window for a moment. That had been intense. Weird, beautiful, and intense. It was nice to see such beauty, when my new world had so far offered me such ugliness and fear.

Then I turned to face Tasha. "You were *snooping* on me?"

The Shadows

"Do you know him?" I stared at the face in Max's sketch, wishing all kinds of nastiness to crash down upon the head in front of me.

"I've seen him before," Tasha's voice sounded distracted. "Can't recall his name, but I have a friend who will know how to find him."

She pushed the sheet of paper into the middle of the table and edged her chair back.

"Where are you going?"

"See a man about an arsonist."

"I want to come."

Which came as much of a surprise to me as it did to her.

"Not sure that would be a great idea."

"Why not?"

"Your hands."

She had a point, but I really wanted to go. I was so bored, and I wanted out of the house – only I didn't want to go exploring on my own. That hadn't gone too well the last time I tried it, and my confidence had taken a hit.

"They're much better," It was a half–truth, not a lie. "I could probably go without the wrap. It's not dangerous, is it?"

"It shouldn't be, but that doesn't mean it won't be. Best not."

"I'll tell."

"You'll what?"

"The detective yesterday. He gave me his card. I'll call him and tell him you have information about the suspect and didn't tell him."

Tasha's eyebrows arched at me. How desperate did I sound? And about eight years old.

"You want to come that much?"

I nodded.

"Well, you can't wear that."

I wore jeans and a snoopy tee. "What's wrong with it?"

"You look like food. What else do you have?"

The answer was 'not much'. Tasha went through my entire bag of clothes without finding anything suitable to wear. She started on my hair, too. What was wrong with blonde, a little over three feet long and ruler straight?

She sat me down and pulled it into a tight braid that made my scalp ache so much I worried she might be punishing me for getting pushy. She looked at the other bedroom door.

"No."

"What?"

"I'm not going through her things."

"What are you going to do with them? You'll have to get rid of them some day."

"Give them to a thrift shop, I suppose."

"And you've never bought anything from a thrift shop?"

If I said no, I'd be lying, so I said nothing.

"Would she rather you had her stuff or a stranger?" Tasha pushed the point, and I raised my hands in defeat.

"You look. I don't want to go in there yet."

Tasha shook her head at me but marched across the room and into Tamsin's bedroom. I didn't care how she looked at me. One day, I would do it, but I still didn't feel comfortable going in there. She was back in minutes.

"We would have got on," she announced. She held up a leather bike jacket, a black tour tee-shirt from a band I'd never heard of, and a pair of ripped black jeans. "This is more like it."

They all fit, though I did need a belt for the jeans. I don't usually go for belts, especially wide ones with chunky buckles, but Tasha liked it and I was damned sure I wouldn't be going with her unless she approved of my outfit.

"I still don't understand why we have to go through all this," I grumbled. "Where are we going to find this guy, anyway?"

Tasha smiled, tight and fierce.

"We're going into The Shadows."

I didn't have a clue where we were, and I had an idea that Tasha might not want me to know. I told her I was checking for messages and opened the prehistoric mapping app on my phone. With luck, it might just be able to track where we went.

We drove through the business district, then down a long strip of malls and shops that turned into auto traders, then repair shops. Tasha turned north, and the zoning shifted toward manufacturing and industry. Everything looked grimy and sinister, and Tasha made a zigzag of turns that took us into smaller and smaller streets.

The last corner took us into a short alley, barely wide enough for the car. I could see the other end open onto the next street, and that was why I screamed when we dropped down a ramp that wasn't there. No trap door, no tilting road, we just tipped down and drove into absolute black.

I looked across at Tasha. By the light from the dash, I could see she wore a wide grin; she had loved making me scream like a teenager at the fairground. I made a note to think of something to get her back.

But I only managed to cope with her driving in absolute black for about a minute.

"Please put the lights on."

She chuckled again. "Sorry." She twisted the end of the turn signal and the parking lights came on. At least now I could see we were in a tunnel. Not a brick tunnel; a cave tunnel of natural stone. Where the hell had she found this place? I almost wished I hadn't asked for the lights.

Ahead, two wooden warehouse doors blocked the way, but Tasha didn't slow down. I gritted my teeth, clenched my hands into fists despite the pain, and refused to react. She had already gotten two rises out of me this trip. Third time was *not* going to be the charm.

The doors turned out to be an illusion, or something. We drove through them like they were ghosts and came into a warehouse district, or that's what it looked like. By the time I turned to look over my shoulder, I couldn't tell which of the buildings we had just come through.

"The Shadows is careful," said Tasha, seeing me looking for an exit. "You either know how to get in or you don't, and it won't let you out unless it wants you to go. Now shut up and let me find somewhere to park."

I didn't point out I hadn't uttered a word. She drove for a few more minutes, then turned into a side road and parked between an ancient red Cadillac with huge fins and something that looked like the car from the Jetsons. We got out, and she clicked the door lock. The alarm blipped and sounded utterly out of place.

"Do you want to explain why it's dark?" I asked as she set off along the sidewalk. "We started out in the middle of the day."

"It's the Shadows," she said, as though that explained everything. I kept my mouth shut until she gave me an actual answer. "Here, you're the odd one out. This is our world."

"Our?" Her choice of words troubled me more than I expected. I had always looked on Tasha as just like me. A few oddities, true, but essentially human. Now I wondered where her allegiance would lay if it came to a crunch.

"Well, I *am* an emophage, even if I haven't turned all the way yet." She looked sad. "It will happen one day. Either by accident, or the craving will beat me. I'll drink too deep and the transformation will complete."

"And what happens to you?"

"Just drop it, okay?"

I felt like she slapped me, and we walked in silence while I wondered if coming here had been a good thing. Didn't guys have a word for this? Bromance? Another guy comes along who is way cooler than they are and sweeps them off their feet. Was that me, crushing on her? Was I confusing that with being a friend?

I'd been aware of a rumble in the air for a minute or so. It had been getting louder, but suddenly there came a real increase. Tasha grabbed me by the arm and pulled me into a left turn. Before us was an orange glow that got brighter the closer we got to the end of the alley. At the end, we walked into a golden market.

The square was enormous, with shops around the outside and a market in the middle. Tents and stalls sprinkled across the central space apparently at random, so close together there were no streets or alleys. Four major roads joined the square at the corners and a forest of tall streetlamps lit the place with a sodium glare.

"He's over the other side," said Tasha, and set off. Her voice still sounded cold, and she didn't look to see if I was following. If I had known how to get home I would have left, but I didn't, and she was my ticket out of here. And it was my own fault I was here at all. I jogged a few steps to catch up, then fell in behind her.

Until I walked right into her back when she stopped, and I was too busy gaping around like a tourist. The woman behind the stall looked human to me, but I was learning. I smiled anyway.

"What can I do for you?"

We both looked at Tasha.

"Your hands," she said, in an 'isn't that obvious?' tone.

I tried to catch her eye for a moment, but she was browsing through a vast collection of tiny jars and pots on the table. I held out my hands. The woman winced and came out from behind her stall.

"May I touch them?"

She didn't look like she intended to drag her nails across my palms, so I nodded. Her hands were dry and gentle, and her fingers touched my burns as softly as the fire demon's. "Arcane or mundane?"

"Arcane, we think," said Tasha, while I was still drawing breath to admit I didn't know.

The woman disappeared into some space behind or under

her table, and emerged with a small wooden box, a little like a matchbox except the lid fit on the top. Plus the bottom was full of a thick ointment, not matches.

"This will help. Apply over the entire hand today, and again tomorrow. Be careful, it can make your fingers slippery."

Tasha handed over coins and waved away the change the woman offered.

"Come over here, out of the way."

We ducked into a space between two open–front tents, and Tasha opened the box. "Give me your hands."

I held my hands out as though she was checking they were clean, but she dabbed a generous blob of the gel on each palm, then put the box in her pocket.

I made to take my hands away, to massage in the gel, and got a curt "wait" for my trouble.

And then her hands wrapped around mine, left first, then right, gently massaging the gel into my skin. The salve tingled, but it didn't sting, and the coolness of her hands was soothing. Then I realized this was an apology, and I understood a little better. It wasn't me she was mad at. It was her life; her craving, her ultimate destiny and her fear.

"Thank you," I said, softly, when she took her hands away.

"No problem," she replied, wiping her hands clean on the fabric of one of the tents. "Now let's go find Jimmy."

The shop front was narrow, just wide enough for the double door fitted into it, and the sign above was almost as wide as the door it hung over: "Jimmy's: Quality Caffeination and Tonsorial Sculpture".

A steady stream of patrons passed in and out. We stepped inside, into a long corridor. Arrows on the floor pointed inward on one side and outward on the other, but people ignored them. Most seemed to get out of Tasha's way, so I stayed behind her and let her take point.

The corridor opened into a vast coffee house. In one corner, on a small stage, a green monster with curled horns was playing 'Freebird' on a Gibson Streamliner, and doing an outstanding job. The bar ran the length of one wall, with four shining six–head Petrocelli espresso machines.

But at the end of the bar, opposite the music stage, was another raised platform. On this one sat an old–style reclining barber's chair, like in the gangster movies.

Tasha slowed as she walked toward the bar and I saw her head move from side to side as she scanned its length. Then she was back up to full cruising speed with a slight change of direction.

"Jimmy."

"Tasha! Not seen you in a while." He looked at her hair and frowned. "You've been letting somebody else cut that."

"Can't always get down here, Jimmy."

He looked hurt. "And I thought we were friends."

"Need a favor."

"Don't you always? Your credit's starting to wear thin, lady."

"The hell it is. You still owe me, and you know it."

When Tasha snapped, I saw a flash of angry fire in Jimmy's eyes. He was built like a bouncer; six feet tall, wide shoulders and no neck. His torso tapered down in a nice V, but he wasn't human. I must either be getting more observant, or just waking up to the obvious stuff that had been staring me in the face for years. His fingers were too thick, and his nails were more like horns. His beard and his hair, though, were perfect. Sculpted.

Tasha raised her hands almost as the words left her mouth. "Sorry, Jimmy. I'm not myself this afternoon."

"So how about a coffee to lighten the mood?" He stared at me for a moment. "You look like a medium latte, mellow roast, caramel shot."

Not my usual, but it sounded delicious. "Light roast Brazilian?"

"Close, little bird, but not from anywhere you have ever heard of. You take your coffee seriously?"

"Used to be a barista."

He held out a meaty fist. "Family," he declared. "You ever need work, you come see me." I bumped him.

"You think she'll want to work in a dive like this?" Tasha laughed.

Jimmy gave her the British two–finger salute, but grinned. "That's better. Now what do you need?"

Tasha slipped Maximus' sketch onto the bar. "Know this creep?"

Jimmy glanced at it. "Sure. Doesn't everybody? Slimy little pledge goes by the name Icarus. Real name Dale, I think. Flames for hire. Likes to think he's a Mage, but he just got taught a little chemistry."

"Any genuine talent?"

"Not enough to light a match." Jimmy sneered.

"How long has he been a pledge?"

"Sixty, seventy years."

I tried not to let my eyebrows rise. He didn't look a day over forty.

"Where can we find him?"

"Five left off North," said Jimmy. "About a block down. He

lives over a rundown repair shop."

"That's on the edge of the dark."

I looked at Tasha, not having understood a word other than 'Repair shop'. She was pursing her lips.

"Are you sure you want to take blondie down there?" He looked at me. "No offence, but you look a little raw. Might be safer if you waited here while Tasha took care of business."

Tasha glanced at me, eyebrows slightly raised, making the offer. But sometimes it's a lot easier to be brave when you don't know how much danger you're walking into. I shook my head.

"No, I twisted your arm to let me come. I go all the way."

Tasha gave me a thin smile that I chose to believe meant she was proud of me, then turned back to the Jimmy. "What do we owe you?"

Jimmy's eyes flicked up to my head for a moment. Tasha laughed, and I turned my eyes just in time to see her eyes coming down from a roll. "Creep."

"Am I missing something?" I asked, looking between them.

"He wants to touch your hair."

Well, that was new. "But it's in a braid."

"Doesn't matter," said Tasha. "Turn around."

I had visions of a knife appearing from under the bar just before he slashed the braid from my head, but I turned.

Weirdest sixty seconds of my life to date. Even more so than being fed. He ran the braid over his hand, felt the weight of it, touched the top of my head and felt the hair there, then tugged out a single strand.

I "hey"–ed and turned to face him again, but his expression wasn't some pervert getting off on his fetish, but a craftsman assessing a raw material.

"Let me cut it." His tone was a mixture of begging and worship.

My hand rose protectively to the root of the braid. "No!"

"Give me a free hand. I'll give you information for a year."

"No."

"And free drinks."

"No."

"If you don't like it, both. For life."

"N–" Tasha's hand was on my arm, squeezing.

"Let her think about it, Jimmy. We have to see a fire bug about his nasty habits. Later."

Tasha turned away, but a memory popped into my head. Not an old one, a new one. "I'll think hard if you can help me out with something else."

They each said a synchronous "Oh?".

"Another name. Justin Sands."

Jimmy gave me a look I couldn't decipher and glanced at Tasha as though asking her permission. "The Sandman? He has a place two right on West. First block."

"Thanks. And I will think about it." I looked past him at something I couldn't see and that wasn't there. "Maybe I'm in the mood for a change."

Jimmy clasped his hands over his heart and grinned at me, and I waved as we turned back to weave our way out of the place.

Interrogation

Tasha took us back to the market, weaving through the crowds until she saw what she was looking for. The stall was bright and businesslike, the being selling from it a slim troll, if your mind will stretch that far. As soon as it saw Tasha coming, it tried to close up shop. Tasha quickened her pace and grabbed hold of the shutter just as the owner tried to pull it down. They struggled, but the troll gave up when the wood creaked.

"Get lost, Campbell. I sell nothing you would desire."

"Silver cross and a fifth of holy water."

"I don't sell that stuff. It's contraband. This is a clean joint."

"And my father dated your mother. Give, Mashra."

"I'm telling you I'm clean."

"Why do you put me through this every time? I know you're not." Tasha hooked a thumb at me. "Hells, she knows you're not, and she's never seen you before. I don't have time to go through this charade again."

But Mashra folded its arms over its chest, and I assumed it was looking stubborn.

"Is there an Inspector for this market?" I asked. They both looked at me and I wished I hadn't started. "You know, someone who makes sure everybody is trading by the rules, that nobody is selling stuff they shouldn't."

"Usually over in Northwest corner," said Tasha, looking confused.

"So if I were to go over and tell them that someone at this stall had tried to sell me holy water, or a wooden stake, or silver bullets, what would they do?"

Tasha grinned and turned back to Mashra. "They would come over here and rip the stall apart. Even if they didn't find anything, the stall would be out of business for a day, maybe more. And I could stand here to make sure the stall holder didn't try to run, or dump anything with anybody else."

"Who is she, your bitch in training?"

Tasha smirked. "Coming on, isn't she?"

Mashra's shoulders drooped. "OK, OK, but make it somebody else next time."

"You don't value customer loyalty?"

"Bite me." Mashra disappeared behind the counter, returning with a brown paper bag and a credit card reader. "Eighteen dollars."

Tasha held out a twenty. "Keep the change. Call it an incentive for next time."

"Wow, a whole two–dollar tip."

"Why the hassle?" I asked as we walked away. "Why not carry stuff like that with you?"

"The wards that hide the entrances don't like it. They try to keep weapons and toxins out. Most times they just don't let you in. But I've heard stories of people carrying who come into the ways and get dumped out halfway around the world. Or worse."

I struggled to imagine worse, then pushed the thought aside.

I had enough to deal with. "*Any* weapons?"

"Blades are ok. Strangely, so are guns. But no garlic on the blades, or silver bullets."

"I thought you said garlic didn't work."

"I said it didn't work on *me*."

"And this stuff will kill him?"

Tasha laughed. "In his dreams. He's a pledge, and still basically human, but he's allowed a vampire to feed off him for half a century. He'll feel something, but nothing like what a real bloodsucker would. Thing is, he so wants to be one of them, his mind will think it hurts more than it really does. At worst, it'll do no more damage than a slap across his face."

As we passed the edge of the market, it was like we went from day to night. There were still lights, but they were ordinary streetlights, not the massive towers in the square. As I looked into the distance, they seemed to get fewer, and less bright. There were shops here too, set back across a wide sidewalk, between or under apartment buildings and anonymous blank walls.

"Is it far?"

"Five blocks."

"What's the dark?"

"What?"

"You said it was on the edge of the dark."

She grunted. "The farther you go from the Market, the less light. Most of the beings that live down here are creatures of the night, of darkness. Go far enough out, beyond where the streetlights work, and it turns into their world, into the Dark."

I felt a trickle of ice run down my back, but it just made me stand straighter.

"Shouldn't we have taken the car?"

We walked for fifteen minutes then Tasha stopped, staring at a building with shops along the bottom and two rows of windows above. When Jimmy said repair shop, I had imagined broken witch's brooms and magic amulets, not toaster ovens and vacuum cleaners. But I suppose even vampires have to clean up the place.

A door sat recessed between the repair shop and the unit next to it. Tasha shoved at it, and it opened. I wasn't sure if nobody had locked it, or she busted the lock. The stairs started right behind the door and went up forever, just like at Docs. Tasha pointed to the edges of the treads and whispered.

"Try to step wide. Not so many noises."

The stairs still creaked. I stepped as lightly as I could, but it was hard trying to be quiet and while keeping up with Tasha, who seemed to float up the stairs she moved so fast.

When we got to the top, something didn't feel right, but I couldn't put my finger on exactly what. A light bulb, brown with the accumulated grime of years, barely lit the landing. There were two doors, an apartment over each store, and whatever was bugging me felt worse when I looked at the door over the repair shop. Then the headache came back, pounding at the back of my skull, and so did the sparkles around the edge of my vision.

Tasha was reaching for the doorknob, but I grabbed her arm. "Wait."

"What?"

"Something feels wrong." When I reached out with my open palm, my fingers started to tingle as soon as they were within six inches of the handle. I looked around for anything helpful and saw the scraps of a broken broom leaning against the opposite wall. They would do. I picked up the snapped-off stick, pulled the sleeves of my jacket down over my hands, and poked at the door.

The door swung inward, but had moved only an inch when the handle exploded in a ball of flame. It was there and gone in a flash, but I felt the scorching heat even from six feet away. Anybody who had been touching the door or the handle would be on fire.

Tasha leaped forward, smashing the door out of the way and running into the apartment. I followed a half–dozen steps behind, still holding the brush handle. Damn, but that woman could move. I burst into the living room in time to see Tasha hauling somebody back in through the window.

Icarus, or Dale, shoved his feet against the sill as he came through, tumbling both of them to the floor and breaking Tasha's grip. I guess he didn't think I was much of a threat. He screamed and ran at me, and I caught a flash of satisfaction on his face as I stepped aside, apparently to let him push past me. He smirked right up until I stuck the broom handle between his legs and tripped him into a full face–plant on the wall.

Tasha was on him in a second, hauling him to his feet. He was moaning and whimpering, and when she turned him around, it looked like he had split his nose when it hit the wall. I was mortified. Not. She gave me one of her tight, fierce grins, and I felt proud all over.

The carpet had holes in it, and he hadn't vacuumed since he moved in. Pizza boxes and other takeout containers stank in one corner, and the sink was full of dirty dishes covered in who knows what kind of mold. He had no bed, just a mattress in the corner and no, I did not want to speculate on what the stains were. A single armchair faced an old tube TV on a pair of cinder blocks. A DVD player and, of all things, a VCR sat on the floor next to it.

The small dining table was covered in crap and had two chairs next to it. It was to one of those Tasha dragged our host.

"Find me something to tie him."

While the mighty Icarus whined like a child, I ripped the cables out of his entertainment system. I didn't break anything; he could put it all back together, but he kept on whining.

Tasha held him down, arms over the seat back. I tied his wrists, then fastened them to the back of the chair. Then I looped another cable around his legs. The little rat tried to kick me. Tasha slapped the back of his head and snapped, "Manners." I tried again, this time from the side, then I used the last cable to link his ankles to his wrists.

It wasn't as bad as it sounded. I've tried to use TV cables as tie-downs before. To keep stuff on my scooter, before you think up anything weird. They're weak, and they stretch. I figured we just wanted to keep him in one place while we got his attention. Then I realized I had left the bag of persuasions Tasha had bought out on the landing. I scurried off to get it.

"And here she is." Tasha said as I got back. "This nice lady has some questions."

"Fuck her, and fuck you too." He tried to sound tough, but his voice shook and his eyes were darting all over the room. Tasha ripped his shirt open, revealing a scabbed and pimply chest, then stood behind him and pushed his head forward. She took out her phone and it made a bright flash as she took a photo of the pledge tattoo on the back of his neck.

"Get off me, bitch."

She cuffed him across the back of the head again. Not hard, just a reminder of who was in charge. "Tell the nice lady what she wants to know."

Which put me right on the spot. What was I supposed to ask? Was this payback for making a thing about coming along? Or was it a chance to get some of my own back?

"Why did you set fire to my house?"

"Don't know what you're talking about, blondie. Why don't you go back into the light and buy yourself something pretty to wear? Maybe come back and show me." He leered, then ran his tongue around his lips.

I saw Tasha's hand tighten in his hair, but I moved quicker than I thought I could. I slapped him across the face, hard, forehand then backhand. "Mind the mouth, vermin."

Tasha pulled his head back so she could look into his eyes. He choked a little, and I saw he was pulling against the cables. I also got a good look at his neck. The scars made my skin crawl, layered over and over each other. There were half–healed puncture wounds on the right of his throat, and signs of infection in the left.

"You are not a gentleman, are you?" Tasha said. "Very unchristian way to treat a lady."

As she spoke her eyes flicked up to meet mine. I took the hint and reached into the paper bag, hiding the cross in my hand as I took it out.

"I asked why you tried to burn my house?"

He spat at me. It missed my face, but it dripped down my jacket. I showed him the cross, and he squirmed, but Tasha put her hand on his shoulder and held him down.

"I don't think he likes it," I said to Tasha. "And after we bought it specially for him."

"His master might enjoy looking at the scar on his neck when he feeds," she replied.

"Where would they see it best?" I asked, getting closer to his face with the cross. Then I reached forward and pressed it to his forehead. "Right up front maybe?" He screamed, and I was sure I heard a sizzle. I lifted the cross after a second, and it left a red mark where it had touched his flesh; something between a mild burn and an allergy rash. The power of wish fulfilment, I guess. I touched him again, just below the hollow of his throat. "Or here."

Another scream. "Please, don't. You don't understand the trouble I'll be in."

Over his head, Tasha mouthed "water" to me. I put the cross in my pocket.

"Then tell me why you wanted to burn my house."

"It wasn't personal. It was just business, a job."

I reached into the bag and took out the bottle of holy water. The label was simple but eloquent – a black crucifix over the skull and crossbones. Salvation for some, poison for others. The bottle was plastic and, when I took off the cap, the thoughtful manufacturer had put a little nozzle in the neck. I pointed it toward the nasty little rat on the chair and sprayed a jet of water at his bare chest. He steamed as he screamed.

"If it was business, someone must have hired you."

"I'm just the small fry."

Squirt

"Look, they gave me the job. I don't know who I was working for."

Tasha pulled his head back. "Then who was the broker?"

I squirted again and got his neck, but Tasha hissed too. "Do you mind?"

Dale found that funny, so I gave him about a quarter of the bottle, right over his face, making sure some went into his mouth. I know I was being nasty, but this creep nearly cost me my house, my new world, and the lives of my tenants. He had stepped over the line. Besides, Tasha said anything he felt was from his own mind.

Tasha let him speak again when he stopped steaming.

"Jessander. Jessander gave me the job. She said I didn't need to know who it was for, and I had to use the code 'Corvax' when I reported back."

I glanced up at Tasha and found she was already looking at me. That was close to the name that Bernie had been working for. Except now every hair on my arms was standing stiff and I had no idea why. The name meant nothing to me. But something about it troubled Tasha. Maybe that was it; I had seen the look on her face and that was why I had gooseflesh. I had to wait until we finished with Dale the drip before I could find out what it was.

"Are we done with this creep?" I asked. "I've got everything I want."

"Jessander will put her own contract out on you for this," Dale blustered. Tasha didn't bother to slap him. She was already walking away, but she stopped and turned to glare at him.

"When Jessander finds out how fast we found you, and how easy we got her name out of you, I don't think it's us she'll put the contract on." Then she muttered to me. "Pour the rest of the water around the door, then drop the cross into it."

I did as she said, then mic-dropped the bottle onto the floor as I turned and followed her out.

I was buzzing. My feet didn't feel like they were touching the ground as we hurried down the stairs and onto the street. I wanted to chatter about it like a kid the first time they got to a carnival, but Tasha marched along the sidewalk, shoulders hunched and head down. My buzz faded into the night like the steam that had risen off Dale.

Had I done something wrong? Had I been too rough with him? Said a wrong thing? I thought I'd done what I needed to. We didn't get as much as I hoped. I wanted for the name of whoever tried to hurt me. But we had the next level up, which was better than nothing.

And it felt good for me, too. Through what life I could remember, I kept my head down, doing my best not to get anybody mad at me, meek and mousey, always being pushed around. Taking things into my own hands felt great, even if it was a little scary. And I had Tasha there as a safety net.

As my mood turned darker, the headache came back. I hadn't noticed it since the top of the stairs, since I sprung the little rat's trap. Now it was grinding away at the back of my head again, relentless, immune to any pain meds I had access to. I felt my own shoulders slouch, and I trudged along, a pace behind Tasha, as we made our way back to the car.

"You're quiet," Tasha said as we drove away.

Maybe I was. I had no idea if my phone map was still keeping track of where we were. If it wasn't, I would have no way of knowing how to get out of the Shadows if I ever visited on my own. Still, I took some exception to her words.

"*I'm* quiet? You didn't say a word after we left Dale's hole of an apartment."

"You think it's smart to hustle some guy then brag and giggle about it as you walk away from his crib? If I had said one word, you would have been gushing like some preppy band nerd all the way back to the car."

176

That hurt. Maybe I would have been chatty. She didn't have to be so harsh.

"Well, excuse me."

Not the most cutting of comebacks, I know, but my head was thumping, and I had no pain relief with me. I put my head back against the seat and closed my eyes.

(Un)Familiar places

When we came out of the Shadows it was late afternoon, which threw my time sense sideways and made my head ache all the more. Tasha pulled up outside the house and made should-she-come-in suggestions, but I begged off. I needed painkillers and a cold cloth over my head, and I didn't need her to do that. She had annoyed me. No, she'd hurt me. And now I was feeling like a puppy she smacked on the nose with a paper when it wasn't me that pissed on the floor.

I guess it sounds redundant to say I wanted to lie down in a dark room after being in the Shadows, but there's a difference between the darks. An enormous difference. It's not just down to the actual light, or lack of it. I think it's down to where the darkness comes from.

The pain meds started to work after a half hour, and I must have drifted off to sleep, because the next thing I knew it was tomorrow morning and I was ravenous. I still hadn't gone grocery shopping or had that chat I promised Amanda and Nathan. The milk carton was close to empty, so it was coffee or cereal, but not both. That wasn't even a contest. I thought about toast until I noticed spots of green mold on the bread –

ew – but I found some cherry pop tarts hidden at the back of a cupboard.

I unbraided my hair and showered, then changed into something less *biker chic*. Not that I didn't like the look, but I still felt odd wearing Tamsin's clothes.

Then I remembered I had laundry in the machine from days ago. I went down to the basement to check out what state it was in. I hoped somebody had pulled it out of the machine and stuck it in a basket, but I expected to find it in a smelly mess in the bottom of the washer.

It wasn't. It was dry, folded, and stacked in a basket for me. On top was a note from Amanda, hoping I was okay, and with her cell to call her when I wanted that chat. I'm not used to random acts of kindness. Felt nice.

I'd just got the basket upstairs and into my room when my phone beeped with an incoming text. I hurried out to the living room, picked it up, and poked it.

Tasha: "Had idea. Wtng outside."

It would be so easy to say I wasn't here – but then she would ask where I was and pick me up from there. I was still pissed from yesterday. If she thought she could pull another stunt like that, I didn't want any of it.

The phone pinged again. "U cmng?"

I glared at the screen for a moment, then shook my head, grabbed my keys, and hurried out the door.

"Sorry about yesterday."

She was apologizing before I had my backside in the seat. I wanted to stay mad at her, but it's difficult to do that when someone 'fesses up. Especially when they sound like they mean it. I grunted and reached for the seatbelt.

"I was a bitch. You did great. Sharp, but not too much nasty.

Asked the right questions. And catching the trap on the door was a neat bonus. Could have hurt both of us. Nasty bloody thing. How did you spot it?"

"Something felt wrong. I didn't know what, but it made sense to me that if he was going to boobytrap anything it would be the door."

Tasha nodded. I left a pause to see if she wanted to raise anything else. She didn't, so I went on.

"Why were you in such on odd mood?" And that surprised me. I'd meant to say something far bitchier.

"Disappointment, mostly. I hoped chasing down that burned out butt of a human would give us something we could follow."

"Didn't it? We know there's a connection to Corvax, whatever that is."

"Or whoever."

"And we know this Jaswinder has something to do with it."

"That's Jessander, and you stay away from anything to do with her. Even I don't cross paths with Jessander unless I can't get out of it."

"Who is she?" I had a problem thinking of anybody who could intimidate Tasha.

"She's the mob. Vampire and wallows in it. Nobody is sure how old she is, but by the speed she can move, she has to be original old country, three or four hundred years."

"There's vampire organized crime in the Shadows?"

She looked at me like I was an idiot, and I felt my cheeks burn. "There's organized crime everywhere, and Jessander runs this city below and above."

"Here?"

She nodded, and the car went quiet while she let me digest

that. I was going to ask why we didn't just go to Jessander and ask who had asked her to kill me. Then I thought about it a bit longer and was glad I hadn't. Jessander sounded like a big wheel. To get anything out of her, we would need more leverage than whoever took the contract out on me, like more money. Even though I wasn't hurting for green these days, I couldn't hope to match that.

The car pulled over, and I looked out the windows. A suburban street, one step away from white picket fences. Two–car garages at the end of every drive, and children's toys scattered here and there. Middle Class Normal–ville.

"Where are we?"

"I had an idea. No more leads to follow at the moment, so I thought we could try to unblock some of your memories."

My heart rate doubled, and I felt a hand squeeze my throat. And I had no idea why. I wanted to get my memories back.

Didn't I?

"How are you going to do that?"

"No idea. Just playing things by ear."

My head was pounding in time with my heart, and the sparks at the edges of my vision were flashing in time. "Where are we?"

"I was thinking you might tell me."

My head twisted back and forth, my eyes scanning up and down the street. I had no memory of it, but Tasha seemed to think I should. What was it supposed to mean to me? I turned in my seat to glare at her. "You tell me where this is, or I swear I will get out of the car and get an Uber home."

"This was the street where you lived. Before the fire."

"And where is the house?"

She shook her head but met my angry eyes. "Doesn't

matter."

"Of course it matters."

"How? Even if you remembered, what's there now wouldn't be the same."

"After ten years why would *anything* be the same." I turned in my seat to face front, arms crossed over my chest. "I want to leave this place."

Tasha started the engine and slid the stick to drive, then pulled slowly away. I stared out the windshield, pretending not to look while my eyes skittered from side to side, desperately seeking for the slightest familiarity. I didn't relax until we had driven two blocks away, but two blocks after that, Tasha was slowing down and pulling over again. My heart rate shot up.

"Now what?"

"Next stop."

"How many of these do you have planned?"

She shrugged. I looked around, but there wasn't much to see.

"You have to walk," she said. "Two hundred yards. And you have to go alone. Is that OK?"

It was a dazzling day, without a cloud in the sky. I pulled the lever and cracked the door, but I didn't undo my seatbelt. What she was doing made a certain sense, but didn't apply to me. She couldn't feel the absence. She couldn't feel the wall, how tall it was, how cold it was. The wall someone stretched across my memories five years ago, hard as diamond and black as a politician's heart.

And if I said no, what then. Would that be it? Would she give up on her pet project? Leave me at the sidewalk and drive off into the sunset in search of something more interesting and more achievable? She was trying, at least. I undid the seatbelt, got out of the car, and started to walk.

I stood outside the high school and stared at it, willing something to look familiar, or for some ghost to speak to me from beyond the wall. Nothing. For all I felt, it could have been Sunnydale or Springfield. It was nothing more than a pile of bricks with a flagpole out front. I heard an engine idling toward me, and a faint squeak from a brake as it stopped. I turned around, opened the door, and got in.

"Take me home."

"Are you sure? I have a couple more ideas that might—"

"Just take me home." I spaced the words out but didn't raise my voice. My headache was so intense even my ears hurt. Everything looked too bright, and yet I felt I was standing on the side of a canyon, me on one side, the rest of the world on the other. "I appreciate the effort, but it's not helping."

We made no conversation as we drove back to my condo. I didn't even look at her, didn't even think about how she felt. That was unfair of me, but I could feel I was burning out. "I need some time," I said when we pulled up outside. "This is all getting too intense."

She said "OK", or something like it. I was already out of the car, so I didn't hear properly. I listened to the car drive off, not wanting her to see me turn and watch, then went inside.

The glass of wine I poured sat on the breakfast bar, ignored, as I perched on a stool and looked out the window at the little garden. It was starting to look untidy, and I wondered if it was my responsibility to maintain it. Probably. Life seemed to work like that. And I didn't know the first thing about it, so there was every chance I'd kill all the plants by trying to care for them.

This was not going the way I expected it to. This was the

dream. I was a property owner with paying tenants. I didn't need to work. I could do what I liked. Hell, I could rent out this apartment, too, and go live the high life in the Caribbean.

Would that stop people trying to kill me?

If it was so easy a fix, why did the idea hold no appeal for me? My mind went back to Dale's squalid apartment, to how empowered I had felt asking him the questions. Did I enjoy it so much because I was that cruel?

Or did I enjoy it because for the first time since Tamsin walked into the coffee shop, I felt in control? Was that why the Caribbean solution, or something like it, didn't sparkle? Because I would still have no real control? Because it wouldn't resolve the issue?

Or because I would spend the rest of my life with half an eye over my shoulder and my doors locked at night?

Could I live like that?

I stopped ignoring the wine.

The Memory Man

I rigged an ear bud from the phone to fit inside my helmet. That way, I could hear spoken directions from the app. I had tried rigging some kind of clamp to hold the phone on the handlebars, but it never felt safe enough. Besides, trying to perfect the clamp was a perfect stalling tactic.

A lot of the route looked familiar, but I would have got lost at least once if I'd tried to do it from memory. I found my way to the alley and rode carefully along it, bracing myself for the sudden drop of the ramp. And when it didn't come, it felt like I had floated upwards. Unexpected and odd.

Obviously, I'd done something wrong. As soon as I thought about it, I realized there must be some kind of trigger, and that I hadn't been paying attention to whatever Tasha had done. I could hardly phone her and ask. I knew damned well that she would frown on what I planned to do and would come screaming down to the Shadows to stop me. And I couldn't allow that.

But this was something I hadn't thought through. The ramp couldn't appear for everybody going along the alley. That much was obvious, now that I thought about it. But what opened it? A spell, or a talisman? If it were either of those

I was screwed, and I'd have to abandon my plan until I could figure out a way to get in on my own. But maybe I was over thinking. Maybe it was a lot simpler.

Circling back around the block I came into the alley again, but this time I thought of the ramp, and of the Shadows, and the market and how much I wanted to be there. I was wishing so hard I almost screwed my eyes up– which would not have been a great idea riding a bike. It felt stupid, like some kid blowing out birthday candles or sitting on Santa's knee.

And then the world dropped out from under me. I squealed like a teen and the bike swayed back and forth until I un-clenched and let it settle itself.

I always ride with the light on – anything to help idiots in cars see me at junctions – but the sudden dark still surprised me, and it took a few seconds for my eyes to adjust. When I could make things out a little more, the relief gave me a huge buzz. This was the same tunnel. I had found my way into the Shadows.

Finding my way in was one thing. Finding my way around was another. I remembered the address of Justin Sands, but figuring out how to get there was more of a challenge – especially when I found the Market was a pedestrian zone. At least I wasn't walking. I think I went around the outside of the Market twice, but I found the right block after twenty minutes or so. I ran the bike up onto the sidewalk and chained it to a railing before I started looking for the Sandman.

The houses were much nicer here than where we found Dale. Here, it was all brass plates and entry intercoms, and it looked like old town lawyers or doctors. Jimmy hadn't given me a building number, so I walked along the block checking entry phones and plaques. 'The Sands Institute', handwritten on a label on a battered entry phone, looked close enough.

I didn't have an appointment and didn't want to make one. I wanted to see him right now, and there was every chance they wouldn't even let me into the building. Didn't mean nobody else would. I'd seen a trick girl scouts use selling cookies. I ran my finger down the buttons, pressing them all and hoping somebody was expecting a visitor or was just too lazy to waste time on a conversation. Voices babbled through the tinny speaker, and I heard the satisfying clunk of the door opening.

The entry phone label said the 'Institute' was on the second floor so I slogged up the stairs, not creeping, but keeping my eyes busy and my wits about me. I saw nothing about the place to make me cautious, but cautious I was. I put it down to Tasha, for good or ill.

Short corridors led back into the building from the landing. The Institute was on the left, toward the back of the building. A light shone through the stained-glass fanlight over the door. I reached for the handle, twisted and pushed. The door swung inwards, smooth and quiet, and I stepped into a waiting room.

It was swanky, with leather button chairs to wait in, bottled water on the table, and a polished wooden desk where the receptionist sat. Except nobody was there: neither clients nor staff. The desk held a computer, and a phone with lots of buttons, but nothing else. When I walked around to the other side, the screen was off. Seemed the Institute was closed for the day. But my brain did wander off for a moment wondering who provided a phone service down in the Shadows.

I came back to the moment when I heard somebody moving around deeper in the office. If it was who I hoped it was, we were going to have a conversation.

I had two options, surprise or good manners. Surprise might

give me the upper hand if Sands tried to make an unexpected exit, but good manners might earn me brownie points and a little cooperation.

"Hello?" I got no answer, so I tried a little louder. "Hello? Anybody here?"

A door opened on the far side of the room, and I saw an office, or a consulting room, behind the mid–sized figure in the doorway.

"Did you have an appointment?"

"No, I–"

"We're closed. No walk-ins, no consultations without an appointment."

He stepped into the waiting room and closed the door behind him. He was exactly what I expected: male, not old, slight, no dress sense, half–moon glasses perched on his nose and advanced pattern baldness.

"I'm afraid I must ask you to leave." He spread his arms wide as if he intended to shepherd me from the room. I stood my ground and played what I hoped was my trump card.

"Grant Peterson said I should come see you."

He stopped, frozen, but his expression showed nothing. His arms fell to his sides, then he took off his glasses and polished them on a handkerchief from a trouser pocket.

"Did he? And why might that be?"

"I have a problem with my memories. He said you were the best in the field."

"That I very much doubt," Sands replied, with hints of bitterness and anger in his tone.

"Well, he did say you were the person I should see."

Sands sighed, put the glasses back on, and peered at me over the tops of the lenses. "And you are?"

"My name is Jane Doe."

As soon as I spoke, I wished I'd lied. I couldn't be sure, but I was sure I saw a flicker of recognition. But Sands went on as though my name meant nothing. "And what is the problem?"

I thought about the long story but settled for "I can't remember anything before about five years ago."

"Yet you remember your education, to speak, to walk?"

"Obviously."

"So what exactly are you unable to recall?"

"My past?" I shrugged. "My life before."

"Before what? Was there an injury, or some trauma?"

"The doctors said there wasn't."

He hummed and polished his glasses again. "Let me check my diary for this evening. I may be able to fit in a preliminary consultation, or I can make you an appointment for next week."

"Today would be good."

"I'm sure it would. Take a seat. I'll be back in a moment."

He disappeared back into the office and I took a seat on one of the button-back chairs. For all its fancy leather, the seat was hard and uncomfortable. At least it didn't squeak or fart when I moved.

Then the air crashed in on me like a thunderstorm just appeared over my head. My eardrums felt like they met in the middle, and my skin tingled all over. I heard, or felt, a thud behind me, not loud but uncomfortably intense. I leaped to my feet and turned around.

It wasn't human. There were horns. And fangs. Not terribly large, but terribly different. Its skin was dark green, thick and cracked all over like dried mud. But it wore black jeans and a leather waistcoat.

Its hands made a shape over its belly, like it was holding a ball, and my skin prickled again, but it flicked his hands, complete with talons instead of nails, open as if it was brushing something away.

"You're not worth gathering the energy," it growled and stepped toward me.

I had already looked around the room. I had nowhere to hide. Everything had a back or an edge to a wall, giving me no chance to play keep–away around a table. It was going to kill me.

It was closer to the exit than me, and it was forcing me farther away from the only way out. I had nowhere to stand my ground – hell, I had no ground to stand on; no weapon, no skill, and no bloody chance. It was backing me into a corner and I had no ideas.

I tried to dodge past it, ducking down and left. Almost made it, too, except it hit my shoulder hard enough to make me stagger sideways and spin around to slam backwards against another wall. I slid to the floor, wind knocked out of me. Before I could draw another breath, it was in front of me, hauling me up the wall by my neck. I deployed the girl's best friend – and it laughed.

"Only works if they're on the outside, chica."

While it was still chuckling, I raised my hands and clapped them over its ears. That got its attention, and it dropped me. I scuttled away like a cockroach, making for the way out, but a ball of fire as big as a tennis ball shattered against the wall in front of me, sending off sparks and a stench of sulfur. When I dodged the other way, a second fireball sizzled past me so close I could feel the heat.

It had me backed up against a wall again, and it was standing on the other side of the room, tossing another fireball back and forth between its hands, making fake throws and trying to make me commit to dodging one way or the other. While it played with me, I rolled off my ass into a crouch. It threw, and I moved without thinking, taking a single step to the left and letting the ball fizzle against the wall.

Then my left hand crabbed like I'd just let go of a bowling ball, though I've no idea why. Fire and fury lit up my mind. Who the hell did this guy think he was? My hand felt like it was on fire – and then it was. Not just the hand, but an inch-wide beam of heat and flame that shot from a point between my fingers, stabbing the demon in the center of his chest.

He screamed, but his hands were still moving, trying to make another of his own fireballs. I tilted my hand, just a little, and the beam of fire moved up to his head. The scream stopped as the fire ate away his face away, then his skull. I clenched my hand, and the fire stopped.

I rose to my feet, looking first at the carnage then at my hand There wasn't a mark on it. The stench from the smoldering flesh of the demon made me throw up. As if there weren't enough disgusting smells or sights in the room already.

Once my gut was empty, I forced myself to go look at this creep. I found a pouch tied to its belt that felt like it held coins, and tucked in a pocket sewn in the lining of his waistcoat I found a pocketknife. It had a bone handle, and a scalpel sharp blade. Mine. I took it, and the pouch.

You can frown if you want. I had nothing down here, and they were spoils of combat. It certainly wouldn't need them anymore. I stood up, wiped my hands on a curtain, and went to the door I had seen Sands duck through before this all started. My first urge was to kick the door in, but it's not something I've had much practice at. Bouncing off the door with a broken ankle exceeded my quota of looking stupid for the day. So I knocked, with my fist, like a demon would.

A lock *snicked* open and I heard a bolt being pulled back, so right call on the kicking thing. The door opened a crack, and I barged against it. I don't weigh that much, but I caught him off guard and he stumbled backward into the room. By the time I had the door open, he was sitting on his backside like a toddler learning to walk. He looked up at me and his face went white.

"But..."

"Sorry, didn't fancy dying today."

"I had no choice. He would have known."

I took the knife out of my back pocket and unfolded it. He was a little man, but I didn't have the strength to just haul him to his feet. I held the knife in my left hand while I held out my right to help him up. That surprised him too.

"So how does this work?" I asked. "Do you need both hands on my head?"

"You still want me to treat you?" His eyebrows rose.

"You want me dead?"

"Not personally, but—"

"Do you get paid if I die?"

"No."

"So you did your bit; you snitched on me." I glared at him. "Now you can do a favor for me and nobody needs to know. Anybody asks, I killed the thing outside and ran away. Look, Peterson said to come and see you. I don't think he was setting me up." I stopped and thought about that for a moment, but then blinked the idea away. Too much to consider right now. "So, do you need both your hands to do this?"

"No, but—"

"But what?" He was annoying me now.

"I don't think I can help."

"Eh? You haven't even looked."

"The person who did this to you may be too powerful for me to undo his work."

"You *know* who did this to me?"

"No, but there's a rumor." He looked away. Liar.

Damn. For a moment I thought I had gotten lucky. He had an idea who had done this to me, but I wouldn't get it out of him. Whoever it was, he was scared of them. I best make sure he was scared of me too. He was still my best hope, and I needed him to step up. But which was the best option: bully or cajole?

"You won't know until you get in there and look. Imagine, you could be the one to poke a hole in that all powerful reputation."

"And you would still trust me to do this?"

I tried for a nasty grin. I think it worked. He flinched. "Trust won't come into it. Shall we?"

I sat in what looked a dentist's chair, and he sat behind me.

"Give me whichever hand you don't need," I said.

"But I need them to–"

"Already asked that, and you said you didn't. Give me an arm. I already set fire to a demon today, and I don't want to get cranky again."

An arm appeared. I took a firm grip on it just above the wrist and pulled it down over my chest. I jabbed the blade of my knife into the dent where the artery goes; not hard enough to cut anything, but hard enough so it would slice deeply if he pulled the arm away. And I put the knife longways, not across the wrist, to make the point it would probably kill him.

"So it works like this," I explained. "I feel anything I don't like, I cut and you die."

"But any involuntary movement–"

"Then make sure you don't tickle me. Get on with it."

It took about five minutes. It was like bugs crawling around inside my mind, but none of them tried to bite or sting.

"I'm finished," he murmured. I think he was trying not to startle me.

My hands were at my side, both of his were on my head, and my knife, still open, rested on my belly. I looked at the clock on the wall and almost an hour had passed. So much for my attempt at being threatening. I poked at my memory. I thought about the idea of 'mom'. Surely that would have brought up a memory?

"There's still nothing there."

"And there won't be," he said. "I'm sorry. I really am. The block is both general and oddly specific, but it is more solid than anything I have seen, and it seems to have bedded in deeper since it was established. Most unusual."

"Would Witchbane have anything to do with that?" I felt sick.

His eyes widened. "In very high doses, I suppose it could. I have managed to thin the block in some areas, particularly around semantic, factual information. Elements of it may return to you in time. Your episodic memory — the memory of your life, if you will — remains unavailable."

I sat up and got a minor head rush.

"What do I owe you?"

He let out a dry chuckle. "You let me live. Most would have killed me for what I did." He looked panicky. "You're *not* going to kill me, are you?"

I shook my head. "Too much effort."

I hopped down from the chair and walked out though the surgery without looking back at him, or the ruin of the demon that had tried to kill me. I did stop for a moment, at the top of the stairs; just long enough to fold the knife and slip it down the inside my right boot. It was a little uncomfortable, but I only had to walk as far as the scooter.

Except it wasn't there.

Stolen Wheels

Bastards. They left the chain still looped through the railing but somehow, someone had stolen my wheels. How was I going to get home now?

I mostly remembered the route Tasha took when we left, but I wasn't keen on walking that far. Besides, we had driven through some places I wasn't comfortable passing through on foot.

At least I still had my cell. I got as far as opening it and calling up the speed dial list before I realized I couldn't call her. Tasha would come and get me – I hoped – but the ensuing *What did you think you were doing* or worse, the chilled silence, wasn't something I wanted to go through.

It was only after churning through that chain of logic that I remembered where I was. Couldn't call anywhere without a signal and in the Shadows there would be no... except there were three bars and the name of a carrier I didn't recognize. When was I going to learn to stop making assumptions? I shook my head and started to work out alternatives.

My best option was Jimmy. He wasn't that far away, no more than a couple of blocks, and he would know what I could do. I unlocked the chain from the railing, looped it around my neck, and set off. Yes, I know it was heavy, and it made me look cheap, but decent bike locks are expensive.

The lights of a major road glowed from my left, so I turned that way. Didn't matter which one it was. I could follow it back to the Market, and it was all good from there.

But I'd gone no more than a dozen steps before I realized my feet weren't the only ones on the sidewalk. I could hear another pair behind me. It wasn't an echo; the steps didn't match mine. They were farther apart. And heavier. A flashback to the demon mage made my heart pound, and I spun around to face my stalker.

But I saw nobody, or nothing, there. The street was empty, though there were a thousand deep shadows where anything could have hidden. I started walking again, hurrying a little while I tried not to look like a victim – and knowing I wasn't doing a good job.

The footsteps followed me as soon as I moved, getting closer with each step. Then I heard more on the other sidewalk. I twisted my head around but saw nothing there either. My heart hammered faster, the thumping in my ears making it difficult to hear the footsteps.

As I stepped out to cross an intersection, something shrieked like an eagle and dove toward me from the corner of my sight. Flinching, I ran, but didn't realize I was running away from the market until I had covered a hundred feet. The footsteps were running behind me now, again on both sides of the street.

Another crossroads came up. If I could turn left, it would take me back toward the main road, and maybe even help. But something like a bat flapped in in my face as I tried to turn. Though I waved my arms over my head and in front of me, they didn't do any good. Something brushed against them, but not very hard. As soon as I squirmed past one, another flapped around my head, and then another on the other side.

Though I had enough light to see the buildings on either side of the road, I couldn't see whatever was attacking me. I found a direction where nothing was flapping in my face and ran that way.

They herded me. I realized what they were doing after another attack at an intersection, but I couldn't do a thing about it. They were disorienting me as well as turning me, and nothing was more important than getting away from them. I had no idea where I was, and less where I was going. Except it seemed the lights were farther apart and not so bright.

The knife in my boot moved and slowed me down as it tried to grind a hole in my ankle. I finally turned into a blind alley and ran to the end because I had nowhere else to run. Only when the wall stared me in the face did I turn and confront whoever had been pushing me around. I didn't know what to expect. Vampire to drain my blood or my mind, or demons to eat me.

What I saw was three empty cloaks with ragged flapping arms. Gliding soundless and faceless through the air, they got closer and closer until their rags wound around me and covered my face. A foul-tasting strip over my mouth stopped my screams, and another covered my nose to force its foul stench into my lungs as it stole my breath. My legs were wrapped, my arms were pinned to my sides, and my chest was crushed. My struggles grew weaker as I fought to breathe, until it was all I could do to force air in or out past the sickening grip. Weeping for the life I never got to live, I died.

Escape?

The afterlife was, it seemed, a chilly gray room with no bed and a door with no handle. The bulb in the bulkhead light over the door barely shone to the back of the room. This suggested the peephole was a bit of a waste of time.

Whatever the horrible flappy things had on their fronds must have knocked me out. Or maybe they did suffocate me until I passed out and they drugged me after. Nasty experience. Either way, I'd no memories between them wrapping me up and waking here.

To add to my discomfort and misery, someone had tied me up. Not like they do in the movies, with some cheesy thick hemp made for holding fishing trawlers to docks. The worst that can happen with that is you scrape your fingers on the fibers as you pull your hands free.

Whoever did this knew better. They used a thin rope, like parachute cord, less than a quarter–inch wide and flexible. Wriggling my hands out of these wasn't an option. I wriggled anyway, more in hope than expectation, and rubbed my boots together.

The knife scraped against my ankle, and I grinned. I'm not

sure why. It's not like I thought I could MacGyver my way out now that I had a blade, but I still grinned. Besides, ropes over boots never seems to work – again, in the movie–verse.

Getting my hands from back to front over my boots wouldn't work, partly because of the way they tied my wrists, but mainly because of the bootheels. I started dragging my heels along the floor, wincing at the damage it was doing to the leather. They weren't designer, but they were all I had, and I liked them.

I've no idea how long it took – it certainly felt like forever – but eventually one heel came free. That was all I needed. Boots off, hands to the front, shake out the blade, cut hands and feet free, boots back on. Easy.

I patted myself down and got another surprise. I still had everything I had been carrying when I had been attacked, even the coins I'd taken as spoil from the demon. Whatever this was, it wasn't a simple mugging, and whoever had snatched me were scared enough of their boss not to rob me.

But now what? Unless the door was conveniently unlocked, because they tied me up and left me unconscious, I was still going nowhere. I checked, it was locked and there was no way I could get the knife into the lock to miraculously pick it. Wouldn't have known how, anyway.

To make things worse, the door opened inwards, so I couldn't try to break it down. Breaking doors down was very much getting to the top of my must try list, though. I looked around the room. Apart from an 8-inch floor vent, there was nothing but plastered wall.

Something was clicking, metal on metal. As I was thinking, I was rapping the blade of the knife on the thumb ring. The gem had changed color again. I didn't think it was the dim light, but the color was different, more orange than the yellow–white it had been before. Like the color of the coil on an electric fire, heated just enough not to melt.

Was that where the power had come from to fry the demon? Had I somehow taken the fire that had tried to torch my home and squeezed it into the ring. I'd given it no thought at the time, but all that heat had to go somewhere. Spectacularly clever if it was true, but I had no idea how I had used it, and without frying myself. I couldn't see a way it could help me now, either, unless I wanted to blast a hole in the door, or maybe set fire to the place. Neither was inconspicuous and, unless I wanted to save myself from another fire, one was pretty stupid.

But then my eyes switched from the ring to the blade. The metal had shone prettily in Sands' office, but not like steel. I tapped it against my teeth. It didn't sound like steel. And then I'm thinking *Idiot. How the hell do I know what steel sounds like tapped against my teeth?* I should stab myself in the hand to see if it cuts like steel, I'd learn as much.

But what if the blade was something magical, like silver? And what if I could channel the fire that fried the Demon through the blade?

My head was thumping, and that nasty, stabbing pain deep inside was back again, poking at me with every beat of my heart. Who was I kidding? I should just sit down with my back to the wall and wait for whoever was coming for me. This was too much.

I even got as far as starting to close the blade of my knife. If the damned thing hadn't stabbed me in the hand, I might have. Because I wouldn't have felt that brief spike of anger, and I might not have seen the glow around the ring. It wasn't much, and it faded as fast as my anger turned to curiosity, but it had definitely been there.

Could it be that simple?

I put the open knife between the door and the frame, resting it on the bar of the lock, then I put the ring against the top of the blade. But when I set to getting angry, it proved to be a lot harder than I expected. How angry was I supposed to get? Fear of my life angry? That was what burned a demon's face off, and I didn't think I needed that much. Did I only need to be mildly annoyed about something?

I ran back through my memories, what little I had, looking for things to get angry about and discovered a weird thing. When you looked back on something, you don't feel the anger. You feel pain, betrayal, hurt. You even feel stupid for letting it get to you at the time. But it's difficult to feel angry.

I banged my head against the wall next to the door. Of all the times not to be able to get pissed off, this would be the worst. Stupid woman, with my stupid ideas and my half-witted conceit that I could do this sort of shit on my own, when I was no better at it than a...

I smelled metal. Hot metal. The blade was melting through the lock like it was ice cream. But as I watched, the metal cooled and, to make it worse, my knife stuck fast. I dug through my memory again and hit pay dirt.

That fat slob of a cop who tried to take me for burning my own house. The same cockroach who snapped handcuffs around my burned hand, who pulled his damned gun on me...

My knife came free. For a moment I thought it had just pulled loose from the half-melted lock, but then I saw it had cut through. All the way through. I put the back of the blade to my hand, intending to close it, then snatched my hand away. It would be hot enough to burn. Except it wasn't. It was cold, colder than the room. As I closed the blade into the handle, I caught sight of the ring. The gem had changed color again and was now surly red. Just about enough left to light a cigarette or set fire to a piece of paper. It had done an outstanding job, but I really didn't want to set fire to my house again to recharge it. I guessed I was on my own now. Terrifying thought.

I listened at the door before I opened it. Not sure what good it did. I had no idea how thick the door was, or what it was made of. I couldn't hear anything, so I eased the door open and found a corridor about fifty feet long, with a row of other doors just like mine on either side. Both ends of the corridor were open, so I used the maze rule and followed the left wall, turning left again at the end.

Dim fixtures bolted to the wall, too far apart for any real use, provided enough light to save me running my hand along the wall as I walked. Big strip lights ran the length of the ceiling, so I figured the wall lights must be for emergencies, or security. Either way, they were better for skulking. I think I might have stayed in my room if everything had been lit up like a shopping mall. I took two more lefts and realized I was going round in a block. So that rule let me down too. I dropped the idea and walked in a straight line.

Seemed I was in a basement. I could see no windows, and the corridor had that dead sound you only got underground. Creeped me out and left me feeling I was the only person down here. No signs or markings indicated what might be behind any of the doors, which was another real help. But after ten minutes of aimless wandering, I found a door with a window in it, and a flight of narrow stairs beyond.

As soon as I pushed the door open, I heard noise. Not close, but a background rumble of life. Oddly, it made me feel a little better. The silence had been getting to me, making me feel like they'd locked me in an empty building and forgotten to collect me. Or abandoned me. On the flip side, now I had people to hide from. Why couldn't life be simple? A nice, straightforward escape through clearly signposted and fragrance–free sewers, maybe.

I eased the door shut behind me. The stairs ended at my level, and I snuck into the middle to look up. I could see at least four floors above me, perhaps five. Shapes and shadows moved around two levels up. I ducked out of sight and tried to bully my brain into coming up with something helpful.

One option was lurking around on this level some more, maybe open some doors. But someone would notice I was missing eventually, assuming they didn't intend to starve me to death. I might find a convenient tunnel that let out to a long ladder and a handy sewer cover. Or I might get caught with all this bumbling around.

The more I thought about it, wandering back and forth looking for something clever would almost certainly get me caught. But there might be a loading bay on the level above. They tended to be lower than the main floor, didn't they?

Or could I walk right out the front door? I saw or heard somebody say the best way to steal something was to walk out holding it like you already owned it. Maybe the way out of here was to behave like I was one of them. I had dressed for the part, wearing much the same outfit as Tasha had bullied me into before we last came to the Shadows. Maybe mix up the two?

I put on a grumpy face, with a touch of sneer, kept my hands sightly cupped, as if I was half–prepared to throw fireballs out of them, and stomped up the stairs. The first landing looked too quiet, so I stomped some more and turned out of the stairwell two levels up.

Result. A hundred feet ahead of me were double doors leading onto the street. I firmed up my grumpy face and stomped toward the door. They had sent me on a petty little errand, and I wasn't pleased about it.

I got a curious look or two, but nobody interfered. Right up to the damned door. Stood on either side were a couple of guys, or whatever, wearing some kind of uniform, and looking inwards. The one on my right stepped in front of me, hand up.

"Where do you think you're going?"

"Errand."

"Staff entrance is at the side. You new?"

I snorted. "Hardly. I know that. But it takes an extra ten minutes to get out front that way, and Jessander wants spice for her blood, so I get to run out to the market to fetch it."

I'd messed up. When I spoke the name 'Jessander', both pairs of eyes went wide like I'd dropped a C−bomb in a playgroup. I raised my hands in apology.

"Sorry. I'm just mad being used to run errands. Now can I please get past so I can fetch the Mistress her spices?"

But the cover−up was too late. Both of them were looking past me now, and I could feel a subtle vibration through my boots, like trees walking up behind me. I was just wondering if I could dodge past both the door guards and get out to the street when a hand closed on my collar and lifted me off my feet.

Intermediary

My shirt bunched up under my arms and dug into my armpits so bad I couldn't raise or turn my head to see what was carrying me. I might have been able to get away if I'd put my arms up, but the next time they caught me they might not be so gentle. Besides, the walking mountain was taking me somewhere other than where I had escaped from, which could be good or bad. I tried to think optimistic thoughts.

We waited outside a double door while something that looked too much like a footman opened the door and slipped inside. A moment later he returned, opened the door wide, and gestured for whatever was carrying me to go inside.

I wasn't sure if it was a drawing room or an office. The decor was aristocratic, with white and gold and glass everywhere. Expensive display cabinets displayed expensive things, like clocks, vases, and something that looked a lot like a Faberge egg. At the far end, a woman sat at a desk. I couldn't see her legs, but up top she was wearing a classy power suit in a red few women could get away with. I couldn't even make a guess at her age; she could have been anything from mid–thirties to mid–fifties. She had long auburn hair with a gentle wave, and she was beautiful.

Until we got closer and I saw her eyes. They were pale blue and ice cold. Cruelest, most ruthless eyes I had ever seen.

"Put her down, then you may leave. Tell the provisioner I granted you an extra bag of blood tonight."

The thing that had grabbed me dropped me, rather than let me down, then it turned and walked away. I looked over my shoulder and frowned. I had expected some mountainous demon, but he was a man. Tall, slim, but unremarkable.

"Please, take a seat."

"Was that for my benefit?"

"Excuse me?"

"The bag of blood thing?"

That got me a thin smile that didn't leave her lips. "No. He is young, and barely able to think. The benefit was entirely his."

"And you are Jessander? Is that the correct form of address?"

"I would expect a 'miss' or a 'mistress' from my staff, or one trying to ingratiate themselves with me. As you are neither, Jessander will suffice."

"So why am I not dead?" I decided to get straight to the point.

"I have no current interest in your death. Current."

I felt like a hick from the middle of nowhere. All right, *more* like a hick from the middle of nowhere She had a faint accent, and I think it was Italian, but she spoke like a princess deigning to converse with a muck–shoveler. I pushed the concept away. She had the power right now, but she wasn't necessarily better than me.

"Then why was I snatched? Why did you send someone to

burn down my house?"

Again, the thin smile. "I brokered the contract with the arsonist, but I had no interest in whether it succeeded or failed, except insomuch as it affects my reputation for finding the right person for each job when asked. I must confess I was most disappointed in Icarus. He is usually so efficient."

"And the demon warlock? You sent him too?"

She raised one perfectly defined eyebrow. "So that was the disturbance. And you survived?"

I avoided the 'obviously'.

"No, Miss Doe. Someone alerted me to the disturbance, someone else recognized your–" she puckered her mouth like she just sucked a lime. "–vehicle, and I became curious about you. I decided it was time we talked."

"Why?" That surprised me. "I'm nothing."

"Whatever you are is enough to make a powerful man want to kill you. And then you become involved with the most renowned neuro–thaumaturgist in western civilization."

"Good job I decided not to kill him then."

"If it was he who summoned the demon warlock, you were generous." She reached forward across her desk and took a thin black cigar from a fancy dispenser. She poked it into the end of a six-inch-long holder before lighting it with a something in a lump of jade big enough to be a murder weapon in a board game. Then she settled back in her chair and looked at me through lidded eyes.

"So why do all these people want you dead, Miss Doe?"

"I wish I knew."

Anger flickered across her face and she looked ready to snap at me, so I raised a hand and gave her some more.

"I know some creep stole my memories, stole my family,

and stole my life. I also know he dumped me in Hicksville, in the state of Nowhere, and tricked me into taking Witchbane for the last five years."

She said nothing, but her eyes widened for a moment. I filed it under 'useful information' and carried on.

"What I don't know is why he didn't kill me five years ago, nor why he is trying now. And I would very much like to know who he is so I can ask him."

I kept my eyes locked on hers. I wanted her to know I realized she knew who he was, and I wanted her to understand that he had not, on the face of it, been open and honest with her. As I had.

She held my eyes long enough to inhale a lungful of cancer and dragon it out through her nose, then she looked over my head in a classic thousand-yard gaze. I guess she expected me to be a polite little girl and stay quiet while mama thought, but that didn't seem to be working for me much these days.

I said: "And the big question now is, what's on your mind."

That got me another sharp look. "You are very direct, human. It's quite charming, in a puppy-like way."

If she was trying to needle me, she was succeeding, but I tried to keep an interested face while she talked down to me.

"One option would be that I turn you over to the one seeking you. He would then be indebted to me, but somehow I doubt he would honor the debt should I call it in."

Another useful snippet. Even the other bad guys don't trust the nasty trying to kill me.

"But I am not beholden to him. Any contracted dealings I have with him I have fulfilled. He has no standing arrangement regarding you." She drew on her cigar and tapped the ash into a jade bowl. "You are interesting. You are a loose cannon. I have heard rumors about you, already, which is why I had you detained. I wanted to see the lengths to which you would go to regain your freedom. Now I see how resourceful you are. You either have substantial power and are wise enough not to squander it or advertise it, or you are running on pure nerve. In either case, you have the potential to cause much disruption. Disruption brings chaos, and chaos has always been good to me."

I could feel she wanted me to ask something, to beg her, so I kept the interested look on my face and my mouth shut.

"So I think our ways shall part. On one condition."

"Which is?" Well, I couldn't let that one past, could I?

"That you owe me a favor. I could have you killed, or kill you myself. I'm sure the experience would be intoxicating, if fleeting. You cannot pay me more than I could demand for handing you over to he who wants you dead, but the future is far from certain. I do not need his money, but a boon from you, even a small one, may be worth far more."

"I won't kill for you."

She held up a hand. "So hasty, so quick to judge. You don't know who I might ask you to kill. He or she may be worth killing. But I'm feeling generous today. You may turn down up to three requests, but you must fulfil the third, if you reject the first two."

I was being bought, and it was my own stupid fault. Now I was playing poker with the devil, and she had all the cards. And she knew it. Agreeing would buy me time, get me out of the current fix, but I could be signing my own death warrant for a month or a year from now. But it was this or get handed over to the monster who had already tried to kill me twice.

"Agreed."

Jessander dropped the remains of her cigar into the jade bowl and placed a crystal lid over it before ringing a silver bell.

"Excellent. Your transport is waiting for you at the rear gates, and someone will direct you to the nearest exit. Considering this is your first visit to The Shadows, you have done well. You survived."

She stood up, flickered, and was standing next to me, her hand around my throat. Her face had changed to a thing of horror, and her canines were now sharp, curved fangs.

"But next time, be better prepared. This is *our* world, day dweller, not yours. Our arrangement grants you no special protection should you venture here again."

Different Track

Tasha texted me late in the afternoon. I hadn't spoken to her after I got back from the Shadows, and I had already decided I could never tell her about it. The trip had been a shambles from one end to the other. Apart from the magic, maybe, though I had little idea how I did it and less how to control it. And I didn't even want to think about her reaction to the news that I owed Jessander a favor. Even if she didn't scold me, I would die of embarrassment.

The text didn't say much, just that she wanted to pick me up at six. It hadn't been a good morning. The headaches were worse than ever, though I didn't get so much of the flashing. Meeting with Tasha made for something to look forward to, a distraction. Besides, I was almost out of Advil.

When I got in the car, I wondered how she would be. I had stormed away without a word the last time we had been together. Sometimes apologizing made things worse. I settled for pretending it didn't happen unless she brought it up.

"How have you been today?"

"Headaches and boredom, mostly."

"You need a job."

I snorted. "Right. With somebody trying to kill me and you

dragging me all over the city at any hour, that's going to work."

That got me a wry grin. "Point."

"What I need is more Advil. Is there a drug store on the way?"

Tasha gave me a sideways look. "Your head is bothering you that much? Have you seen anybody?"

"Haven't had time."

"Would you like me to help?"

Wow. Awkward. How did I answer that? If I said no without a good reason, I would hurt her. On the other hand, even though it was Tasha offering, the idea of her feeding on me was uncomfortable, and made me think of Icarus – or Dale – the pledge. I didn't know if this was the same thing, and I couldn't imagine Tasha doing anything to hurt me, but I didn't want to end up like him.

"I can't keep using you like that, Tasha. It's just a headache."

"It's no trouble, but get it looked at. Soon."

I nodded, though I wasn't sure if she noticed. "So where are we going? You taking me to the movies?"

"I mentioned a client I was working for?"

"Didn't tell me much about him, though."

"Client confidentiality. But we're going to see him."

"Oh. Why?"

"He says he has some more information for me, and I need to update him on a few things."

"And I'm along for the ride because...?"

"Let's wait until we get there. He can go over the story again. I like clients to do that. It can help them remember stuff they didn't mention before."

We were only in the car for thirty minutes before we pulled up outside an apartment block. The area had that up–and–coming young professional feel, with tables outside bistros and wine bars along the street. Aspirational.

Except someone had busted open the security gate.

Tasha raised a hand for me to stop, then took out a gun I didn't know she carried. I assumed that last time she was here the gate had been just fine.

She held the gun behind her back, and we edged through. The place had a Mediterranean feel, with terraces and steps and doors on various levels, and plants and ferns scattered about. Attractive, but it made for hiding places everywhere. Tasha walked more or less normally, though I could see her head moving constantly as she scanned the different levels. Figuring four eyes were better than two, I concentrated on the shadows, and places behind plants where someone could lurk. I kept a lookout behind us as well.

Then we were outside an open apartment door, and the gun wasn't behind her anymore; it was in front of her, raised and ready, index finger resting along the top of the trigger guard.

"Wait here. If anybody but me comes out, do *not* try to stop them. Let them go."

I waited.

As long as I could.

I hadn't heard anything, so either a silent assassin had executed Tasha, or she'd found no threat. I peered in through the door. Open stairs ran up one wall, but this level was a single open space, with a breakfast bar separating off the kitchen from the rest of the room. Generic layout, but nice. Lots of bare wall with thick, swirled plaster. No blood sprayed around the walls, no signs of turmoil or struggle.

Apart from the guy sprawled out on the floor with his head looking way too far over his shoulder.

Tasha saw me and waved for me to come in. "Sorry, should have called you sooner." She jerked her head toward the body. "You okay with this?"

"More than he is," I replied. "Was he who you were coming to see?"

She nodded. "Kyle. He was my client." She handed me a pair of latex gloves and I put them on.

"So why are we here? Why don't we just call the cops and get out?"

"Kyle said he had some information for me. I want to see if I can find it before the boys in blue hide it away in an evidence locker."

"Again, why? He's dead. Why would you keep investigating?"

"I don't like it when people kill my clients. I'd at least like to know the reason. Besides, case isn't closed. I have a strong hunch there's a connection between his story and yours."

"Huh?"

She stopped looking around the living room and perched on the back of the couch. "Thirteen−year−old, A−minus student drops to a C in a semester. Truancy goes up, then the school gets a notice to say she is accepted into a gifted student program and she'll no longer be attending. When the school try to find out more, they get vague nothings from the parents and a letter warning them off interfering in a government program. Except one teacher, that would be Kyle here, who also runs a couple of extra−curricular clubs, knows the girl is mad about chess. Okay, not the most glamorous sport, but this girl takes it really seriously. So much so, she was in line to represent the state in the national playoffs. And she just drops it. No note, no message. And nobody will listen to him. Sound familiar?"

I shrugged. It did, and I felt uncomfortable.

"And if I add that the house fire where we met was this girl's family home?"

That stopped me cold. On the outside, at least. Inside, my brain was screaming so many things at me at once that I couldn't think for all the thoughts. I took a 10-breath and tried to steady myself. Tasha was looking at me, questions in her eyes, and perhaps the hint of a challenge, or a dare.

This was the girl Tamsin had sensed. The other victim, being pulled out of her life and manipulated to do who whatever it was I had failed to. I held my breath as guilt washed over me, then I pushed it aside – as best I could.

"And what was this chess nerd's involvement?" I jerked my chin toward the body.

"He didn't believe the stories. He wanted me to find where she had been taken and why. Guess he wanted to see her and get the word from her own lips. He got even more serious after the fire. The police report said there were four bodies. In Katherine's room, was a bag like she had just arrived home. A pair of hair straighteners were plugged into the wall and rested on what was left of the bed. They were the ignition point of the fire, allegedly. Except she had short hair and wore it spiky."

"Could have been her sister's, or her mother left them there."

"True," but Tasha's eyes said she didn't believe it. "My guy in the fire department said the ignition point was arcane, not chemical, and that there were no accelerants."

"So back to what are we doing here with a dead guy?"

"I told you. He said he had fresh information. Let's see if we can find it."

It didn't take long. I noticed a manilla envelope on the breakfast bar, letter size, that reminded me of the one Tamsin had left for me. I hesitated, then picked it up and slid my finger under the flap. Inside were fifteen or twenty sheets of paper. I held the envelope out to Tasha.

"Is this what we're looking for?"

She was also wearing gloves now and snatched the envelope from my hand. "Don't mess with the evidence."

Except she pulled the contents from the envelope and spread them out on the breakfast bar. Talk about do what I say, not what I do. She took out her phone and started photographing them. Halfway along the row of paper, she looked up at me.

"Call the cops, report that we found a body." She gave me the address, and I dialed 911.

I looked back just as Tasha was tidying some of the pages away, and one caught my eye. I reached out to pull it from the stack she had finished with.

"Leave it, we don't have time."

But I wasn't listening. My whole attention was on the logo on the top of a letter to the school. It, and the company name underneath it, sent jangling waves of panic down my spine. Tasha snatched it from my fingers and put it with the others, then slid them all back into the envelope. "Where did you find this? Exactly where?"

I pointed, then adjusted the angle when she put it back. Sirens were getting closer, and she pushed me toward the door.

"Stand outside, hands open and away from your body. Make no sudden moves."

We got outside the door just as two uniforms appeared, weapons out and raised. Tasha had her license open and in her hand.

"Registered PI," she called. "Handgun with concealed carry permit in shoulder holster. We called it in."

One uniform held back and covered us while the second approached and took Tasha's gun before he checked her license.

"What's with the gloves."

Tasha gave him a surprised look. "Do I look like I got this yesterday? Body on the floor, neck looked broken. Had to check he was alive and didn't want to contaminate the scene. And we're waiting here for forensics, or to be told to report to forensics later."

"You got that down pat." The uniform at the back was fidgeting and kept resetting his grip on his gun. He was terrifying me.

Tasha sounded bored. "Not the first time I've found a body. Just stuff you pick up. OK if we sit on this wall while you call it in?"

The wall was in the shade, out of the way of the door, but where they could keep us in view.

"Who's she? I don't see her waving no license." Twitchy was staring at me and my palms began to sweat.

"Intern," Tasha sounded bored. "Training visit to a client. Didn't expect it to break like this."

"ID," he snapped, glaring at me. "Slow and easy."

I 'slow and easy'ed my ID and driver's license out of my hip pocket and held it out for the uniform that looked like he didn't want to shoot anybody today. He opened it and chuckled.

"For real?"

I managed to grin at him. "For real."

"Jeez, your mom and dad must have hated you."

My heart froze, and so did my face, but he hadn't meant

anything. He had no idea how deep his words cut. His partner continued to be an ass.

"Got to be fake, man. We have to cuff her at least."

"Chill. Can't beat on someone because you don't like their name, Leo. I'll stay outside, call it in and keep an eye on them. You look around inside."

Soon more sirens screamed down the street toward us. Uniforms unwound police tape and knocked on doors, and eventually a suit walked into the condo.

"Well, this is either good or bad," muttered Tasha.

I looked at her, then at the plainclothes, then looked at him again. It was the same jerk who had tried to use me to boost his arrest rate after Icarus/Dale tried to burn down my house. When he saw us, his face set into angry lines.

"Again? This time I am going to bust you both for–"

"What? This guy was my client. I had an appointment with him to discuss a case. Where's your probable cause, doofus?"

"Then what's she doing here?"

Tasha looked sad. "Is there something going on? Dammit, you used to be a good cop, really good. Now you're looking to bust someone just because you saw them at the scene of an unrelated crime? She's with me because this client and she have – had – things in common. I told you; she's connected to the Paulette Tipton case. My ex–client has been trying to get you guys to look into something that smells the same to me. No tricks, Eddie. All cards on the table here."

I may have imagined it, but for a moment I was sure Detective Eddie looked ashamed, but then he hardened up. "You turned your back, Nat, and walked away over nothing. That means you don't get to tell me, or any of us, that we're not living up to your standards as police officers. You're one of *them* now."

"One of them who just reported a crime then stood here and waited for you to turn up. I know enough not to leave any trace you could link back to me, and I could have been away from here and not even called it in. You think the DA will go anywhere near anything like that? Pull either of us in and you'll have the department on the wrong end of wrongful arrest and unlawful detention cases in a couple of hours."

She dropped her voice, but not so low I couldn't hear it.

"Dude, she has Walcott as her personal lawyer. You want him in the mayor's office tossing your name about?"

"Don't threaten me, Tasha."

"I'm not threatening you, doofus. I'm trying to help. And I'm getting annoyed. You want us to wait for forensics, in which case I'll give you thirty minutes, or do you want us to come by the station house to give samples and statements, in which case I'll give you five. After which I walk out of here and the only way you'll stop me is to arrest me or shoot me. Then all hell breaks loose."

Eddie glared at her for a good ten seconds, but Tasha wouldn't drop her eyes and glared right back. The detective made a disgusted noise and turned away. "Get out of here. Statements and samples by the end of the week."

We retrieved the stuff that the first cops on the scene had taken from us and walked back to the car.

What I saw on the letterhead shook me. The logo, the name, were buzzing around in my head, louder and faster until it seemed I didn't have space for anything else.

"I wish I knew what was getting into those guys," Tasha muttered. "It didn't used to be like this. Sure, we all felt the pressure when I was a cop. There's always somebody pushing for results, but this is getting crazy. Everybody seems to be a suspect." She shook her head as she opened the car. But I wasn't listening. I hadn't been listening for a while.

Freak Out at Tasha 's

Tasha lived in an apartment on the edge of the financial district. The building was impressive. I remember a passing thought that it must cost her a fortune in rent, but I wasn't paying that much attention. I was freaking out and trying to keep it inside. Since the moment I had seen that logo, the ever–present headache had escalated to broken glass scraping inside my skull.

Everything sounded wrong. Echoes phased and shift from ear to ear like a prog rock band. The trembling was worse, and it felt like I had been fighting it forever. If the cops had seen me shake, or if my walk had been unsteady, they would have pounced like hyenas on a baby antelope.

But now it was coming out. As we rode the elevator up from the underground garage, my arms and legs trembled like I was struck with a chill. The elevator pinged and the doors opened, but I was stuck to the wall. I knew if I moved, my legs would fold under me, and my arms wouldn't be strong enough to get me to my feet. I tried calling to Tasha, to ask for help, but all that came from my mouth was "Tuh...tuh...tuh". Tasha had left the elevator and was standing at a door, digging through her purse for keys. She turned around, looking for me, and dropped her purse. Her eyes opened wide, and she got to the elevator just as it was about to close. The door hit her arm, then reluctantly opened again. She caught me just as I fell.

"Jane? What's wrong?"

I must have looked like I was having a seizure. I wasn't. At least I don't think I was. I'd never spoken to anybody who suffered from them. But I was lucid, in a way. My brain was too busy to communicate with my body. I was drowning in the cacophony of broken images from the past and emotions very much of the moment. That cursed symbol, the name, the fear, and the anger. Memories flickered into existence, then disappeared again. A flash of a burning house, but not burning with natural fire, like the one I had watched. This one was burning white hot, consumed before the fire department could get to it.

I could feel the sound of Tasha talking to me, but none of the words lived long enough in the inferno of my thoughts for me to understand them. I felt her lift me, then drop me onto something soft, then tugging as she pulled off my jacket before she lay me down.

And whirling ever louder behind my thoughts, as a sound-track to the inferno movie of my home, was a dry British accent telling me it was my fault. All my fault.

Icy fingers touched my face. Tasha. She was speaking, but the words were arriving in the wrong order. It took me forever to put them in a sensible sequence.

"Let me take the pain away. Jane? Can you hear me? Let me take it away. Please."

No, she mustn't. I'd lose it. The pain was the memories; the memories caused the pain. Take one and the other would go too. And now that I had something, agonizing though it was,

I had to keep it. Nothing could take it from me. I managed to control my cramping arms enough to bat her hands away, but she forced them down to my side and kept repeating her words, louder and louder. They hurt, burning into my thoughts.

Her icy fingers touched my face again, but now she had stopped talking. I could feel the cold seeping in through my skin and into my mind. She was doing it anyway, taking my fears without asking, and stealing my anger.

I got my hands under her and tried to push her away. They wouldn't work, and the cold sank deeper into me. Anger boiled up beside the fear. She would ruin *everything*. I pushed again, and my mind held together for one co-ordinated second, burning a blinding white as I felt my hands shove into her chest, driving her away from me.

The effort cost me. My mind exploded in searing pain, and I disappeared into the brightness.

When I woke, I was cogent. Kind of. My thoughts were straight, calm, and my hands didn't shake when I held them out in front of me. Yet everything felt unreal, or distant. Not by a gulf, but by a millimeter. Enough to feel odd, detached.

Tasha was on the other side of the room, huddled in a mess at the bottom of the wall. I walked along the line of carnage she had left and touched the skin at the side of her neck. It was as cold as death, but then it would be. How the heck was I supposed to tell if a vampire was alive? If she didn't turn into dust, did that mean she was all right? She said she recovered from anything that didn't outright kill her, so she should recover from this.

I dug into my head to see if I felt bad about what I had done to her. The answer seemed to be 'not really', which horrified me. She was my friend, and I had hurt her enough to knock her out. I should be more upset than this, more worried, but it seemed my emotions were running on empty. My thoughts were cold, rational, even brutal. I asked her to stop, and she didn't. She made me push her away.

I thought about that for a moment and decided it was a little harsh. I could apologize later.

She had taken pictures of the sheets her client had left her, and remembered I wanted to see them. The laptop was screen locked, and I didn't stand a chance of guessing her password. Her phone was locked too, but it was new enough it had fingerprint unlocking as well as a passcode. I carried it over to her still limp form and held her thumb against the button.

The screen unlocked and I took a moment to add my own thumb to the list it would accept. Then I called up the photos and looked at the last images. Most of them meant nothing to me, but then I found the letter I had glimpsed, the one telling the school that Katherine was being taken out of class for education at a special unit.

It could've been a copy of the one sent about me, almost word for word. Again, just a meaningless but familiar scrawl instead of a signature, and no typed name. If this bastard was the supervillain he was supposed to be, why wouldn't he be doing something different from last time. But what I wanted to see again was the logo, in the top left of the page.

It didn't look right, not on the screen. I tapped and slid with my finger until I found the option for a printer. Either I would get my copy, or someone else in the complex would find a very weird printout on their machine.

I found the printer by following its purr to other side of

the room and snatched the sheet as it hit the collection tray. When I held it up, I got a connection, like a jolt of static frying my spine. But in my mind, the image wasn't on paper. It was on marble, amongst a list of other businesses on one of those signs in the foyers of office blocks. And I could see the block, and the street it was on. I didn't know the address, but I knew beyond doubt that if I drove without thinking about it, somehow I would get there.

Tasha was still showing no signs of life, or whatever her version of it was, and I knew nobody I could call to help her. Certainly not 911. I patted her down, taking her car keys and the automatic from her shoulder holster. It was matt black, square, and ugly, in that way of all things that deliver death are both ugly and beautiful at the same time.

I had no idea where the safety was, but I jammed the gun down the back of my jeans and walked out of the apartment, letting the door lock behind me.

The Night Before

I drove on autopilot until I found the building, and it took less than an hour. That should have freaked me out, but my emotions – well, most of them – were taking a break. Moving the BMW around the block, I pulled up far enough away to not get noticed, yet close enough I could sit and stare at it. It was the strangest feeling. The sight was as familiar as the back of my hand, but overlaid above that was the certainty I had never seen the building before. Yet I knew a guard sat in the foyer, that there were ten floors and a penthouse, and that out back was a street level parking lot with a loading bay.

But I wasn't ready. I put the car into drive and moved off. There was another place I needed to visit, and it wasn't far away.

Two blocks north, I turned in through a set of wrought–iron gates. The sign over them said 'Ashbury Gardens', and beyond was a tidy parking lot big enough for a couple of dozen cars. This time I switched the engine off and, after a moment, got out.

Ashbury Gardens was a recreation space, a miniature park I guess the city put in to enhance the lives of its citizens, or some such political blah blah. But I had a shadow of a memory about it. He allowed me to come here to walk, sometimes to run crazily around the place, burning off uncontainable energy. Other times just to sit in the sun. And there again was the whisper of a clipped British accent. The hairs on my arm rose and my heart thumped.

I found a bench by the edge of the lake and sat. It was a fake lake, but during the day a fountain made it look pretty. Ducks muttered to each other in the dark, disturbed by my presence. Maybe I would come feed them to apologize. If I was still alive tomorrow.

I leaned back and felt the automatic slide up in the waistband of my jeans. I grabbed for it before it fell out and looked at the thing. The fancy street lamps didn't give off much light, but it was enough to see the word 'Glock' near the nasty end, and the number '19'.

It was heavier than I expected. The matt finish made it look plastic, which I figured ought to make it light. It didn't. I knew there were things you needed to do to make a gun ready, so I put my hand on the top and pulled it back. A bullet flew out sideways. I stamped on it to stop it rolling too far away, and my leg cringed. Could it have gone off under my foot? And had I just flicked out the only bullet in the gun? I looked in the hole and there was another one waiting, so I eased the slide slowly back into place. I picked the bullet – or was I supposed to call them 'rounds'? – off the ground and put it in my pocket.

There ought to be a safety switch, too. I looked all the way around, but I was damned if I could see anything. All I could do was trust that the people who made it wouldn't sell a gun you couldn't fire, and that wouldn't go off by accident. Footsteps approached, slow and measured, and I stuffed the Glock into my jacket pocket. It didn't quite fit, but if I held it there, it looked like I was keeping my hands warm.

A cop turned out from a side path. I looked up at him and smiled, then groaned inside as he turned toward me.

"Evening, miss."

He looked like an old style beat cop, getting on toward retirement but still able to walk his neighborhood. He struck me as a community guy, not someone playing precinct politics or sucking up for promotions. Didn't make me trust him any more than any other cop, but I was prepared to go along with the stereotype. After all, I might be wrong, and he might be genuine.

"Little late to be sitting out here, young lady."

I nodded and grimaced. "I know. Needed somewhere quiet to think."

"Fella issues?"

This time a shrug. "Life issues. Just get on top of me sometimes, you know?"

He nodded and gave me a sad smile. "I certainly do, miss. I certainly do."

For a moment I thought he was going to sit down next to me for a 'friendly chat', and the Glock in my pocket felt the size of an assault rifle.

"You aren't thinking of doing anything to yourself, are you? If you were planning to drown your sorrows in the lake, I should warn you it's only a couple of feet deep."

That made me laugh. "No, officer. Drowning wasn't on my list for tonight. I just wanted somewhere to get away from the noise."

He nodded, "Then I'll leave you in peace. That your car up in the lot?"

My turn to nod. He looked up and down the lakeside. "It's

safe enough around here at night. Not too many crazies. But I'd hightail it out of here if you hear anybody else coming." Then he tapped the brim of his hat and wandered off on his beat.

Nice guy.

Why couldn't I live in his world? It sounded simpler than mine.

And it seemed I had come to a decision, or a determination, and without even thinking about it. I had to do what I had to do. If I didn't, I had no life. Losing it by fighting for it didn't seem so crazy, and if I managed to stop someone else being made into another version of me – or into what I was supposed to be, which felt worse – that came out as a bonus.

This couldn't be how Tamsin had intended things should play out, but I didn't have her to guide me. I hoped she understood why I had to confront the bastard who had been pulling my strings, and was now trying to cut them.

I walked back to the car. There was one last thing I needed to do.

Jimmy's wasn't much quieter than on my first visit, and the man himself wasn't at the bar. A two–piece band on the stage was doing a decent job of covering Dire Straits and were working their way through *Where Do You Think You're Going*. Uncomfortably apt. I marched up to the bar, people fading out of my way left and right, and got into the face of a girl in B–movie vampire gear, right down to the fangs. Unless that's what she was.

"I need Jimmy."

"He's not working right now."

"Fetch him." Her eyes narrowed and she bared her fangs at

me. I remembered my manners. "Please."

"I said he ain't here."

Disappointment tried to crush me, but I held it at arm's length – for now. "Get word to him. He wants my hair. Bad. It's his, but only if he cuts it right now."

"Boss don't take orders, except for coffee."

"He'll take this one. Please. It's important."

"To whom?" One side of her lips twisted into a sneer, but she walked to the other end of the bar, picked up a phone, and punched a number into the pad. She had a brief conversation, then slammed the phone down too hard. She walked back toward me, thunder in her face.

"Boss'll be here in ten minutes. He says to get you what you want."

I nearly said coffee, and probably should have. "Jack on the rocks. Two fingers."

The drink arrived, and I turned my back on the bar and the scowling barista. Again, I was being unfair to her, but I had stuff on my mind. I glared out over the clientele, then wound my neck in when more than one looked back at me as pissed as I was looking at them. I didn't want a fight. Yet.

There was so much to see, just letting my eyes graze over the people doing whatever it was they needed to be doing right then. Less than a third looked anything like human. The rest were from fairy tales and horror movies. Except they weren't. There were some cold eyes being exchanged between groups, but here, in Jimmy's, a peace reigned. And I wanted to know more about it, about them.

Another layer of cold anger wrapped itself around my heart. I was going to lose it, lose it all, before I'd had a chance to taste this wonderful, unknown world. He was going to take that from me too. Unless I could find a way to stop him. And who was I kidding about that? Still, he wasn't going to face the *me* he thought he left cowering in a backwater.

I saw Jimmy barging his way through the crowd like an icebreaker and tossed down the rest of my drink. Bad idea. My eyes were watering, and I was still trying to hide my cough when he greeted me.

"Is it true?"

I still didn't trust my voice not to croak, so I nodded. I got a beaming smile thrown back at me.

"This is wonderful. Magnificent." He hugged himself for a moment, then threw his arms wide and gathered me up in them. The hug made my ribs creak, but it was wonderful. When he let me go, his face was serious.

"There are rules. The only place this will happen is up there." He pointed to the chair on the platform. "And you can be sure there will be an audience. You will not see anything until I finish the work. Do you agree?"

I nodded and got another smile.

"I will not disappoint you. May I ask, why now?"

I looked Jimmy in the eyes long enough that he started to fidget. I liked him. He had warm eyes and seemed more genuine than most humans I knew. I decided he deserved an honest answer.

"Because I expect to be dead by dawn."

He took a half step back, then put his hand on my arm.

"Deep, dark words, little one."

I drew in a breath and pulled my shoulders back, still looking him in the eye. "Someone stole my life, my memories. This is how he left me. I have to confront him. If I can't beat him, at least I'll spit in his eye for what he did to me. And I want to do it as *me*, not the meek, weak thing he left me."

"Do you *wish* to die?"

I shook my head.

"Then run."

I shook my head again. "And sleep with one eye open for the rest of my life?"

He nodded, a long, deep gesture. "This I understand. Then I will dress you as you should be, my young warrior, so you can face your doom as the person you have become."

He motioned me toward the empty chair on the second stage and gestured to the vampire behind the bar. I was sure I saw her roll her eyes, but she reached under one of the shelves and fiddled with something.

The lights went out. All of them. The amps fuzzed the guitars into silence, and even the conversation faded to an expectant hush. A single spot snapped into life, tight and focused on the chair, and a soft *Ahh* rose from the patrons. Red emergency lights flickered into life behind the bar and along the front at floor level. On the sound stage they switched to acoustic, a single guitar fingerpicking Bowie, starting with *Changes*.

I climbed the steps to the stage, suddenly very aware that the chair was facing out into the crowd. I would be a spectacle, and I felt the first tremors of stage fright. Until I got to the top and realized the spotlight was so bright I couldn't see anything – and if I couldn't see them, they weren't looking at me. I know, bullshit, right? But it worked for me.

He pulled off the scrunchie I'd used to pull my hair back in a loose pony and started with brushing; he used long slow strokes, crown to tip, teasing out the odd snarl. By the time he finished, it must have gleamed. I felt a lurch, and the stage began to revolve. Spectacle didn't cover this. I wondered if

233

there might be a couple of cameras looking down on me, and whether there was much demand for hair porn.

Jimmy gathered my hair in his hands now, scraping it back tight against my skull like he was going to put it into a ponytail. Then he stopped, and my heart did the same. He was going to take it *all*.

"Last chance," he breathed into my ear. "I don't usually offer an opportunity to back out, but your hair is divine, and I want no regrets."

I swallowed hard. "What will happen to it? Do you throw it away, or burn it?"

He gasped. "Never."

"Then what?"

He didn't answer. The crowd couldn't have heard our conversation, but a restless whisper threatened to overwhelm the lone guitar. I tried to turn my head, to see why he wouldn't answer, but he held my ponytail firm and I got nothing more than a glimpse from the corner of my eye. He looked embarrassed.

"Is it that important to you?"

"I'm curious."

"I make wigs," he confessed. "For sick infants of all races. It's not much, but sometimes it helps them cope."

My hair had been shoulder-length when I had walked into the hospital five years ago. I hadn't cut it since. I guess it was some kind of mute protest I wasn't aware of. And this way, maybe a part of me would live on, helping someone. I settled into the chair.

"Cut."

The sound of the shears slicing though my hair went on forever, through it couldn't have lasted for more than ten seconds. Jimmy stepped around the chair to stand in front of me. As he raised half the length of my hair into the light, his huge voice called "Sacrifice" to his congregation below. It glittered like a waterfall of liquid gold. The invisible watchers let out a long sigh, then erupted in thunderous applause, intermixed with whistles and cheers.

I heard the *snick snick* of scissors, used like a gavel to call for order, and the crowd fell silent. Let the styling begin.

There was lots of snipping, then a lot of tugging. It was very weird, not seeing what the stylist was doing, but at the same time it was cathartic. I was putting myself into the hands of someone I barely knew, yet implicitly trusted. That trust got stretched to the limit when he pushed a cart alongside me, loaded with makeup and brushes. *That* I wasn't expecting. Still, go big or go home. As he wiped my face clean with remover on a pad, the guitarist shifted to Zeppelin – old school, but classic. I did wonder if Jimmy allowed anyone to play music less than fifty years old.

"In my people, you would be *sa–warrein*, a she–warrior." His voice was soft, for my ears only. "Feared more than the men for their great hearts and their skills. Never beaten, never defeated, only killed. You have such a heart. I feel it beating within you."

Wrong time for him to say such a thing, just before putting on eye makeup, but I swallowed the lump in my throat and kept the tears out of my eyes. It took him fifteen or twenty minutes, then he stepped away. A moment later, he handed me a mirror.

Well.

Fuck.

Me.

Tight braids ran along either side of my head, just above my ears. My eyes were dark, smoky without being goth. He had used darker lip gloss than I would have chosen, but it brought out the brown of my eyes. I loved it. All of it. He had even woven metal rings into the braid that ran down the back of my head. I raised my hand and brushed one with a finger.

"My people believe they bring strength," said Jimmy. "Others say warriors used them to hold spells of protection, or to confuse their enemies. The hair will stay like this until you touch the bottom ring of the center braid. Touch it again, and the braids will reform." He whipped the sheet from around my neck with a dramatic flourish. "Stand."

I walked to the edge of the platform, spot still tight on me, and from behind, in his magnificent voice, Jimmy called to the masses.

"Behold the *sa–warrein*."

The crowd screamed their approval. I turned back to Jimmy and bowed.

Preparation

I parked a block away, then burned my fingers trying to put the keys in the exhaust pipe before I settled for hiding them on top of the rear wheel.

Expecting to fail was no place to start from, but what else did I have? This was my fight. I didn't want Tasha getting hurt in a battle that wasn't hers. I wasn't sure where I stood with her anyway. Client, employee, sidekick, or friend? Tick any of the above or write in at the line.

But I was going in. Maybe it didn't need to come to a fight. Maybe we could negotiate a solution. However it turned out, it would be better than this half-life of constantly watching my back for someone else trying to kill me.

I stopped at the corner, before the open lot at the back of the offices I wanted into. If a camera watched the lot, I didn't want it to see me loitering.

They set the fence ten feet back from the sidewalk, and in the middle was a section on rails, maybe even remote controlled. But where the fence ended, on both sides, there were deep pools of darkness. Seemed stupid to me, but exactly what I needed to give me cover while I climbed over the fence.

Problem was, *inside* the fence the light was better, and I saw cameras. I scanned back and forth, looking for a path that would keep me out of their eye, even if it was only mostly. The cameras didn't pan left to right, and I had no idea if they had a wide view, but if a blind spot existed, it was on this side. This was where I would go over the fence. I stepped forward.

A hand grabbed my collar and hauled me back, hard and fast. Another grabbed my arm and spun me around, while a foot stamped into the back of my knee and sent me to the ground. My wrist got yanked up between my shoulders, my hand held flat and twisted around until it felt like every joint from wrist to shoulder inclusive would pop out of its socket.

I bit off a scream and tried to turn my head, but the arm lock twisted me up so bad I couldn't even do that.

"Borrowing my car is one thing, but don't you ever steal my gun again. *Ever.*" My wrist got an extra painful twist to make sure I got the point. She released the armlock, replaced it with a hand at the scruff of my neck, and she marched me away from the corner. When she threw me into the wall, I felt her take the Glock from the waistband of my jeans. I turned and faced the furious Tasha.

"Don't ever carry one of these like that. There's no damned safety and you can shoot yourself in the ass, or the spine. Now what the hell are you doing?"

"My fight. I don't want to get you hurt."

"But you want to get yourself killed?" She did a double take. "And you took time out for a *make-over*?"

I didn't have an answer she could understand, not without taking half an hour to explain. I shrugged.

"What the hell was your plan? Did you even *have* a plan?"

"Of course I didn't have a plan," I hissed. "I was just going to get into there, find this bastard, and shoot him if he won't leave me alone."

She hit me. She actually cuffed me across the side of my head.

"And kill the security guard too? Or two or three of them? And this girl you say is up there?"

"I don't know what I would have done, will do, whatever. But I'm doing this tonight. I can't take any more of the half memories and headaches, the flashes in my eyes. And I've had enough looking over my shoulder every minute I'm awake, and not sleeping because I'm waiting for somebody else to torch my house. I've had *enough*."

Tasha let go of me, raising her hands between us. I think she was trying to get me to calm down, but it wasn't working. She said nothing, her eyes lost in thought, then she pulled me away from the wall and pushed me away up the sidewalk, only gentler this time.

"Back to the car, idiot."

I stopped and turned. "I said I'm not leaving."

"Did I say we were going anywhere? I have an idea. It's a bad idea, and will probably end up getting us both killed, but it's an idea. Back to the car."

Entry

We pulled up opposite the front door of the building. "Are you mad?"

"Just follow my lead and don't look nervous," said Tasha.

"How the hell am I supposed to do that?"

"Want to go home so you can find your big girl pants?" She gave me no more than a second. "Thought not. Now get out and go back to the trunk."

She punched a button on the dash. The lock made a soft thud in back and a motor whirred as the trunk opened. Cool night air breezed through the car as I opened my door and got out. Tasha pulled two bags out of the mess in the trunk. The one she gave to me looked like a laptop satchel and had computer cables spilling from it in all directions. She took something that looked like a toolbox, and threw a black, single–strap sack over her shoulder.

We walked across the street and up to the door while the car closed and locked itself. Tasha tapped on the glass door until the guard looked up from his desk. He shook his head and made a shooing away gesture.

"Come on, sir. Don't make me stand out here in the street

shouting."

She lifted an ID card hanging from a lanyard around her neck and pressed it up against the glass. The security guard looked at us a moment longer, then sighed visibly before folding his paper and letting his feet fall from whatever he had propped them on. He ambled over to the door, placed a practiced foot to stop us ramming it open, and pressed a button at the side of the door. It opened an inch.

"Can I help you ladies?"

"Network service," said Tasha. "We got a call out to this address."

He shook his head again. "No notification. And no notification means no access."

Tasha nodded. "Usual damn story. Monitoring center in Bangalore picks up an overnight transient and hits the panic button before they check the site procedures. Then I end up banging on the door of a building and security knows nothing about it. Mind you, this one probably knocked the phones out too. Outgoing would be fine, but it could be nobody can call in. Network room is in the basement here, right?"

The security guard was wavering. I could see his suspicion fading. Tasha kept the patter going.

"Hey, can we just come stand in the foyer? Standing out in the street at night makes me uncomfortable, and the stuff in this case is worth most of my salary for a year. I can dig out the number you need to call our response center once I have my hands free. You can go through your security check with them."

The guard looked at us a moment longer, then he stepped back and held the door open. Tasha shifted her bag to her left hand and stepped forward first. As she passed the guard, her right hand flashed out like a rattlesnake striking and clamped around his wrist. The guard gasped, let out a moan that was frankly disgusting, and sagged to the floor.

Tasha dropped her case and caught him before his head hit the floor. Then she dragged him behind his security station. She handled him as though he weighed no more than a child.

"Shut the door, then move the bags back here." She looked a little annoyed, and I cussed myself. I should have through of that. I scurried, and got back as she patted the guard down. She took his revolver and emptied it into her hand, then dropped the bullets into the bag I had been carrying. A moment later she did the same with a speed loader, then she relieved him of his keys and a swipe card. A quick search through the desk drawers revealed another speed loader, which also went into the bag. Experience at work; I would never have thought to look in there for anything.

"Are there any more of them?"

Tasha shook her head. "I doubt it. No radio."

A semi-concealed door behind the desk opened into a closet, with enough space to sit the guard on the floor. "Is this any good?"

Tasha looked up then nodded. She dragged him inside and made him comfortable.

"How long will he be like that?"

"This will all be over before he wakes up, whichever way it goes, but he'll wake before morning." She stood up, face very serious. "This is your last chance to back out."

I shook my head

"Then let's get on with it."

An elevator waited in the lobby, door open. We walked over to it, but Tasha put an arm out to stop me stepping inside, then pointed to the buttons in the mirrored wall across the back.

"Key switches. One for the penthouse, which you'd expect. But why level 4? Can you read mirror?"

Each button had a black in gold plaque next to it, announcing the company for each level. I could read in a mirror, but I didn't need to. I knew what it said, even though I didn't have a clue what was there.

"It says *CORVAX Research*. Can't we see if one of the guard's keys fits?"

"Good point, but then anybody in the penthouse might hear the lift motors. They may know we're here already, but let's not make it too easy for them."

I looked around for stairs. There are always stairs, even if the architect hides them away. What I found was a service door on the other side of the lobby. I pointed to it.

"Let's try back there."

The stairwell smelled funky, like most do. Not the subtle background of public toilet, but the aroma of dirty mop water. The air breathed like someone needed to open the doors and let a fresh breeze through.

We didn't talk. When you're climbing that many stairs, you save your breath unless you have something important to say. You get into the rhythm, blank your mind, maybe get an earworm at the same beat.

I almost walked past the door on level 4. Tasha grabbed me by the arm and pulled me back. There it was, bold and brazen on the doors. That hated logo and the words "Corvax: Research Dept." Underneath it, in red, "No Access to Unauthorized Persons." I stood and stared for a minute or two. I hadn't seen it in the foyer. Maybe it was smaller, or maybe I had been too busy. Here, it was impossible to miss.

"Can you feel any traps or alarms?"

Tasha broke the spell, and I drew in a breath that felt like I hadn't taken one for minutes. A tight pain clamped across my chest, while my legs felt cold and weak. "How?"

"I thought your abilities might have made something of a comeback, after the way you threw me across my living room."

I pulled a guilty face but shook my head. "Nothing I can rely on."

But it left me thinking. *Were* things starting to come back to me? They must be, even if I wasn't sure how. If so, what would be the sort of thing I would need to do? It was a long shot, but pretending I knew what I was doing had worked on the door lock at Jessander's.

I took a breath and tried. Nothing clever, just letting my thoughts calm and allowing anything that wanted to happen the freedom to do it.

Nothing. Well, not quite true. I felt no strange sensations, but I did understand something. There would be no traps on the door, and no alarms. He knew I was coming. He knew we were there. And he wanted me to see what was behind this door. I wasn't sure if he was hoping it would scare me away, or if it was an invitation, but I knew I had to go inside.

I snatched the card from Tasha's fingers and swiped it through the reader.

Laboratory of the Arcane

I pushed through the doors and into the 4th floor elevator lobby. Lights flickered on, woken by our presence, but all the elevator doors were closed here. At the end of the lobby was a double door, with frosted glass panels and a repeat of the 'Corvax Research' and NO ENTRY signs. By the door was another card reader, and I walked straight up to it.

"Alarms?" Tasha sounded alarmed herself.

"Doesn't matter. He knows we're here."

"Then shouldn't we just get up there and sort this out?"

I shook my head. "Then he would have locked all this off. He wants me to see something here."

"Doesn't that mean we shouldn't?"

I got her logic, but I wanted to see it as much as he apparently wanted me to. The closer I got to the door, the more ghosts of memories flickered inside my head. I had spent years here and knew nothing of it. Was that what he was trying to do? Get me to remember the good times, how we were once such best buds? If so, it wasn't going to work. I walked up to the next set of doors and swiped myself in.

Like so much, it was familiar yet brand new to me. In some ways, it reminded me of Tamsin's workshop. Shelves full of old books ringed the room, but instead of old wooden bookcases, they were modern wire units.

It smacked of a school science lab, but instead of pictures of atoms and the periodic table on the wall, these posters showed astrological projections and a diagram of alchemical symbols.

A circle marked the floor here too, made of metal just as Tamsin's was, except where Tamsin's silver looked hand beaten and shaped, this looked cut into place with a laser. But I remembered it.

I remembered it like it was now, empty and clean – because I had just polished it. And I remembered it full of symbols that I partly understood. I had spent hours sitting in it, but I couldn't remember why.

All this tip of the tongue stuff was maddening. I almost stormed out of the room, but something held me back. I had something to do here, though I didn't know what, and I was becoming more certain by the second it wasn't him that needed me to do it.

I went around the bookshelves again. Was there something here I needed to see? Was he playing with me, and if not him, who? Had he left something I should recognize, something I should be able to use to defeat him? Just to taunt me, so he could say to me later *If you had any wits left you would have recognized the doohickey, and if you had brought it with you, you could have frammitzed me to death*? I didn't have any reason to think that, but somehow I knew he was that sort of person.

The shelves of equipment were meaningless to me, so I moved on to the bookshelves. I had only scanned them before, but this time I read each title, and ran my finger down each spine. Some felt soft, others rough, and some made my finger prickle the way it does when you run your thumb across a sharp blade. Then I touched one that my fingers knew. It was leather bound and hand stitched, and when I pulled it off the shelf, I saw from the edges that the paper was made by hand, not machine. What stood out was that it didn't look old.

The outside held no markings, no title, so I opened the book at a random page –

And nearly dropped it.

It was full of my handwriting. The book was *mine*.

"You all right? You just went a funny color."

I held out the book for her to see, and wanted to snatch it back when she misunderstood the gesture and took it from me.

"Special?"

"Mine."

She raised her eyebrows and flicked through. "Looks like some kind of exercise book."

"Book of Days," I corrected, then wondered where the hell that had come from. Tasha kept flicking through, then stopped.

"Hmm."

"What?"

"Somebody didn't think much of your last assignment."

She held the book up to show me. Six or seven pages were torn out, right where my writing stopped. I got sad and angry about a book I had only known of for five minutes. Or for half my life.

I flicked through it again. I had known some cool stuff once, and it looked like I had been pretty good at it. Tasha took the book from me, closed it, and put it into her pack.

"Not the time to let this distract us. You can read it through when we get out of this."

But I didn't think it was there as a distraction, at least not in the sense of costing us time. I thought it was there as a reminder of what I lost. Maybe a goad, to show what I could have done if he hadn't raped my mind. Or maybe to remind me of what I once was capable of.

And that was the decision I came to. There was nothing here for us to look at. He didn't want us here to slow us down, he wanted me here to demoralize me. He was trying to beat me before I ever looked him in the eye. I went over to the circle.

"Careful of that," Tasha called. From another unbidden memory, I knew a subliminal vibration, cold and angry like a wasp, was missing and that told me nothing lurked on or in the circle. I stopped thinking and let my body move on autopilot. It walked me straight to the center of the circle. I turned until I felt a direction I liked, then sat down and crossed my legs.

"What are we doing now?" Tasha's voice was quiet, but I heard her impatience.

"Nothing." I cleared my mind and focused on the quiet in the room. "Waiting. He'll let us know when he is ready, and there won't be a thing we can do until he is."

And then I felt it, drifting up from the circle. I couldn't tap it, couldn't collect it, and what should have been blasting up from the earth like a geyser was no more than the gentle steam that rises from a damp field on a summer morning. But it was there. My body remembered it too, like a scent in a garden that touches your soul with the memory of a loved one, or the petrichor scent of fresh rain on dusty, dry ground.

It might have brought me no strength, no power, but it brought me calm, and it brought me peace. I closed my eyes and let it wash over me.

Until an elevator chimed in the lobby.

Battle

The door of the elevator was open and stayed that way. "Must be in maintenance mode," Tasha muttered. "Someone sent it for us."

"No prizes for guessing who."

We went to the elevator and peered in. I looked at the panel in the back wall mirror and pointed it out to Tasha. A key was in the switch next to the Penthouse sign. "Yup, definite invite."

She pulled me back and turned me to face her. "You have an option here. We get in, head for the lobby, and run like hell. You've found the book, and we can take other stuff. You can learn, give yourself more of a chance."

It was tempting, but I shook my head. "Even if we do get out, which I doubt, he'd never leave me in peace. I couldn't stop running from the second my feet hit the sidewalk. Besides, it gives him more time to train whoever he has up there to replace me. Maybe enough so she can do whatever he wanted me for."

She put her hand on my arm. "What have you got? What can you take to him that makes you think you stand the tiniest chance of walking out of here?"

She wasn't helping, but she was right. "I got nuttin," I

admitted, trying for a little humor and failing. "But I can't live looking over my shoulder. I can talk to him, maybe talk to her." I took her hand from my arm and held it. "But you should go. This isn't your fight."

She grimaced. "Kind of is. I don't like people killing my clients. Means I don't get paid."

"I'm not planning to turn him in."

She pulled her Glock from its shoulder holster. "Neither was I."

We stepped into the lift, and I turned the key.

The doors closed, and it wasn't until the elevator started to rise that I realized I was holding my breath. Half of me expected the bottom to fall out of the car, or for a cable to come whipping down and cut us both in half. Tasha pushed me to the side, then pressed her back to the other side, keeping us both out of the line of the doors. Made sense, and it annoyed me I hadn't thought of it myself. Tasha held her gun in a two-handed grip, barrel pointing down at the floor, while I did nothing and wondered what I was doing here.

What the hell *was* I doing here? If I had listened to her, we would have been on our way out through the doors and running for the car, with a bag full of magical booty, not standing in an elevator wondering if we would still be alive in five minutes.

The elevator slowed. I saw Tasha settle her grip on the gun. Her eyes were closed, but her face was calm. I wished I felt the same.

The car jerked as it locked into place and pinged politely. I held my breath as I waited for the magical equivalent of a 12–gauge shotgun blast to rip through the doors. It didn't, they just opened.

Tasha's eyes opened but she didn't move. I was about to

peek around the edge of the doors when I saw she was staring at the back of the elevator, I felt like an idiot again. I looked at the mirrored wall and checked out the lobby the elevator opened into. It was empty. Not even any planters or occasional seating. Not even a door.

Tasha caught my eyes in the mirror, then began waving her hand at me and pointing her fingers at her eyes. I don't know any cop hand sign crap, but I got the idea. Poke our heads out, her looking to the left and me to the right.

We went on three.

"Nothing my side," she whispered when we pulled back into the car.

"Corridor, maybe twenty or thirty feet. Pictures and pots. Opens into a room, I think."

She relaxed but kept the gun in the ready position. "OK, I'm guessing no obvious or immediate booby traps or welcoming committee. Let's go find our hosts."

We stepped into the hallway, Tasha with her gun shoulder high, and me feeling like the spare guest at a dinner party. I could hear a fire crackling in the distance, and felt a little spark of hope. Maybe I could use it, like I did on the demon. Then I remembered I had to have it in the ring first, which I almost certainly wouldn't have time to do, and I felt sick again. I concentrated on what I could sense again, to stop myself panicking, but other than that the only thing that disturbed the air was our shoes hitting the marble tiles and a faint smell of orange blossom.

But as we walked down the short hall, I felt my back straighten, and my steps opened out and had more purpose. I was not going to walk up to this bastard like a victim. He could have killed me half a dozen times since I walked into the building, but I wouldn't hunch my shoulders and cower in fear. He didn't want me dead yet. And that might be his biggest mistake.

Tasha got to the corner and flattened herself to the wall, ready to do a quick peek, and from the corner of my eye I saw her horrified face as I walked straight into the room beyond.

I wished I hadn't. My head spun, and I almost missed a step. I got a massive *deja don't* – I knew the room so intimately, and yet it was utterly strange to me. The crazy log fire pit that wasn't logs at all, the kitchen counter off to the right. The massive flat screen on the left wall was new and jarred even more. And right in front of me the three doors; his room, mine, and his office in the middle.

And that was where they stood, a few feet in front of the middle door. Him, salt and pepper hair, sharp-edged beard, and eyes the pale blue of deep ice. Mid-height, but wearing an expensive suit and standing like he was six feet tall. Next to him, the girl. My heart broke for her as soon as I saw her. Nobody but she had cut her hair in years. It was clean, but matted, almost meshing into blonde dreadlocks. She wore oversize sweats and sports socks, but no shoes. She held her hands in front of her, clawed, chest height, and I could see she'd bitten the nails almost to the quick.

But it was her eyes, or maybe her entire face, that tore at me. Her eyes looked solid black and her expression was a mask of fear. She was maybe sixteen, and I hated him a thousand times more for what he was doing to her right now.

"Hands in sight and away from your bodies, please," Tasha said as came around the corner, Glock raised and slightly to the right. She was looking down it like a rifle sight, rather than a typical cop pose. "Jane, look for something to tie their hands."

He laughed. Not a Bond villain 'mwa–ha–ha' laugh, but like he just got told a smutty joke. "Oh, how melodramatic. Katherine, dear child, would you?"

Fear turned into intense concentration, and the girl's arm shot out as if she was delivering a heel–punch. I felt the edge of it, like somebody walked into my shoulder, but Tasha took all of it, head on. It lifted her off the ground and threw her at the wall behind us. There were two cracks, the first from the Glock as Tasha managed to shoot off one round. I saw the puff of plaster from the wall, a foot over the girl's head.

The second crack was Tasha's skull on the wall. I turned my head in time to see her sliding to the floor, leaving a trail of blood down the wall. The Glock ripped itself free of her hand, then flew back down the hall toward the elevators. I turned back to see him dusting his hands like he had touched something dirty.

"Now, dear girl, I want you to pay attention."

That cut–crystal British accent scratched at my ears like nails down a chalkboard, and for an instant I thought he was talking to me. Still, I looked at the girl, Katherine, the same moment she looked at me. The fear was back. She had the slightest trace of blood under nose, and she was rubbing her thumbs across the tips of her fingers. Her skin was paler, too.

Hell, it had *hurt* her. When she used magic, it caused her pain. And he was forcing her to learn more, do more, even though her body was rejecting it.

"Study her. This is the embodiment of failure. This is the wretch who had the opportunity I have given you, and she squandered it. She didn't practice, she didn't follow my instructions. She broke the rules.

"But then, she was a poor choice. She didn't have the talent you have, or the ability, and when she realized she would never live up to my expectations, she betrayed me."

Katherine soaked up his lies and looked at me like I was a bug. When she glanced up at the man, I saw worship. She was under his spell, but I couldn't tell whether that was true magic, or just his charisma. I had been going to call him out, argue his lies, but I saw it was pointless. Nothing I said to her would change her mind, not while he stood next to her. Anything I said would be brushed aside as spite.

"Will you deal with her for me, my dear?"

She looked up at him again, her face clouded with uncertainty. "But Master, wouldn't that be, well...?"

"Murder?" He pretended to look thoughtful. "I suppose it would, and you are right to weigh it carefully. You should never undertake an action without a full understanding of its costs, as well as its benefits. Perhaps it would ease your mind if I told you that jealousy has possessed this creature since she learned I had taken a new apprentice. This, dear Katherine, is the monster that has been trying to kill you. *This* is the beast who destroyed your home and killed your parents."

I should have run as soon as the words left his mouth. Down to the hall and into the elevator, praying that it would get to the bottom before she burned through the cables.

But his words stunned me. I raised my hands. "Wait. no..."

But her face was a flat mask of hatred and rage, and before I could blink, she held a ball of fire between her hands. She flung it at me.

I leaped to the side and felt the heat as it passed. The fire struck the wall beside me while I was still in the air and threw me farther away from the hall and deeper into the room. It trapped me. I had nothing to hide behind, and wherever I tried to run, she would still get a clear shot at me. My fight with the demon at Sands' office echoed through my head.

She sucked another ball of fire from the heat of the room and hurled it at me, but she faked me and threw after I dodged. I flailed my arm and batted the fireball away. I don't know why I tried, but something came into my head about gesture and action, and I tried it. It worked this time, but that could have just been luck.

Katherine twisted up another fireball and the temperature in the room dropped so hard I got goosebumps. It was smaller, too, so again I swatted at it. The fireball bounced off me a few feet away and exploded somewhere in the kitchen.

"You said she wouldn't know. You said you took it all away." Her voice was plaintive, whining, and terrified.

He slapped her across the back of the head. "Focus, you cretin. She knows nothing. Take her down but don't kill her."

"That's all you'll get from him, Katherine. Lies and bully-ing."

"You're the liar," she screamed, and held her hand toward the fire. The flames leaned toward her, fading as she stole their heat. When she had enough, she threw another fireball at me. I batted this one away too, and it seemed to get easier each time.

"Vary your offence," he snapped, and she flinched. Her hand reached out in a different direction, and an arc of electricity shorted from a socket to her hand. This time I got a sparkling blue–white ball, and it moved much quicker.

I caught it.

Remembering the ring, and the fire in my house, I reached out and snatched the sparkling ball from the air. I squeezed my fist closed around it and forced it into the ring.

Next, she pushed her hands toward me like she was shoving a box. Without thinking, I raised my hands like the bow of a ship. The wall of air flowed past me on either side, though it did force me back a step. I was working on instinct now, letting my body do what it knew even though my mind had forgotten.

Fire, air, fire, electric, air, battering at me, but not defeating me. But it was defeating her. Blood ran over her mouth and sweat plastered her hair to her head. She gasped for air and took longer to prepare each attack. One fireball was so slow I had time to move side on and whack it back: not at her, but at *him*. It bounced off something while it was still four feet away, and that gave him another laugh.

I caught another ball of electricity in the ring while he wasn't paying attention but had no idea what I was going to do with it. I couldn't strike back, not at Katherine. This wasn't her fault. She didn't know better, and she would kill herself for him. I couldn't add to that.

She drew more heat from the fire and spun it into a ball, but before she could throw it, Katherine's eyes rolled up in her head. She dropped to her knees, then fell forward over the fireball. It detonated beneath her, flipping her over onto her back and setting fire to her clothes.

He looked at her, his face full of disappointment and disgust, then he extinguished the flames with the slightest nothing of his hand. Then he turned to me, and I understood. He had been using her to test me, and was willing to let her kill herself so he could see if I had anything to strike back.

"She's even weaker than you are." He brushed some imaginary speck from his sleeve. "But at least she's more gullible. She'll work until I make her do what you wouldn't, or she'll die and I'll learn for next time."

He made another gesture, no bigger than that to brush away an annoying bug, and I smashed into the wall. I fell to the floor beside Tasha, stunned, but not unconscious.

He had played me, and won.

Defeat?

He laughed again. Perhaps he saw the realization on my face. Then he strolled toward me. My head spun, but I sent frantic demands to my arms and legs to do something. They flailed, trying to get me to my feet.

"Ah, ah." He wagged a finger, and a weight settled on me that drove the breath from my lungs and pinned me to the spot. My ribs creaked. "It would be so rude of you to distract me while we are having this conversation."

"Just kill me, you bastard." I could barely gasp the words.

"I have something much better in mind. Don't be in such a hurry. We have so much to catch up on."

He crooked a finger; a footstool slid across the floor toward us. His abilities crushed me. How had I been so naïve to think I might have been able to stand up to him? Even so, I slid my left hand up against my thighs, hiding the Magni ring. No point giving the spoils away for free, or before I was dead.

He put the stool over my legs and sat on it, staring at me while he chuckled. "I assume that's what this is all about? You wanted to know why?" He put his elbow on his knee and leaned forward. "Actually, it's not all your fault. If that meddling old bitch hadn't started digging, and if that incompetent troll I placed to watch over you had done what she was told, you would still be living out your meaningless existence in that hotbed of banality I dropped you in. Leamington?"

"Clifton."

He made a whatever gesture and a flash of irritation sparkled in his eyes. I had dared to interrupt him.

"Unless, of course, this useless bitch proved to be of no worth. Then I would have come back for you, and sweet–talked you into being my little puppet all over again."

"Never." The word grated its way out between my clenched teeth, and he slapped me hard across the face.

"Don't interrupt. You aren't important. Not anymore. You turned into an experiment, and now the experiment is over." He smiled. "I suppose there can be no harm in letting you have your memories back. Some of them, at least. I shall sit here and enjoy as you rediscover them."

He reached forward and flicked my forehead.

My life unrolled in my head like a movie pastiche; not minute by minute, but all those important scenes like first bikes, and my puppy George. All the emotions flooded in as a background, like the soundtrack to the movie; how much I loved my mom, how I idolized my dad. His crazy fascination with old motorcycles.

Then things turned darker. I changed after my twelfth birthday. Not just teen hormonal, but deeply introverted. God help me, I even started to dress like a Goth.

Visits to the school counselor, the psychologist, threats of expulsion. Being offered the special school, hating the idea and fighting it with all my soul, but being dragged here, to this building, day after day. My pop fighting back his own tears as he made me get out of the car and delivered me to the fourth floor, all because he believed it was the best thing for me.

Tears were running down my own cheeks now. I didn't hate my father for it anymore. At the time, I just wanted to go home and prove I could be good. That they didn't need to punish me by sending me to this place and this man anymore.

He didn't abuse me sexually, but that was about the only thing he didn't do. Looking at it now, I could see he was trying to break my spirit, to make me dependent on him, just like he had done to Katherine. And there was something he was trying to teach me, something powerful. I fought him all the way and just wanted to go home.

Then he let me.

And everything was fine for a week. Right up until I had a shouting match with my sister about nothing. Right up to the moment she was engulfed in white-hot flame. I heard her screams, and I cowered in the corner with my arms over my head. It didn't blot the screams out, nor the roar of the fire, nor my parents, terrified, shrieking our names until their screams, too, turned to agony. The house burned around me, white hot, destroyed in minutes, while I huddled safe in my little bubble, the flame boiling six feet away from me.

I had killed my family.

Me. My anger, my selfish loss of control. My refusal to learn how to manage the terrible power that could rip out from me at any time.

His finger was under my chin, lifting it, so he could see my soul rip itself apart and throw itself on the fire of the memories.

"Ah," he said, with a smirk and a malicious glitter in his eyes. "There it is."

He watched as I wept. I tried to turn away, but his thumb rested on the front of my chin and held me in a vice.

The movie rolled on. Four years of trying to please him, four years of trying to atone for what I had done. Four years of him beating me over the head with what a danger I was, how I would kill people again unless I could learn to control it, and the only way to learn that was to summon it again – but I never could. Memories of looking just like Katherine; the same hair, the same clothes, the same empty desperation in my eyes.

And all the time I could feel him, his face two feet away, watching my fresh agony.

Relishing every second of it.

He let me stew in this horror of my own making. It felt like an hour, but it could only have been a minute, perhaps two. Then he leaned closer. "Shall I tell you another secret?" He whispered.

I probably looked at him. My mind was numb, and I don't really remember.

"*I* set the fire. *I* killed your mother, and your father, and your pretty little sister. Even your annoying little dog." He jerked his head toward the still–prone lump of Katherine's body. "Just like I did hers. Just like I told her it was her fault. She sniveled about her family as much as you did about yours. Begged them to let her come home, just as you did. I needed to get their meddling out of my way and stop both of you hoping they would rescue you rather than turning to me for guidance."

My mind froze, then shattered into a million razor sharp fragments that spun like a hurricane and tried to shred me. I howled, and all the time he held my chin and stared into my face with his satisfied little grin. The hatred grew inside me, but the razor–sharp horror stripped it apart before it could do anything.

Until icy fingers touched my hand and cool calmness seeped up my arm.

"And now you've had time to digest those fond recollections, I am going to finish with you. Don't worry. I shan't kill you, or your friend." He was staring deep into my eyes again, and I forced myself to look back. He mustn't see what Tasha was doing.

"But I shall make a few alterations. Oh, inside you'll both be just as you are now. People might see a few changes outside though. Drooling, no control over your bowels or bladder. Both of you will need a nasal tube to feed through. I'll leave just enough connection to the world so they have to declare you minimally aware, and you can spend the remainder of your lives stuck inside your own heads, screaming out the rest of your pathetic existence. But for you I have one more, special treat for *daring* to *interfere with me*."

The last words came out as a screaming shout that flecked spittle over my face, but still I held his eye. Tasha's calmness was siphoning the horror and the guilt away, but leaving me the anger. Most importantly, leaving the hate. And yet I wasn't ready, not quite, and I was damned if I knew what I was waiting for. But I knew I had to wait for something.

"I shall leave your friend for the moment. Don't worry, I'll bring her over later, so you can watch the light of reason vanish from her eyes and smell the piss as she loses control of her bladder. So you can get an idea of what you will look like when I'm done with you. But first, the Lord giveth and the Lord taketh away. Having let you see your pathetic, insignificant life, I'm going to take it all away from you again. Except this time, you will know *what* I have taken. You will remember that you knew things, but that I took them from you, as a fitting reward for your treachery."

He shifted his weight forward to rise from the stool, then

lifted his left leg, reaching forward and again flicking my forehead.

I punched him in the balls with every ounce of my strength.

And, as an added bonus, I was inside whatever he was using as a shield, so I threw everything left in the Magni ring into the punch as well.

He flew twenty feet through the air with a ball of electricity and fire burning on his cock.

But it was too late. I could feel my memories draining away, starting with my family. I wailed like a broken-hearted child, knowing there was nothing I could do to stop it, knowing that I would never remember any of it again and terrified of the torment he had promised me.

But the fear fanned the embers of my anger, and something ignited inside me. Something deep, something ambiguous, from a place where good and bad got snarled up with each other. From far, far below, a dark energy swirled up to embrace me.

I brushed aside the force he had used to pin me in place and lifted myself to my feet. Without any idea how, I reached inside me and killed the worm he had set to eat my mind. I could analyze the damage it had done later. For the moment, I had bigger issues.

"Kill her," he screamed. "Kill her before she can use the Bloodfire."

That was it! *That* was what he had been trying to get me to raise all those years. And that was what he was killing this poor girl to do – except she never could. I could feel it wasn't in her, no matter how hard she tried.

She was, bless her, on her knees, trying to summon the strength for a spell and screaming at me to leave him alone. I couldn't help her with that right now. What ran through my body was war magic, not healing. I pushed her aside.

She took off like a football in a place kick. Realizing what I had done, I built a cushion of air behind her, but not fast enough. She hit the wall with a crunch and slid to the floor. She would have been strawberry jam if I hadn't tried to soften the landing.

But for what came next, I didn't need control. I just needed to be able to slowly fry this son of a bitch into ash.

I turned back to him just as he threw a wall of solid air at me, hard enough to turn me into a bloodstain on the wall, too. My fist slammed into it as it arrived and scattered it around the room. Before he could try anything else, I threw air back to him, but in a lance, not a wall. He brushed it aside, but the effort showed on his face, as did the fear.

Excellent. Exactly what I wanted.

I aimed my open hands toward him and unleashed the Bloodfire.

His shield held, and within it he drew another around him, then another, then another. Layer after layer, an onion of protective walls. The outer wall failed, but as soon as it did, he drew another around himself.

Impasse. Which of us would weaken first? Because whoever did, it would be their death.

And it wouldn't be me. Something, perhaps a half-erased memory, told me there was more. I threw one hand up and blasted a hole through the ceiling, then clenched my fist and drew down fire from on high to match what I was already using. I hadn't a clue what these things were, but I knew how to use them.

Light shone down on me through the roof, and smokey

energy swirled up my legs from below, winding together along my arms in a helix. I stretched my arms wide, let the energy flow out and around his shield. Then I *squeezed*.

He tried, but I burned through his protections faster than he could raise them, and within seconds he was down his last shield. I crushed harder, while he pressed outwards, trying to support it against my strength.

It wasn't a fair fight. I decided I would have my revenge. I decided that he wouldn't do this to me, or Katherine, or any other girl every again. And I decided he was going to die, right here, and right now.

It was as though the Bloodfire felt this too. The flames around my hands grew hotter and brighter, and the evil bastard's last shield began to glow, first a sullen red, then up through the spectrum like metal in a furnace until its blinding brilliance matched that of the Bloodfire.

The shield wavered, pulsing in and out.

Then it collapsed.

And the world exploded.

Exit

I bounced off the wall again, which was becoming a habit I thought I should probably break. My head whacked hard into the plaster and my vision was full of sparkles. I tried to lever myself back to my feet, but neither my arms nor my legs were taking orders. They let me get as far as my knees though, which was helpful of them.

Where he had stood was now a hole. Two, actually; one in the ceiling and one in the floor, which made three if you count the one I punched through the roof. I stopped counting as I crawled closer, staying well away from the ruptured gas line where the fire had been. It was busy spraying a flame twenty feet across the room.

I hoped I would see the bastard's charred corpse when I looked through the hole, but all I could make out through the dust was a pile of debris. But he was gone. I felt it. Then the concrete under my right hand crumbled away, and I backed up from the hole real quick.

Over at the wall, Tasha's eyes were open, and she was looking around the remains of the room with raised eyebrows. I made it up to my feet and stumbled over to her, then held out a hand to help her up.

"Are you done here?" She didn't take my hand. "Because if you have more shit to lay down on this place, I think I'll just stay here until you've finished."

"All done," I said, hoping to any gods who were listening that it was true. Whatever had possessed me had left. I couldn't find a trace of it, nor any clue of how to reach it again if I needed to. "You want help or not?"

Tasha slapped her hand into mine and we managed to get both of us on our feet with only a little leaning on the wall.

"Are you ok?" we said at the same time. I nodded and pointed to the huddled lump that was Katherine.

"We need to check on her."

"Are you sure? She tried to fry you."

I nodded and pointed to the flare from the gas line. Other things had caught fire, and there were only a few minutes left until the flames would cut the girl off. I'm good with fire, but I was a ruin and this was more than I could handle. "Can't leave her here to burn. Not her fault. He used her, just like he used me."

Tasha looked at the spiderweb of cracks in the plaster. "She hit this hard."

I felt bad, but only a little. Like Tasha said, she had been trying to kill me at the time.

"If we move her, we could do more damage."

"And if we leave her, she dies, even if we call 911 right now. Can you lift her?"

Tasha gave me a put−upon look, but nodded and hauled Katherine into a firefighter's carry. I went ahead, kicking the worst of the rubble out of the way so Tasha didn't trip on it, and remembering to pick up her gun when we passed it. We piled into the still waiting elevator and Tasha eased Katherine to the floor. "Let's go."

I stared at the panel a moment, finger touching but not pressing the button for street level, then I reached up, snatched the key from the penthouse switch, and twisted it in the switch for level 4.

"What the hell are you doing? We need to get out of here, and she needs to get to a hospital."

Tasha reached past me to press for street level, but I grabbed her wrist. That earned me a glare until I let go.

"There's irreplaceable stuff in that lab. We have to take what we can. What we don't take is lost forever if this place catches fire."

The doors closed, and the elevator dropped.

"The building is already on fire, in case you hadn't noticed," Tasha was snippy, and I couldn't blame her. "And there's a broken gas line. Not a good mix."

"Five minutes. Ten tops. We snatch what looks good and run back to the elevator."

She looked at me, but I wasn't going to back down. I didn't remember everything, but I had vague images of things that had been important. I was determined to try, and I think Tasha saw that.

"Five minutes. Not a second more."

She pulled her backpack around to get at a zipped side–pocket and pulled out two squares of fabric. "Here," she said as she swung her pack back into place. "Open these."

I thought they were handkerchiefs at first, but they kept unfolding over and over again until they were twice the size of a pillowcase.

"Good for fifty pounds each, but if you can't lift both, leave one behind." The elevator stopped, and the doors opened.

Tasha slid Katherine forward until her foot was between the doors. "Just in case. Let's go."

We walked up to the doors and I swiped them open with the guard's card. "Remember, I can carry her and one bag, if it's not too heavy. You have to manage all the other doors and the gun while carrying the other. Be careful what you take."

I ran to the shelf of artifacts, and Tasha held a bag open behind me. I kept putting things in it until she called enough, then we dropped that bag and I moved to the library.

"Five books, tops," she snapped. "And two minutes."

This was harder. So very much harder. My eyes went from spine to spine, trying to judge which were of greatest value, but I couldn't make a choice. Right up until Tasha snapped "Sixty seconds. Come on."

I closed my eyes and grabbed six books – two were really thin, honest – and I dropped them into the second bag. She was running for the elevator the instant I let go of the books, and I was only two steps behind her after I grabbed the other bag.

The fire alarm sounded as we burst through the doors of the laboratory, and we saw the elevator trying to close against Katherine's leg.

"Quick. They go down to street level and stay there if the alarm goes off."

Tasha pushed the doors open again, and I slid into the car under her outstretched arm. The doors were already closing by the time I turned and hit the button for the street. I probably didn't need to, but I wanted the thing to know which way we wanted to go. A sign lit at the top of the panel. "Fire. Do not use elevators." I started praying the wonderful thing would keep going downwards, and that it didn't roost at the top.

269

By the time the elevator stopped, Katherine was over Tasha's shoulder again and we each carried a bag. The doors opened and we ran, but I got a prickle on the back of my neck. I looked over my shoulder and a security camera winked at me. The cops would be all over us for this, and this time they'd have a good argument for pinning a murder on me.

I swung sideways, toward the reception desk. "Keep going. I'll catch up at the car."

Tasha slowed down. "What the hell are you doing?"

"Security."

Her eyes told me she hadn't thought of that. "Not worth your life, Jane. Get out."

But I was already at the station. I didn't expect it all to be there, nor any convenient VCR I could pop the tape from, but I found a box that controlled the camera and the views and a few other things, and I had a hunch. I put my hand on the controller and sent a wave of confusion and erasure though the system. The box erupted in a satisfying cascade of sparks, and both screens fuzzed with snow.

I ran out from behind the desk, but Tasha was still at the door. "It won't open."

Blast. I had fried the door locks as well. I pulled the Glock out of my waistband, pointed it at the window, and pulled the trigger twice. The first bullet went more or less where I wanted it, but the second took out the window above. I'm not sure what made more noise, the sharp barks of the Glock, or the crystalline waterfall of the granulated glass.

"Warn me next time?" Tasha grumbled, but she was running as fast as I was to the car. I opened the trunk, then the back door, and was just opening my own door when a terrible problem crossed my mind.

"What about the guard?"

Tasha had just put Katherine on the back seat of the car. She looked up at the flames roaring skyward from the roof, gave me a worried glance, but took off before I could change my mind. As she ran, I walked back toward the building. I didn't know what I could do to help, but I couldn't stand so far away. What if she needed me?

I was halfway across the street when the top of the building exploded, a rolling fireball climbing up into the night. Sirens were already getting closer. Tasha had picked the guard up and was starting back when a horrible thought struck me. The elevator shafts. If the fireball was also burning down through them...

A vague how-to memory shone in my mind and I threw up a wall between Tasha and the elevators – just as the fireball blew two doors out of one shaft and boiled into the lobby. Was that how this was going to work? Memories hidden until the moment I needed them. Fine, so long as nothing turned up late.

I got most of it, but I was sure Tasha felt some heat. I know she wasted a second or two looking at it before she picked the guard up and ran.

That was when I realized the flaw in my plan. The fire had moved faster, but the debris blown off from the explosion was about to crash to the ground around me.

I swung the shield up, over our heads, and spread it out as far as I could. The strain was incredible. Knives stabbed into the backs of my eyes, and I could feel something warm running over my lips. Blocks of masonry and burning beams bounced off my shield, and their force came through to me like a hammer on my brain. Tasha flew past me. I pulled the shield in, keeping it over the car and us while she tucked the guard in to a doorway opposite the building.

"Get in," she called. "Let's get out of here."

But I had to keep the shield up. Some of the stuff still falling could crush the roof of the car. I staggered to my door and climbed in. The engine was already running, and Tasha floored it so hard the door shut itself.

"Belt," she snapped.

I tried, but I was more worried about the heartbeat in my ears. The one that was getting slower. Damn drummer was missing beats too...

Light at the End of the Tunnel?

"... don't care what appointments you have this evening. I've got two major traumas in this car and you will clear everybody out and have someone on the sidewalk to help me get them up into your surgery, or the whole story about you with the two dryads in the hot tub will be all over the Shadows by morning...
"

"... Carefully. That one got thrown hard against a wall. This one? No idea. Alive. Of course she's alive, cretin, she's *warm*. I'm a frigging emophage, that's how I know. Now get her up those stairs before I prove it..."

"... can do for her. That one I can help. Flail chest, torn spleen, pneumothorax. All stuff I can cope with right here and now. This one? I don't know what's wrong. What in all the hells was she doing...?"

"... at least think about it. I have nothing left. I can find no trauma, but she has barely enough life to keep her body functioning. No, not turn her. Of course not, not without permission, but something lesser, like a pledge..."

Cold and thick on my lips, almost sticky, running down my tongue to the back of my throat. I have to cough or swallow, or I choke, and my body hardly remembers how to do either. But it decides. Swallow. The chill runs down through my chest and...

Boom.

Safehouse for Katherine

I woke, in my own bed, and had the whole *Was it all a horrible dream?* thing before I moved and found out it hadn't been. Then I spent a few minutes trying to get out of bed, grumbling that my life was just a cliche. I made it to the bathroom, did what a lady still has to do. It wasn't two seconds after I flushed the toiled that Tasha stumbled into the room, disheveled and sleepy and wearing silk pajamas.

When she saw me coming out of the bathroom, she looked desperately relieved, then covered the lapse with grumpy.

"You're awake then?"

"Nope, just sleepwalking." I looked at the curtain and saw light glowing around it. I'd been asleep for a few hours.

"Must have crashed in the car. Don't even remember walking in."

"You didn't."

"Aw, you carried me in."

"No, two big guys who work as orderlies for Doc brought you in, and that girl who tried to kill you. You need coffee?"

I thought about it. "And food."

We started to walk toward the kitchen, but I was no more than a step outside the bedroom door when I had to stop and put my hand on the wall to stay on my feet. In that short space the strength drained from me, especially my legs, and my head spun.

Tasha caught me, putting a hand under each of my arms and holding me until I steadied. I smelled jasmine. It suited her. "Maybe I should bring you dinner in bed."

"Dinner?" I shook my head. "I feel stiff, like I've been in bed too long. Help me get to the kitchen."

Tasha dumped a mug of coffee in front of me, with creamer, then set a pan of water to boil pasta while she nuked frozen carbonara in the microwave. Simple, fast, and half of it disappeared from my plate between two blinks. I was starving.

"Where's Katherine?"

"In the old woman's room. I've been sleeping on the couch."

I choked on a mouthful pasta and Tasha got a cloth while I coughed.

"Here?" And then another penny dropped; the way she said, 'sleeping on the couch'. She hadn't meant just crashing for a night. "Wait, what day is it?"

"Sunday."

I put my fork down before I dropped it. "But we went into the office Thursday night?"

She nodded, then looked pointedly at the pasta. "Eat, or it'll go cold."

I picked up the fork, twirled it in some pasta, and put it down again. "So why is Katherine here?"

Tasha pointed at the fork. "That has to go in your mouth. Two reasons. First, I didn't know what you were planning to do with her, and I guessed you wouldn't want to leave her in a hospital. I took you both to Doc. He fixed you both up but had nowhere to keep the two of you. We brought you both here and I promised to play nurse. He came by a couple of hours ago.

You slept through it."

She rose from the breakfast bar, taking my mug with her, and fixed us both another coffee. She put creamer in mine again before I could stop her, but maybe that wasn't such a bad idea. It tasted more comforting, somehow.

"Her stuff was just trauma, and that makes for good healing. You were in much more danger."

"Me?" I squeaked. "I wasn't hurt."

Tasha shrugged. "Your heart stopped. Almost. Doc said it was like you hadn't enough life left in you to keep everything going. He couldn't heal it, because nothing he could find was actually broken."

"Well, he must have found something," I said, all up–spin and bright.

"He didn't."

Tasha looked somber. I saw fear there too, and I was all kinds of worried.

"What happened?"

"He had run out of ideas, and he said you wouldn't survive transfer to a mundane hospital. Not that they would have been able to do anything for you either."

"What happened?"

"Your skin was gray, and your lips were blue." She was hedging around the answer, but I trusted her enough to know she would get there in the end. "I couldn't just leave you like that and wait for your heart to stop. You saved my life." There were tears pooling in the bottom of her eyes, something I would have bet money I would never see, and certainly not over me.

"What did you do?"

Her mouth moved, but no words came out. Whatever it was,

she was afraid of how I would take it, afraid of what I would think. But she saved my life. Why would she feel bad about it?

"Just tell me." Reaching across the counter, I put my hand over hers.

"I fed you my blood."

I managed not to snatch my hand from hers, but my entire body wanted to draw away from her, maybe even huddle in the corner.

"And that means?"

"I don't know. It's how I was turned when I was dying, but my Dam opened her vein, and I drank my fill. I gave you a teaspoon, no more, just to keep your heart beating."

Fear tried to swallow me, but she clearly felt worse. For someone who came over so calm and assured, Tasha looked broken into pieces, as though this had been gnawing at her for days. I gave her hand a squeeze then drew mine back, then took another mouthful of my cooling pasta.

"Does that mean I'll become like you?"

"I don't know. I don't think so. Doc doesn't think so."

I looked her in the eye and gave her the hardest smile of my life. "Beats being dead."

I got Tasha to help me down to the workshop, then told her I needed to make a call. She asked who, and things got a little awkward when I didn't say anything. A second later she raised her hand and backed toward the door.

"Sorry. Prying. I'll just go up and check on the girl. She probably needs food and the toilet."

I smile. "Thanks. Don't know if the person I need to speak to wants to be known. But put that stool in the doorway before you go. I don't want to be locked in down here if something happens."

She waved her hands a little as if to say *look, already gone,* and left the workshop. I felt bad that I waited until I heard her feet on the stairs before I found the crystal and the stand I had used before. I put them both on the table and rolled back through my new memories, looking to see if I had ever learned how to do this. The knowledge clicked back into place like it had never even been gone, and I focused my mind on everything I knew about Grant Peterson.

It took three or four minutes and, by the time he answered, I was exhausted. The crystal shone his image into the air on the other side of the table.

"Who the hells... Oh. You. Still alive then?" He didn't seem that pleased, but I sensed he was a little impressed.

"Harder to kill than I look."

"Apparently. What do you want? My head is still aching from your firework show on Thursday. That was you, I assume?"

I nodded.

"Wouldn't do that too often if I were you." He leaned forward and peered at me. "You shouldn't even be doing this. Your aura looks like you're half dead. Seriously, you should stop. Now."

"I need your help."

"Quickly. I mean it, or you could do yourself serious harm."

"He was using another girl, like he used me. She has nobody, just a half−assed knowledge of combat magic and a heart full of hate. If I turn her over to the authorities, she'll drop me in it, or try and kill me, and I don't want to have to hurt her any more than I already have. It wasn't her fault. She's just another me. Do you know of anybody who can help her, who can keep her safe?"

He glared at me, then his face softened. "You and she had a lot in common. She would be trying to do the same." It took me a moment to realize he meant Tamsin, not Kathrine. He pulled his shoulders back and looked all grumpy again. "Can you get her down here?"

"I think so."

"What time is it there?"

"Sorry don't know. Seems I've been out for a few days."

He nodded. "It's two here, so about four in the afternoon there. Get her down here around six, your time. I'll see what I can do. Make sure the circle is empty. For now, you go rest."

The crystal flashed and his projection disappeared, and I slumped forward on the table.

Tasha shook me awake, and I looked up to see panic draining from her face.

"What are you doing?" she asked.

"Sleeping, it seems." I pushed myself up from the table, stiff from the awkward position. "What's the time."

"Half past. It took me a half hour to deal with the girl, and I hadn't noticed you weren't back up. I'm so sorry."

If there had been a comfortable chair in the workshop I would have stayed there, but I didn't fancy perching on a hard stool for the next hour and a half. I pushed myself to my feet and wobbled until Tasha got an arm under my shoulders, then we made our way back to the living room.

"I've found somewhere for her."

"Who?" Tasha held my hands as she lowered me backwards into the couch, then made me lie down. The pillows smelled of jasmine and I snuggled into them.

"Katherine. We need to get her downstairs around six. Can

we do that?"

"I can. You can rest."

"Kinda what I had in mind," I muttered as I drifted off.

Being woken by the smell of fresh coffee is something I would never get bored with. It's so much more civilized than an alarm clock shrieking at you. I got my arms tangled in the comforter that wasn't there when I went to sleep, but I fought free of it and pushed myself up until I was sitting. Tasha wasn't there, but the coffee was, so I sipped until she came back.

"She's down there."

"You left her lying on the floor?"

"Of course not. She's sitting on a stool."

"Awake?"

"Sort of. Doc called it 'Fenwycke's Somnambulance', I think. She's essentially in a coma, but you can bring her out of it to the point she can follow basic instructions."

I grinned. "Ain't magic grand."

Tasha gave me a lopsided grimace that implied she doubted my sanity. "Are you ready?"

"Sure. I can manage."

She snorted. "Riiight. I go down in front and you keep one hand on my shoulder and the other on the handrail."

"Yes, momma."

But I did as I was told, mainly because she wouldn't let me go down the stairs until I did. Once I took a seat at the table, Tasha turned to leave.

"You don't have to go," I said, holding out my hand. She took and squeezed it.

"I'll stay if you want, but you can tell me to go anytime. It won't offend me."

She drew up another stool and sat next to me, still holding my hand, and we looked at each other for the longest time.

"You look tired," I said. The smile lines at the corner of her eyes were deeper and longer, and there were hints of gray in her hair.

She smiled. "Things have been busy. I haven't had a chance to feed."

"We could have shared the pasta."

"Not that kind of food." She looked sad and her body tensed as if she was waiting for me to pull away.

"But you took so much in the penthouse."

She shook her head. "Some emotions are more nourishing than others. Besides, I was pretty broken up. I needed everything I took from you just to keep myself alive."

"It was pretty intense, wasn't it?"

We both laughed, then she squeezed my hand tighter. "Can I ask a favor?"

"Sure?"

"Try to take life a little easier. I like to get to know my friends before I have to watch them die."

A lightning–bright flash filled the room. Tasha leaped up from her stool and stepped away from me, crouched, wary. A column of light formed in the center of the circle, taller than a man. It broadened out into a rectangle, then the center cleared, leaving just a frame glowing outline. Inside the frame stood Peterson. He was shorter than I expected, and fatter, and the room filled with the smell of cigar smoke. He stepped through the sizzling doorway and into the workshop.

"This her?"

I nodded. "Her name is Katherine. She's fifteen. He killed her family, just like he killed mine."

Peterson nodded. "I know somebody. They're good with troubled kids."

"Please don't let them take her memory." I blurted out the words before I thought about what I was asking.

He gave me a look, slow and calculating. "Might be the easiest thing."

"But might not be the best. It does things to you." He was still looking at me, judging me. I thought about what I was asking. "How about only as a last resort?"

He nodded. "That's fair. Hopefully, it won't come to that, but I'll pass it on. You need to be prepared she may never forgive you for your part in this."

That twisted me a little. I didn't think I had done anything I needed forgiveness for, but I didn't know how much alike our lives had been. I shrugged, and Peterson approved.

"Fenwycke's?"

For a minute I didn't know what he was talking about, but Tasha nodded. He placed his finger on Katherine's forehead, muttered '*ambulus*', then pointed at the portal glittering in the circle. The girl rose, empty eyed, walked around the table and through the portal.

"There's somebody waiting for her on the other side," he said, then he stomped around to take the stool Tasha had been sitting on, glaring at her as he passed.

"What's a lust–sucker doing here?"

"That's a truly offensive term." Tasha bristled and folded her arms across her chest.

"Accurate though," he snapped, without looking over his shoulder. His eyes locked on mine. "Well?"

"She's a friend. She saved my life."

He looked over his shoulder at her, then back at me, but I

didn't have the complete story. After an few awkward seconds, Tasha began to fill in the gaps.

"After the drama of Thursday, Jane collapsed while we were driving away. She shielded me from a gas explosion and from falling debris. I took her and the girl to Doc."

"Quack, but he knows what he's doing." Peterson wouldn't look at Tasha, but I could see he approved of what she had done.

"The girl had simple trauma, but we couldn't help Jane. Her pulse was twenty, and her blood pressure was unmeasurable. Doc didn't know what to do. So I fed her some of my blood."

He twisted on the stool until he faced her. "You did *what*?"

"It was that, or she wouldn't be here talking to you. It wasn't much. A teaspoon. She rallied straight away."

"You could have turned her."

"Does it look like I did?" Two spots of color appeared on Tasha's cheeks and her voice rose. "I couldn't leave her to die."

"The risks."

Tasha drew in a deep breath, and I saw her fight to regain her cool in her eyes. "Were minimal. I'm an abstainer."

Peterson snorted. "For now. You all lose in the end."

He spun back to face me, so he didn't see the hurt in Tasha's eyes, and I doubt he would have cared if he did. I was starting to think I didn't like him, but apart from Tasha, the miserable old bastard was all I had.

He held out his palm, four or five inches from my chest, just above and between my boobs. "May I?"

It felt invasive, but his eyes looked serious. I nodded.

Whatever it was, it went both ways. I felt him as a deep, deep pool of still water, with just a minor ripple of irritation on top.

I had no idea what he got from me, but whatever he was doing, his lids were closed and he looked like he was concentrating. Eventually he opened his eyes. I accidentally looked into them and saw much more than I wanted to. Years in a flash, good and bad, sorrow and joy. I looked away, and he lifted his arm from my chest.

"There is no trace of the virus within you," he announced. "Though you might find some interesting and unexpected effects show up later. I wouldn't recommend sharing her blood again, no matter how unwell you are. Some things are not worth risking your soul over."

"Also, you are much sicker than you think. Two weeks rest, at least, and no magic at all during that time. Not even research. That's assuming you intend to do any. Will you? Have you decided who you are?"

It wasn't until he asked that I realized I had. Consciously, I had been avoiding the subject. Corvax had raped my mind again. When I let myself look into it, so much was only stick figures and shadows. The beast had tried to erase himself, but all he took was his face; his name, and an echo of his voice, remained. But I had more than I had when Tamsin found me, and I'd bet a lot more than Corvax would have been comfortable with me knowing.

"This is who I am. My life has brought me here, to this point and this place, and I can accept that. Plus, I have this ability. There are things I know, and stuff I can do, but I know I still have a lot to learn. And I have a responsibility."

I sat straighter on my stool.

"I'm Jane Doe."

He smiled, and it changed his face. He stuck out his hand, and I shook it.

"Pleased to meet you, Jane. I wasn't sure Tamsin was doing the right thing, but I'm glad she did what she did. You will need a mentor, and I'd be honored if you would accept me, at least until you have found your own way?"

"Guess you'll do until someone better comes along." I grinned.

"Thank you. And remember, two weeks. I don't want to hear from you before then."

We shook hands again, and he left through the portal. The room seemed dim and tiny after the sparkling frame of light collapsed in on itself and disappeared.

I pushed the stools under the workbench and turned to face Tasha. We stood in front of each other, not quite sure what to do next. Then she stepped closer and wrapped me in her arms, hugging me so tight I could hardly breathe, and yet I didn't mind. Even when the hug went way past the usual two-Mississippi of casual convention.

"I'm glad you're staying," she muttered in my ear. "You're fine just the way you are."

All over?

asha babied me up the stairs again and we walked into the living room, sitting next to each other on the couch, not speaking.

Still so much for me to process. I had told Peterson I was fine with who I was, and that was true, but I hadn't come to terms with it – not even close – and speaking about it had torn the scab off.

"You're hurting." Her voice was soft, almost a whisper. I hadn't noticed she was still holding my hand from when we had climbed the stairs together.

"It's finished. I have so much in my head that's changed. I haven't found a place for it all yet."

A stray memory of sitting like this with my sister, holding hands on the swing seat on the back porch. She was crying because someone had run over her cat, and I was crying because she was hurting, and I loved her so much and I couldn't take the hurt away. But I couldn't see her, even though she was sitting next to me, or remember her voice – and yet I knew that the memory had been given back then taken again. That was the cruelty of it – he didn't just take things; he left markers, outlines, to remind me what he had stolen. It wasn't a blank wall anymore. The beast had left me with a thousand bleeding wounds in my mind.

I started to cry. Not sobbing, just tears running down my face as memory after memory slotted itself back into my world, or showed me what I would never know again. And I cried.

"I can make it go away," she whispered. "I can take the pain from you. Take the pain *for* you."

I shook my head. "No. Thank you, from the bottom of my heart, but no."

"Why not?"

"Because I have to grieve." But I wasn't telling her what I was grieving for.

That was why I had decided to stay Jane. Paulette Tipton wasn't really here. I had her memories now, or the empty shells where they had been, but I felt that I didn't have her soul. I could live with that. There was enough of me, Jane, to make this all work, and I kind of liked myself, or who I had started to become. It was going to be all right.

I wasn't grieving for my parents, or my sister.

I was grieving for Paulette Tipton, and the realization she had truly and finally passed from this world.

The tears turned into sobs, finally, and Tasha's arm curled around my shoulder. She held me until I cried myself to an exhausted sleep.

New Pages

C onvalescing sucks. I felt fine after three days, and ready to kick ass after five. That was when Tasha went home. I think we had both had enough of each other by then and had seen all the movies we both liked.

I cleaned house. Nothing too strenuous, nothing frantic, but I needed to change the sheets on Tamsin's bed anyway, and on mine. I think that was what started it, looking at the unmade bed. I worked my way through the rest of the room, putting stuff into bags for the thrift stores, for trash, and the stuff I wanted to keep. It wasn't much, and I was sure she wouldn't mind, but by the time I had finished, the room was no longer hers.

I started to reverse the process, bringing my bags from the guest room, putting my things into the cavernous closet, and realizing how much more I needed to buy. That was when I found the two bags we had rescued from the Corvax laboratory. I carried them downstairs – it took me two trips – and emptied them onto the bench.

It was tempting, but Peterson had been very sure in his warning. I settled for finding space on some shelves to store the new stuff, where I could keep it away from what was already here. I found my Book of Days, too.

But going through the artifacts, I found one that didn't make any sense. I didn't even remember taking it from the shelves in the laboratory. It was scale model of a motorbike, on a plastic base. It looked very like the poster now stuck on the guest room wall.

At least I had a reason for it now. I had no emotional memory left of my father, but I had a few more facts. Like I knew he had been a motorcycle nut. Half the garage was taken up with whatever restoration project he had taken on. He liked old Harleys, and had rebuilt an Indian Scout, but his real love was old British bikes, and his pride and joy was a Norton. And that's what the plaque on the bottom said this was.

I had no memory of buying it and was surprised Corvax let me have it at all. Why would he allow me a memento of my family? Unless he hadn't realized that's what it was?

It wobbled when I put it down, so I lifted it and looked underneath. One corner of the base plate was raised compared to the other three. I pushed it to see if it would click into place, but it caught something behind it. I slipped a fingernail under the raised corner and pulled it toward me.

The base popped out, and from it fell some paper, tightly folded. I picked it up from the floor, held on to the table while the head rush from standing up too fast faded, then I spread the sheets on the workbench.

They were the missing sheets, torn from my Book of Days. *I* had taken them out, not him. I started to read them, but I remembered Peterson's warning – absolutely no magic, not even research, for two weeks – but that didn't stop my eyes flickering across them. It was all in a language I didn't remember, or in code, but the last line made my blood go cold. The writing was plain, but hurried, ragged, and reeked of urgency.

"He must not know. He can *never* know." I had underlined it. Twice.

I folded the paper up and slipped it back into the base of the model. This time the base clipped properly into place, and I put it on the shelf with the other stuff I had taken.

Was that what had turned him against me? Was that the act of defiance that had cost me my past, and five years of my life? How brave had the other me been to do that? She must have known what he would do to her, how brutal he could be? Had he tortured her before discarding her?

I wanted to call someone, but Tasha said she was busy on a new project, and the only way I could contact Peterson was by magic. His phone number came up as disconnected now.

Sitting at the breakfast bar, I stared out the window into the tiny garden. Alone with my thoughts and my fears, my heart ached with how proud I was of Paulette Tipton. She was stronger than me, and braver, and I hoped one day she would be proud of me, too.

It was about a week after that, when I was technically out of convalescence, that Tasha got in touch. Just a text. Was I free for coffee? I said I was, and she told me to wait for an Uber. As I walked out to get in, I heard a dry rattle from across the street, and caught a glimpse of a large dragonfly, glorious in metallic purple. I smiled. Nice to know someone had my back.

The Uber dropped me outside a deli at the corner of 10th and Cherry, called Leo's. It was a nice place, with a small outside seating area. The place reminded me a lot of Betty's coffee shop, back in Clifton.

Tasha was sitting outside, a stained espresso cup and an

empty plate in front of her, and beside her, a latte and a bear claw. Lucky me. I sat down beside her just as a server bought her out another espresso. Tasha looked nervous about something.

"I'm not interesting anymore so you dump me?" I made a fake scowl.

"And good afternoon to you too. I told you; I was busy. Besides, you needed to rest."

"Well, I'm rested and very bored."

"Any thoughts on what you're going to do about that?"

I shrugged. "Get a job, I suppose. Maybe go work for Jimmy?"

I meant it as a joke, but Tasha was deadpan. Tough audience.

"Did you sort things out with your tenants?"

I nodded, surprised she remembered. I hadn't, and it had taken Amanda slipping a note through my door with a lunch invitation before I got around to it. Amanda was in healthcare and Nathan worked software development from home. I went over the arrangement with them again, and promised I had no intention of selling the condo and that they were safe as long as they wanted to live there. Lunch turned from an hour into an afternoon. "I thought about going back to school, too."

"Aren't you a little old for school?"

"They have mature students, adult colleges, and I have the money."

"But what about a proper job?"

"Like what?" I bit a chunk out of the bear claw, chewed and washed it down with latte. "I have no qualifications, didn't finish high school, and have five years' experience waiting tables which I am in no way interested in adding to."

A server clearing a table near us shot me a mean look and I

glared right back at her until she turned away.

"Look, the house is paid up, and I have two tenants paying me more than I need for utilities, insurance, and living expenses. Plus, as soon as Peterson clears me, I want to get back to learning the m— the stuff in the basement, you know?"

She nodded and called for the bill. I swilled down the last of my coffee, and Tasha left a twenty and the junk from her pocket. I expected her to get her phone out and call me another Uber, but she gathered me up with a jerk of her head and we wove our way out of the tables.

"So what's with you?" I asked.

It was a bright day, so Tasha was in her sun wear – gloves, hat, and oversize shades. She scowled.

"Too much day work. Meeting clients, checking things out. Then trying to find time to do the real snooping once the sun has set."

We carried on along Cherry, and into the next block. Nice enough. Bookshop, hardware store, mom and pop kind of stuff. A nice wide road for plenty of parking.

"So, I was thinking about hiring an assistant."

"Like a day shift?" I chuckled. "Some bottled blonde who spends most of her time on YouTube? Orange foundation and plumped lips?"

"Something like that. Blonde, anyway. The skirt and the heels would be optional." She stopped and turned to face me, and I realized she wasn't laughing. Smiling, but not laughing. "I was thinking more leather jacket, torn jeans and boots."

She stepped aside. Nestled between two shop fronts was a door, and the sign work said, "Campbell & Doe" and underneath it "Investigations."

Then she laughed and reached out to put a chin under my

finger and close my mouth. "Interested? The hours are atrocious, and I can't guarantee how good the pay will be, but it should be fun. You'd have to be my trainee at first, and there are some hoops to jump though before you can get your license. But it comes with a company vehicle."

She took me by the shoulders and turned me around. Parked just out of sight behind a tree was my old scooter. I laughed. "I'll take the job, but I'll want better wheels."

"Like those?"

Her hand was on one shoulder, and her head was next to mine over the other, and I was distracted for a moment by her nearness, and the familiar scent of jasmine. Then I followed along her pointing arm, to the sparkling red Norton Commando Roadster on the other side of the street. I turned round, and she dangled keys in front of my face. I snatched them, then threw my arms around her neck and kissed her.

But then I stepped back. "Oh damn. Now I have something else to learn."

"What?"

I looked back over the road at my beautiful bike and stamped my foot.

"I've never ridden a bike with *gears*."

oOo

Hi. Jane here. Thanks for getting to the end of this. Hope you enjoyed it. The author says people will be interested, but I'm not convinced. I'm nobody special. I'm just Jane.

But, if you want to show the writer you liked it, why not leave a review. I'm told they are pretty important. Click on this link here: REVIEW BOOK (or go to http://bit.ly/ReviewJane)

And, as if that wasn't enough, there's a bunch more stories that got dragged out of me. Pizza and a bottle of JD were involved, but I swear its all true. You can find the next book at getbook.at/BloodHunt

Oh, and the writer says I have to say there's a mailing list. I got a promise that its nothing spammy before I said I would mention it, but it will have lots of stuff like when new stories are coming out, and special deals for mailing list members. You can sign up here at the author's web page: www.robinmarr.com

Gotta go. Tasha has me doing a dozen different things for training to be a PI, but Jimmy has said I can work a shift at his place too. I kinda miss being a barrista sometimes.

Jane xx

Printed in Great Britain
by Amazon